TO SAVE A SISTER
MAJESTIC MIDLIFE WITCH BOOK 1

N. Z. NASSER

HANORA SKY PRESS

To Save a Sister: Majestic Midlife Witch 1
Copyright © N. Z. Nasser 2023
Published by Hanora Sky Press

All rights reserved.

No part of this book may be reproduced, stored in a retrieval system, or transmitted, in any form or by any electronic or mechanical means, without prior written permission from the author, except for the use of brief quotations in a book review.

This book is a work of fiction. All characters, organisations and events in this novel are products of the author's imagination. Any resemblance to real people, living or dead, or to real companies or occurrences is coincidental.

eBook ISBN 978-1-915151-18-6
Paperback ISBN 978-1-915151-19-3

CHAPTER 1

Our sister Sitara was in deep trouble, not that anyone else had noticed. She washed her hair twice a week like clockwork, spoke to the neighbours and laughed when the rhythm of conversation demanded it. Except she was out of sync, like a violinist who couldn't keep time with the musical score. Her hair, though fragrant, retained clumps of shampoo from hurried rinsing. Her eyes held no light, only impatience when she conversed with the neighbours. Her half-hearted laughs petered out like a choked car.

Sitara might have fooled everyone else, but she couldn't fool me. When three women lived under one roof, secrets were impossible to keep. Sisters knew each other's patterns. They knew how to coax out vulnerabilities, soothe hurts and yank each other's chains. Our eldest sister had discarded parts of her identity like an old coat.

I just couldn't work out why.

To figure it out, I had come to the garage adjacent to the ramshackle old house we inherited from my parents. Once, our father had indulged his passion for cars here, tinkering for endless hours. Now it was home to my pottery business.

The whirr of the potter's wheel helped me unscramble my thoughts. Round and round went the wheel as I shaped the clay beneath my fingers. Despite endless hours of practice, the process called for patience and care.

I pushed down a deep sense of foreboding as earthy scents filled my nose. Sitara was ripe for a midlife crisis and dealing with menopause to boot. Perhaps she was reassessing her life and wanted space of her own. Maybe that was why she'd shut me down time and again when I'd reached out to her. In fact, for close to a year, Sitara had abandoned all emotional labour, like she'd unplugged from us.

Her withdrawal hurt, but I understood the need for space.

Sharing a house with sisters in midlife was not for the fainthearted. There was the sigh of contentment over cups of tea, shoulders to cry on, borrowing from each other's wardrobes but also mismatched moods and wishing that we could be queens of our own domains. There were also niggling worries and minor annoyances to address. This morning, the bathroom bin overflowed with wax strips evidently used by a yeti. What is more, Sitara had adopted a hare who couldn't control his bowels. Clusters of hare droppings trailed all over the house, despite her insistence that he was house-trained.

I was grateful for my studio, with its terracotta-tiled floor, pretty displays of ceramics and its window facing out onto the sands and sea of Boundless Bay. Pottery was so much more than how I earned my living. It was my release valve.

A football slammed against the shop front, making me slow the wheel. The crockery in my window display rattled precariously. It wouldn't have been the first time local louts had targeted the shop.

A pimply local boy, all mouth and no trousers, stuck his finger up at me. "Weirdos. Lonely old crones." His antics prompted raucous laughter from his friends.

Group dynamics were a bitch at that age.

"Nothing wrong with being weird. Or choosing ourselves over bad relationships," I shouted. "Do yourselves a favour. Pull up your jeans before you moon the whole bay."

I continued to work the clay, ignoring the middle fingers they raised like masts. Three sisters: the first with green eyes, the second with hazel eyes, and the third with brown ones. All with our own strengths. But our strengths didn't attract as much attention as the fact we lived alone.

A lapse in concentration spilt worry into my fingers. I groaned as the teacup caved into an unsalvageable heap. "What a mess." I tossed my attempt into the already full slop bucket. I had no hope of finishing the order in time. My customer had asked for ten perfect teacups and saucers for her little girl's birthday party, glazed in a design that reflected our coastal town. Not misshapen lumps of differing sizes. I'd be at the wheel all night unless I sorted my head out.

My younger sister peeked around the door, a flash of blue scrubs and a messy bun. "Your grunts are scaring the seagulls, Kiya. Rough workday?" Her deep brown eyes, thickly lashed like my own, glimmered with relief at being home.

"You could say that." It had crossed my mind to get an internal bolt for my studio door. Or a sign spelling out *Bugger Off (Unless You Have Snacks)*. Although that went against the vibe of what Soul Pottery was all about. "How was yours?"

Leena slumped on a dusty stool. Boundless Bay was too small for a hospital of its own. Leena was an emergency nurse in the next town. Judging by the time, my rebel-at-heart sister had floored the pedal on her way back. "It was nonstop. A hedge cutter went haywire. Severed digits everywhere. I'm bone-tired, but nothing a hot bath and a day in bed with a sapphic romance novel won't solve."

I unhooked the tray of my potter's wheel and took it to the sink. "Actually, I think Sitara needs us."

My sister frowned. "You're fretting. Let it go. Sitara's prickles will smooth over like they always do."

There was nothing unusual about this scenario: my sisters and I had always been in a noisy battle of wills and stormy, steadfast affection. Born over a span of six years, the three of us had never lived apart except for when we went to college. Even then, Sitara meddled in my affairs, poking her nose into my dorm room to check I was changing my knickers and eating enough vegetables.

Now forty-three, forty-five and forty-nine years old, respectively, our lives were humming along just fine if you overlooked our clashing personalities, codependency issues and romances that fizzled out before they ignited. My sisters were my primary relationships, and Sitara was our weather vane. The truth was, she was more than a sister to us: bossy, exacting, a mum, almost.

It wasn't her choice. She stepped up after our parents died.

Leena and I ran every big decision past her. We wouldn't have made it without her, which made it all the more concerning that she wasn't ticking quite right.

I rinsed the tray and stacked it at the side of the sink before turning to face Leena. Then I took off my apron and leaned against the work bench a few feet away from her. "Aren't you worried at all?"

Leena unlaced her shoes, mentally already soaking in a hot bubble bath. "Of course I am. But she'll be fifty soon. It's a milestone, you know? Menopause is hard to come to terms with. So she's had an increase in bodily whiffs. Maybe she's mourning what could have been or the perky boobs of her youth. Just give her time."

Right now, Sitara's menopausal grumpiness was off the scale. Think Godzilla on a bad day, minus the reptilian skin. Unless you focused on her heels.

I shook my head and picked at the caked clay around my

nail bed. "This isn't about the funky smell coming out of her room. I'd be far worse with all the hormonal changes."

"Yeah, you would. Maybe what Sitara needs is an additional pump of HRT gel, a decent fan, quality vitamins and stronger deodorant."

Outside, blue waters lapped across Boundless Bay, but intuition told me a storm was coming. "I can't shake the feeling she's hiding something bigger."

The stool wobbled as Leena folded her arms across her chest and leaned against the wall. "I'm listening."

I met my sister's eyes. There was no point beating around the bush. Not in your forties when you knew how fleeting time was. Especially with sisters who had witnessed every aspect of you: warts, halos and everything in between. "Why would a woman obsessed with her job turn her nose up at attending an archaeological dig she had dreamed of? Why would the self-appointed matriarch of the family withdraw?"

"You have way too much time to think," Leena shot back. "It could be that she's just sick of us."

"Think about it. This past year, she's not sat at the table to eat dinner with us once. Have you noticed how furtive she's been about the books she's reading? Why would someone who revelled in sharing every aspect of her life with us clam up?"

"Maybe she's reading smut and is uptight about it. You know how Sitara always likes to be the guiding light around here." Leena snorted. "That's it. We should throw her a sambuca and smut party. Show her it's nothing to be ashamed of."

I rolled my eyes. "Smut might solve your problems, but Sitara is built differently. Don't you think it's odd how her walls have gone up? How Merlin is allowed in her room, and we're suddenly not? Sometimes I swear she's talking to him in the middle of the night."

"Kiya, you do realise you sound jealous of a bunny? It's

not like he's supplanted us in Sitara's affections. The trail of hare droppings is a bit much, though." Leena paused. "I really shouldn't have taken off my shoes, should I?"

A lump gathered in my throat. "Don't you get it? Sitara is the one who holds us together. If she falls apart, then we all do." I wasn't strong enough to hold this family together if our big sister went off the rails.

"This is just another curveball." Leena spoke with the supreme confidence of the youngest child whose siblings always protected her from life's harshest knocks. Her eyes softened as she stood and pulled out her bun, releasing golden-brown hair into its blunt-edged asymmetric cut. "But if it's that important to you, I'll back you up."

I sprang into action. "You're the best. I'll ring the chippy and get them to bring over our usual order while you have a bath. We'll have a boozy lunch to chase away her midlife blues. Sisters shouldn't have secrets. Whatever's going on, we'll pull her back from the edge."

"Don't you have a pottery class this afternoon?"

"Not until 5 o'clock."

"A quick dip, and I'm all yours then." She picked up her shoes and ventured back to the main house.

Turning Soul Pottery's door sign to closed, I gave my utensils a quick rinse and picked up a mop. Hatching a rescue plan with Leena eased the heaviness in the pit of my stomach. Across the bay, the mild summer's day morphed into frothing seas and howling winds.

I jumped at a flash of inky night in the display window of my studio.

Merlin. With his soft black and tan fur, arched back, erect ears and powerful hind legs, he was four kilos of mischief. His watchful liquid-gold eyes gave me the heebie-jeebies.

Sitara and the hare had formed a bond from the get-go. He belonged in an enclosure, but our oldest sister was adamant that Merlin could roam the house and garden. Only,

I'd seen him in the town too: on the beach, at the pub, outside the Post Office, even at the pop-up library. Unless I was losing my marbles.

Before Merlin, Sitara didn't even like animals.

My sister, once so rational and loving, was now unrecognisable.

I set back my shoulders. Today, we would find out why.

CHAPTER 2

I found Sitara elbows-deep in soapy water at the kitchen sink. A foul-smelling tea brewed in a cast iron pot on the stove. She wore a simple linen shift dress in faded orange. Silver roots glinted in the afternoon sun amongst the mass of her midnight hair.

At my approach, hesitancy crept over the heart-shaped face she had inherited from our father. She dried her hands and turned my way, stiffening like a robot. "Hi." The word was flat, unwelcoming, maintaining her barricade against unwanted attention. Her sea-green eyes flicked to an escape route.

I bulldozed in, my tone sunny. "Hey, I've ordered take-away for lunch. You'll join us, won't you?"

Sitara's mouth tightened. "I can't. I'm in the middle of something."

Crouching, I retrieved a Sauvignon Blanc from the sturdy dresser that housed our wine collection and set it on the kitchen table, steeling myself against further rejection. "When was the last time we unpicked our worries? It's been so long since we talked properly. Stay, please."

A wistfulness swept into her eyes, and her resistance

thawed. "I can spare half an hour. That's all, Kiya." Emotions danced in her eyes: pride, determination, fear and love.

The doorbell reverberated through the halls of our house.

"That must be the food. If you get the door, I'll hurry Leena along. She'd spend her whole life in the bath if she could." Hope brimmed for an end to the discord between us.

A deep inhale. "I've been thinking. How about we put the house on the market and move somewhere else?"

I jerked in surprise. Some orphans wanted to escape their roots. Not us. We felt an invisible tie to this land and this house, with its sprawling rooms and high ceilings, bay windows and old Aga, wisteria climbers, my pottery studio and the memories of our parents. At least, I did. "I couldn't bear the thought of leaving."

A shadow passed over her face. "You know mother wanted to leave. She wanted us all to go elsewhere. She craved new adventures."

"Mum and Dad barely travelled. I can't remember one trip apart from that anniversary weekend. The weekend they died." The two decades in between had muddied my memories. Trauma and healing were a process of forgetting and rebuilding, and the three of us had come out of that period changed in different ways. Sometimes I questioned whether my memories actually existed or whether I had made them up. Sitara's memories had remained intact. She'd been closer to Mum. I envied her for that.

Merlin hopped into the room and cosied up to Sitara's feet with a furtive glance at me.

I gave him a wide berth in case he used his teeth on me. It wouldn't have been the first time. "If you want to experience something else, we won't hold you back."

Her laugh was the hollowed-out husk of an oak. "What if I'm trying to hold everything else back?" The doorbell rang again, insistent. Sitara shook her head, scattering dark thoughts like arrows. "I'll get the door."

She had always been cryptic, but then what else did you expect from an archaeologist? I thudded up the back stairs, puzzled at her mood. As far as I knew, she wasn't on drugs. Even in our twenties, Sitara had been more of a sipper than a guzzler of alcohol, needing a tight rein on the controls. Whatever it was, we had weathered storms before. When the three of us confided in and supported each other, nothing could stop us. Our lunch would mend the breach.

I found Leena in her room, already dressed in a slouchy T-shirt and leggings, her wet hair beehived in a towel. "Come on. Sitara's laying out the food in the kitchen. It's just arrived."

"She said yes?" Leena raised an eyebrow.

"Yeah. I think she's in the mood to open up."

Leena followed me back downstairs past framed family photos on the winding walls: sisters splashing in the ocean, celebrating college graduations, baking cupcakes in a cloud of flour, beaming at the opening of Soul Pottery. The most recent addition was our paint-splattered attempts to refresh the façade of our house.

I frowned at the sound of raised male voices. Tommy and I had been childhood sweethearts long ago. He owned the local chippy. "No wonder Tommy's Fish and Chips Shack is in trouble when he sends out both lads to do deliveries."

"He's a saint for putting up with those potheads. I gave them an earful the other day when I caught them keying a car. In revenge, they called me a sexless crone."

"Funny you say that. I had a run-in with them this morning."

"Their mums should have a word." Leena harrumphed. "Maybe I should show them my kinky drawer."

"Their brains would explode. It'll take them until their thirties at least to understand how to satisfy a woman." I stalled at the bottom of the staircase and held up a hand of warning to Leena. Apprehension prickled in my belly. Deep, melodic timbres ruled out the voices from belonging to the grunting monosyllabic adolescents Leena complained about. These voices were older, self-assured. They bristled with anger.

"Give it to me," barked a stranger in low tones of menace.

"No." Sitara's response rang with clarity.

My mind flashed back to our teens when she'd placed herself between us and a growling Doberman, though the salivating dog bared its teeth and made ready to leap. Sitara had picked up rocks from the beach and fended it off under stormy skies. Afterwards, her limbs trembled, and her voice cracked with terror, but at that moment, she had been calm because if she had crumbled, what would have become of us?

We weren't children anymore.

With glances at each other, Leena and I plucked two compact travel umbrellas from a pot in the hallway.

I wielded mine like a baton as we rounded the corner into the kitchen. "Who do you think you are speaking to my sister li–" The words died on my lips.

Next to me, Leena gasped in astonishment. Not two but six strangers stood in our kitchen. They were unlike the usual men in our coastal town, the sort that hung about in the pub slouching over beers or licking their fingers after a portion of vinegary chips. Unlike the rough-round-the-edges types who worked a trade in small towns with calloused hands and weather-beaten skin. Unlike even the pastor's sons, who wore shirts with their jeans and shoes polished to a shine.

My throat constricted. These men stood out like poppies in a field of wildflowers. A bestial power coiled in them. They brushed the door frame in height, their posture straight and uncompromising. They had warm brown skin, the colour of chestnuts faded in the sun, like our mother's. Heavily embroidered ivory dress coats in raw silk clad their muscular frames. Thighs bulged through trousers. The belts at their waists held daggers of various sizes: daggers that belonged on battlefields, not in our peaceful town.

Four of the men had trained their eyes on Sitara, following her every move.

Our older sister jutted out her chin. No surprise clouded her face, only defiance. Her teeth gritted. "Run!" she said to us.

I fumbled, my mind frozen. We couldn't leave her.

Too late. Two of the men stalked to our side. They didn't flinch, although I unleashed the full force of my travel umbrella, extending it and walloping the one nearest to me in his washboard stomach. As if I were a mere fly and not a woman capable of inflicting damage.

One of the men turned coal-black eyes on our eldest sister. A topaz ring glinted on his finger as he stalked towards my sister, opening his palm. There was an aloof handsomeness to him, from the wayward curl of his longish black hair to the cut of his cheekbones. His dress coat was more ornate than those of the other men, with saffron yellow cuffs and a higher turn of the collar, marking him out as their leader. His mouth, sensual and cruel, twisted to acknowledge Leena and me. He spoked with a clipped formality, his accent foreign, yet familiar. "They are not going anywhere unless you hand over the jewel."

Only then did I notice how Sitara clasped her hands tightly at her chest. What jewel could she possibly have ferreted away, and from where? Beyond the house and memories of a fairy-tale childhood, our parents hadn't left us anything of note. Our jewellery boxes contained mere trinkets bought as holiday keepsakes or from Annie down the road, who had started a business to support herself with buckets of passion but little actual know-how.

Two things dawned on me at once: Sitara wasn't showing any signs of giving the men what they wanted, and this wasn't any old robbery. These men were organised, well-equipped, and disciplined. They had the air of a military unit rather than a rabble.

My stomach clenched. My sister was in real trouble.

Sitara raised her chin higher still. "I'm not giving you anything."

Leena trembled, her voice a mere whisper. "Don't rile them. It's not worth it."

Their leader let his open palm fall to his side. With a smirk, he prowled across the kitchen to our kitchen dresser, stacked with my pottery creations. He picked up a plate I had made long ago at a summer holiday camp when I had first discovered pottery. Though nothing special to look at–oddly shaped and uneven in form–it held emotional value because it bore tracings of our parents' handprints entwined with ours. "This is where Hansa was holed up all these years. She gave it all up for this." He studied the plate, turning it over in his hands, then dropped it with wanton carelessness.

A cry left my lips as the plate smashed on the tiled floor. "No!"

The love imbued in it by dear hands, warm flesh long cold, evaporated into the air.

My pain exploded into dread. I started forward, momentarily evading my surly captor, a grizzled, moustached man who towered over me. "Just give them what they want, Sitara."

My captor lunged, catching me around the waist with a curl of his lip as if my clay-marked overalls were beneath him. His voice was hot against the back of my neck. "Listen to the little lady."

I still had the umbrella. I lifted my arms over my head in a rush, striking the man holding me with force borne of rage and fear for my sisters. How dare these men break into our home? How dare they come and exert their will over us in our sanctuary?

My mind freewheeled through possibilities—six

imposing men against three small women. We could make a run for it. Knee them in their little peckers, claw their eyes out, throw plates at them like flying saucers, and scream like banshees until the neighbours heard or Tommy's boys arrived with the fish and chips. They would drive for help in a screech of tyres even though they didn't like us. That's what small-town people did. We helped each other out. It would be okay. Until then, we could hide in the basement and bolt the door, though the lock sometimes stuck fast and needed greasing. There were rusty rakes down there that would make fine weapons. It's not like the men were really going to do anything to us. That would be a ridiculous thing to risk. They had the law to answer to. Their clothes were too fancy for real manoeuvring. They were show ponies, that's all.

All hopes of a defence withered away like the last of the tulips in spring when I looked at my sisters.

Leena was frozen, eyes wild. She wouldn't be any help.

The strangers formed a wall between us and Sitara that we couldn't bridge. She was on her own.

"The jewel, or we'll take it forcibly." The leader's strong fingers played with the knives on his belt. "Will you risk flesh and blood for an inanimate object? You know what we can do."

A shudder washed through me. We bore witness, aghast.

Sitara straightened her spine and planted her feet in a wider stance as if my silent schemes and will to fight had sparked new strength in her. Her eyes on us were full of longing: to scold us, cook for us, and protect us one more time. The hint of a smile drifted over her lips as she faced the men, and though the leader relaxed, thinking she had given in to his demands, I knew the intricacies of every fleeting expression on Sitara's face. I knew the darkening of her brow, the set of her jaw and thinning of her lips meant she was digging her heels in, and there would be hell to pay.

A feeling of exhilaration came over me as she opened her hands to reveal the gleaming jewel the men coveted: a palm-sized bronze-hued stone that matched the ring the leader wore. Outside, through the picture frame of our kitchen window, the brewing summer storm broke at last, darkening the skies and unleashing a torrent of rain that saturated our garden lawn within seconds. Neither the leader of the troop nor his men spared the turn in weather a second glance. Their leader gave the signal, and the brute closest to Sitara surged forward to retrieve the prize.

Sitara's sea-foam eyes narrowed like they did when we played darts at the pub. She launched the jewel directly at the brute. Bull's eye. It clunked against his forehead, and he dropped to the ground, disoriented and moaning. The jewel ricochetted in another direction. Their leader dove to catch it with the prowess of a jungle cat, his dress coat a blur, but the smoothness of the jewel made it slip from his fingers despite his efforts.

It smashed into smithereens, chunks scattering across the floor.

In a corner, Merlin quivered, his inky ears pinned back. His body tensed as if he were about to spring at the attackers, but a subtle shake of Sitara's head stilled him.

She drove her hands into the sink of soapy dishwater. When she lifted them out, the mass of water had grown unfathomably large, larger than had been contained by our battered old Butler sink. All at once, Leena and I were no longer restrained. My heartbeat thundered in my ears. Now was our chance to get the upper hand. Shouts of warning and wrath echoed through the kitchen as a wall of soapy water crashed into the men. It swept them across the slippery floor, taking kitchen chairs and the dustbin with it. Yet Merlin, Leena and I were unharmed. How had she done that?

The men clambered to their feet though water sloshed

around their ankles. Two spun through the air like superheroes. Except these men weren't heroes, they were our enemies, trained martial artists with balled fists or glinting blades in their hands.

"Run!" shouted Sitara. "Don't look back. Go!"

My heartbeat clamoured in my ears. There wasn't time to think.

We ran, though every cell in my body demanded I stay.

CHAPTER 3

Our escape through the front door was messy, a tumble of limbs and swallowed sobs, the strangers' cries at our backs. I clutched Leena's hand as she hiccupped with fear, our bare feet cold against the gravel driveway. Driving rain soaked her T-shirt and my own.

Leena swivelled to face me. "We can't leave her alone."

I nodded. Of course, we couldn't. How could we live with Sitara battling intruders while we fled? We didn't have our phones with us to call for help. Mine lay on the kitchen counter. "Come on."

We grabbed an old broom from the side of the house and a metal watering can. Alarm for our sister overrode any sense of self-preservation. Under the thunderous sky threaded through with gunmetal clouds, we pressed ourselves to the outer walls of our house as we made our way to the kitchen window. A film reel of disturbing images rolled through my mind: brutish men dressed to the nines; our memory-laden plate smashed to dust; Sitara unleashing a flood across the kitchen; her boldness in enduring danger to save us.

Our muddied toes squelched on the wet lawn as we peered inside the kitchen, hearts hammering in our chests. I didn't understand why they still concerned themselves with us when the jewel they coveted had shattered on the floor. Sitara fought fiercely for us, just as she had always done.

All *hows* and *whys* evacuated my mind, leaving only the scene before me.

Our sister, whose every secret had once been mine, stood at the centre of a tempest though she was indoors, calm, resolute, doing what should have been contrary to the laws of physics. Her dark hair whipped around her head, and water swirled around her as she swept her arms in a circle with a dancer's grace, her linen shift dress plastered to her body.

Her hare stood at her side, ears alert to every movement. Sitara had the upper hand, using the water as both a shield and to attack the intruders: it rose as a flood, transformed into icy arrows at her command or a cloud that dispersed in boiling, blistering droplets. But her body curved with exhaustion, and I willed her to finish it, wondering if she could drown them. If she would.

Before I'd formulated a plan of how to assist her, the breath left my chest in a whoosh.

A bejewelled dagger travelled through the air from the hands of the moustached man. Sitara made a clumsy attempt to avoid it, twisting awkwardly. The hare made a siren noise of anguish, but the warning came too late. The dagger hit her with punishing force in the centre of her chest, becoming lodged there to the hilt. Her expression in profile was one of surprise before she crumpled to the floor, taking all her water magic with her.

I watched, rooted to the spot, as Merlin prodded Sitara with his foot, but she didn't move.

He nestled against her, his head on her chest.

The leader cursed, eyebrows knitted together as if hurting Sitara hadn't been part of the game plan. Her limbs lay at an unnatural angle, but she'd never had the patience or flexibility for yoga. He reached down to take her pulse, but she was motionless. He shook his head, dark eyes gleaming.

A fierce need for revenge flared in me.

A brief moment of clarity: this had happened on his watch. I would watch them all burn.

Then I was screaming and crouching on the muddy lawn. Leena held my face in her hands, shouting that we had to go, that the men had seen us and they were coming, and there was no time to grieve. I heard the words, but they didn't penetrate when my mind played Sitara slumping on repeat. Sitara, with a red rose blooming across her orange shift dress. The light dwindled in her eyes. Her dear face, so like our father's, stilling on the floor of the kitchen, where water pooled and mixed with red. Our sister, who could do impossible things. Our sister, our everything, who had mopped our tears, held us together like we were the bricks and she the mortar. Our sister, who had done everything first and now, was also the first to die.

We were out of our depth from the moment the troop of costumed men stepped onto our property. We just hadn't known it. How much had I not known? What good were our makeshift weapons when Sitara could raise a tempest from a sink and still lose her life? Far better to disappear without a trace than to face those brutes. Is that what Sitara had meant when she asked if I would leave Boundless Bay?

I came into my body again, sluggish, my mind fractured.

Leena shook me, spittle flying in my face in her urgency for me to listen to her. Her face was white with terror, her voice a wrangled sob. "We have to leave her now. Please, Kiya. We have to run."

She dragged me up. In bare feet under the pouring sky, hearts broken, our progress was slow. We zigzagged, unhinged in our loss. Boundless Bay was our turf, and yet our options for escape were limited. Our car keys hung safely in the hallway cupboard. With our home situated on the outskirts of the bay, it would take ten minutes to reach neighbours at a brisk jog. Instead, we ran past our cars and hid behind a thick tangle of hedging a few hundred yards away from the house, hoping for a smidgeon of luck. Seagulls circled overhead, squalling. Deep cuts from the gravel driveway mangled our feet, dirt seeping into the wounds. Heaving chests, grief mingling with adrenalin, skittish eyes.

Let them not find us, I prayed. Now there were only the two of us.

Leena's fingers latched onto mine like she'd never let go. Her brown eyes mirrored my own bewilderment. "Who are they?"

Though the summer rain was warm, I shivered. "I don't know." Perhaps I could rewind the last hour like a movie reel. We could decide to go out to lunch instead. Maybe this was a nightmare. Any moment now, the three of us would wake and tut about my nightmare.

Leena burrowed closer to me as heavy boots crunched over the gravel towards us.

"He'll not be pleased," drawled their leader in dark tones of menace. "We don't even know if she excavated any more of them."

The second man sniffed. "You did order us to stick to our ordinary abilities, or we might have captured the woman without the unnecessary kerfuffle. We might have saved the jewel."

A grunt. "We couldn't risk exposing ourselves."

"Forgive me, General, but our very clothes make us stand out in this backwater place."

"This *backwater* place is the root of our magic."

General? Magic? A shudder ran up my spine. What the hell had Sitara got us mixed up in? My heart plummeted like a stone in a well. I couldn't even tell her off about it. It would never be one of those stories that turned out okay in the end because she was gone.

"We'll find her sisters. They can't have gone far," said the second man.

The general gave a husky bark of surprise. "They are right under our noses."

Leena, who had moulded her body to mine, stifled a gasp. I wrapped a protective arm around her. My heart ricocheted against the walls of my chest as the general loomed over the hedge. His coal-black eyes glinted with amusement as he reached for me, all broad shoulders and musky scent. He lifted me over the foliage as though I weighed nothing, as though Leena wasn't trying to anchor me to the ground.

I struggled against him, hissing all manner of curses. The rain added unwelcome intimacy. While his dress coat retained its form, the wet cotton of my T-shirt made for a flimsy barrier between my skin and his calloused hands. A sudden intensity in his eyes told me he had noticed, too.

His lip curled. "This is nothing. I've seen you in the nude before. Oh yes, I remember. It took me a while to put it together. I'll give you that."

I flushed. What in heaven's name was he talking about? Yet somehow, he looked familiar, like the echo of a buried memory or a ghoul from my nightmares.

The general circled my wrist with an iron grip. His tone was casual, utterly at odds with the desperate clamour of my heartbeat. "It'll be easier if you don't fight us, witch."

My eyes flicked to his waistband with its array of bejewelled daggers. "I've been called far worse than that." Hatred surged in my breast. Next to us, Sitara's killer had his murderous hands on Leena.

Her face drained of colour as she recognised him. "Murdering bastard." She launched herself at him, landing a kick to his jingle bells. Her nails clawed his face like she wanted to do permanent damage, even though she'd always been a healer.

Angry track marks sprang up on Mustachio's skin. "You little–" His fist flew through the air.

The general caught it with a smirk. "You deserved that."

I used the distraction to slip a blade from his belt. It sat strangely in my palm, an alien weight and hilt compared to a kitchen knife and my potter's tools. A blade meant for death, not cooking or creating. I twisted under the leader's arm, though he still imprisoned my wrist. A move that belonged on a ballroom dance floor more than an alley fight. With a jerk, I lunged forward, pressing the serrated edge of the blade to Mustachio's belly. "She was everything to us." I spat, on autopilot, not thinking how it would feel to spill a man's blood—only thinking of Sitara, lifeless on our kitchen floor.

"That's enough." A vein throbbed in the general's jaw. He disarmed me with a flick of his hand, and his hands closed around my neck, subduing rather than suffocating me as if I were an animal. He cocked his head at Sitara's killer. "Come. The men must be almost finished. We will wait for them at the vans."

My hatred for them left me dazed: red-hot anger and white spots in my eyes.

The general took me by the forearm, hauling me away from our house to the next field. Mustachio followed suit, bundling Leena into a fireman's hold. She railed with clenched fists against his back, so he punched her. She fell unconscious against his shoulder.

Rage clamoured in my chest, building to an explosion. It threatened to consume me. The cogs in my head wheeled in wild disarray, searching for a way out. I could taste my fear —metal and salt and acid on my tongue. I'd watched enough crime documentaries to know we'd be in more danger if they moved us.

I cast a frantic look over my shoulder, where the rest of the men exited our house carrying boxes of books piled high that I recognised as Sitara's. Some limped, and others had bandaged wounds presumably inflicted by Sitara's arrows of ice. Two men carried a large object wrapped in a sheet between them, passing beneath drooping wisteria. Bile rose in my throat at the realisation that it was my sister's body. Molten-gold eyes followed Sitara's final journey from the porch. The men stormed past Merlin, oblivious to his presence. With his black fur and tan undercarriage, he was a mere shadow when he wanted to be.

And I was mere cargo, dragged along like a sack of potatoes. My bare, bloodied feet slid against the mud. One sister dead; the other slack over a murderer's shoulder. Maybe if I stalled long enough, the fish and chips would arrive, and Tommy's boys would raise the alarm.

I had to try.

I tugged in the opposite direction, back towards the house. "The hare."

The general stopped short under the thunderous sky. "Excuse me?"

"That hare was Sitara's. We can't leave him to fend for himself. You owe us that much, at least." As soon as the words left my mouth, I knew they weren't a lie or a desperate ploy. They were the truth: I would care for Merlin because he had been important to Sitara.

He bellowed a command to the man nearest Merlin, who scooped up the hare with the gentleness of an axe murderer, crossed the green and dumped the squirming ball of fluff in the general's arms. The general turned impatient, unfeeling eyes on me as he thrust Merlin at me as if we weighed nothing at all. "Satisfied?"

I held Merlin's trembling body against my chest and glared at the general.

I wouldn't be satisfied until I killed them all.

A sleek grey van swerved across the green, its side door already open. Near the house, a second van picked up the remaining men, the boxes and Sitara. A wave of nausea came over me. What good was resisting when Leena remained unconscious? It's not like we could run. Sitara's killer bundled Leena into the van without ceremony. I crawled in after her, clutching the hare. When the doors slid shut, I put him down and watched as he sped into a corner, whiskers twitching. Then I edged towards Leena, cradling her head in my lap as the engine roared to life. The two vans raced off together with us as their prisoners.

Bile rose in my throat as I stared out the blackened window. A battered old pickup truck meandered up the road in the distance, emblazoned with the logo of Tommy's Fish and Chips Shack. They were too late to be of any help.

There would be no perfect teacups today, no pottery class.

No nattering with my sisters over soggy fish and chips.

Only heartbreak, sinister magic and a journey into the deep unknown.

CHAPTER 4

The van bounced across the field of long grass, slowing only to allow the other vehicle–the one carrying Sitara–to manoeuvre ahead of us. The purr of the engine blocked out any voices, and there was no viewing window into the driver's cab. I swept back damp, mussed hair from Leena's face and leaned forward to check her breathing. Tears of relief prickled my eyes. A blue-black bruise had sprung up on her cheek, but she would be fine.

I looked around, reeling with loss. The shiver in my bones burrowed deep as if it was there to stay. Nothing lined the van's floor, and no possessions filled its interior. It was sterile, as though it had been deliberately emptied in preparation for a crime. Merlin flipped out in a corner, whimpering and stomping his hind feet, a relentless whine and thump, as if he knew Sitara was gone and wanted to communicate with me.

My imagination was in overdrive. The hare probably didn't have a clue what was going on. He was probably freaked out by the van or carsick. At this point, he could hurl out the contents of his stomach, and I wouldn't even complain. I had to stay focused for all our sakes. Protecting us had always been Sitara's job. I didn't know if I could do it. "Quiet, Merlin. I need to think."

The internal door handle had been doctored, making escape impossible even if Leena roused. I had to believe the intruders wanted more with us than to silence witnesses and make hare stew.

I shifted Leena in my lap to get a better view out of the back window. Rain sluiced down it, and a wiper squeaked over the glass at intervals. I clung to the last vestiges of hope. Tommy's boys would notice muddy tyre tracks on the pristine green. He cared for us. He'd follow the tracks. But the tyres left no trace. The verdant grasses sprang up, their stems juicy and unbroken.

Magic, whispered my mind. Yet I clung to logic. Whichever way I turned them, I couldn't decipher the clues: Sitara's violent end, the jewel she had given her life for, thugs dressed like Indian royalty, a complete disregard for the law, why they had taken us. It didn't make sense.

We hit a dirt road I'd never paid much attention to and drove at speed for less than ten minutes, past a dead-end sign. There was a ribbon of a road there. The sort of blink and you'll miss it kind, one that hadn't been depicted on any atlas or map I had ever seen. I shimmied closer to drink up every detail from the back window. I needed to know our orientation for when we escaped. Trees thickened around us, a cocoon of eucalyptus, banyan and mahogany trees that I'd somehow overlooked on my hikes around the area. That I could have sworn didn't belong in chalky English earth or on this continent. They stretched upwards and inwards, narrowing until their branches scraped against the sides of the van. We pushed through a shimmering curtain, or maybe it was just a play of the light as the sun crept through the clouds. It sickened me that the sky had cleared when the heavens should have lamented Sitara's death, should have reflected the churning tumult in the pit of my stomach.

After a few hundred metres, the van passed some sort of checkpoint before cruising to a stop. The general and his second-in-command exited the vehicle. Car doors slammed, and footsteps approached.

Leena stirred in my arms. "Where are we?"

My pulse hammered in my throat, voice grim as I helped her up. "I think we're about to find out."

The side door to the van swung open to reveal new faces: a quartet of men and women with hands folded neatly in front of them, carrying no visible weapons. But it was the general, at their helm, who commanded my attention.

The hazy light illuminated a silvery scar through his right eyebrow. His hair had dried with a slight curl that gave him a boyish look, but his mouth was stern, eyes dispassionate, as if his mind was already on his next task. He leaned in and reached out a hand resplendent with his topaz ring. "Come. This is your home now."

The bastard. I flinched from his touch, jerking us both further into the vehicle so he couldn't reach us.

Surprise flashed across the sharp angles of his face. "I won't hurt you."

Fury filled me. "Your men killed our sister."

He stiffened. "It was a retrieval mission that got out of hand."

"Sure, that's an excuse for murder." I balled my fists. "When our cars don't move, a neighbour will check on the house. They'll see the signs of struggle. It won't be long until people come looking for us."

His eyes narrowed. "We have a cleanup crew."

Leena moaned in distress, causing the hare to dart from the van.

The general caught him with lightning-quick reflexes and turned his back on us. He handed Merlin to a young woman amongst the waiting staff and addressed the group in clipped tones. "Settle them into the turquoise chamber.

See to their every need, but guard the doors." Then he turned on his heel and strode away. The droop of his damp collar revealed the etchings of a geometrical tattoo on his back.

I tugged my gaze away with difficulty and studied the new arrivals. Their hair was tidy, and their manner was less confident than the soldiers. The youngest woman could have been a boy at first glance. She had plain features, a figure that was all angles rather than curves, and ear piercings glinted on her cartilage. Like the two men beside her, she wore a simple uniform of red cotton shirts with trousers. While the other three studied us with unabashed curiosity, the youngest woman kept her eyes lowered to the ground and hummed a song to Merlin. Her melodic voice eased his distress, and the traitorous hare nestled into her arms when he should have gnawed her nose off.

A buxom older woman in her sixties with a silver pixie cut completed the quartet, though her clothing set her apart from the rest. She wore black harem trousers strung so tightly that her midsection bulged and a faded, formless T-shirt depicting a 1990s Bollywood film. Her canny look of interest made me shrivel.

A scream built in my throat as the van dipped and the two men clambered into it.

I braced myself against the back wall of the van, scrambling for a reason for them to let us go. "Don't do this. My pottery class will raise the alarm with the police." I thought of the yobs at my window a few hours ago. "We are much-loved members of the community. No one will stand for this."

Leena was still unsteady, her voice thin. "The hospital will report me missing as soon as I don't turn up for my shift tonight."

The men didn't listen. They gripped our elbows and guided us out with firm resolve, lips in a thin line as if they had been forbidden to speak. As if it wasn't worth their while to engage with us.

We could make a run for it, but what would that achieve with these footmen attached to us? No, we would have to wait for the cover of darkness or try to commandeer a phone to call for help. I interlocked my fingers with Leena's. "Come hell or high water, I won't let them separate us."

We emerged from the dark confines of the van, blinking as we adjusted to the sunlight. I sucked in my breath. Although only a short drive from Boundless Bay, we could have been in another country. An imposing palace with glistening white walls and a series of domes, turrets and balconies stood before us. Wondrous gardens in a symmetrical design surrounded it, abounding with colourful blooms, a multitude of ferns and trees, expertly trimmed hedging and bubbling fountains.

I swept my gaze over our wider surroundings, my chest tightening like a vice. Armed soldiers guarded the gates encircling the palace complex. A few hundred dwellings stretched beyond the palace in an architectural style unlike England's array of Victorian, Edwardian and 1930s housing. These houses were single-storey and made of red stone, with eerie sculptures on the rims of their roofs. Wide streets bustled with golden-brown-skinned people in colourful Indian dress going about their business. Many hurried towards a temple, from which the sound of bells and singing came.

None of them batted an eyelid at the comings and goings at the palace.

None of them cared that Sitara had been killed and we had been taken against our will.

Worst of all, stone walls at least fifteen metres high encircled the settlement, adorned with embellishments but also spikes, making them impossible to scale. I shuddered at the thought of being trapped within them. My fingers tightened around Leena's, making tiny moon imprints on her soft flesh. She didn't even wince, too wrung out to notice. Too wrapped up decoding the sights before us to react.

My breathing quickened at the sight of two men carrying a stretcher into the palace. "That's Sitara."

Leena gave a quiet moan. "How can life change so quickly? I don't understand."

The splendour of our surroundings seemed vulgar in comparison to the rising tide of grief in my breast.

"Quiet," said one of the guards, our feelings of no concern to him.

Our captors nudged us forwards, flanking us like prison guards. We shuffled forward through the palace gardens towards the main building, accompanied by the strains of the youngest woman's humming as she held fast to Merlin. Trumpeting elephants and pretty peacocks roamed in pairs, their serenity at odds with the turbulence of my inner world. A male peacock fanned out its tail of iridescent blue-green feathers and strutted towards the female, making a bell-like whoop. He didn't notice the tiger prowling towards him until the last moment. My heart thundered as he attempted to flee, willing him to survive and resume its mating ritual. When the tiger clamped his jaw around the showstopper's plump body and settled down to feast, Leena cried out.

I bit down on my lip, drawing blood. My fingers kneaded Leena's, willing her to be strong. My whisper in her ear was fierce. "These people don't deserve our tears." I would cry when alone, not before.

"Another one bites the dust," said the portly woman beside me darkly. "Come on. Let's get you cleaned up. The raja wants to meet you, and you can't very well turn up looking like a pair of wretches, can you?"

We passed through winding halls that were a marvel to behold, decorated with intricate tapestries and paintings depicting scenes from Indian mythology. Each room and courtyard we passed was more grandiose than the last, with smooth marble floors and furnishings draped in embroidered silks and deep velvets. Chandeliers sparkled in the light, made from gold and precious stones.

I couldn't have retraced my steps if we tried.

Palace staff passed us with disinterest, carrying bronze jugs of wine and water, trays piled high with Indian sweets, or musical instruments that twanged in transit. The heavy stones and sumptuous decorations of the palace were like a mausoleum compared to our home by the ocean, with its simplicity of form and function and possessions chosen for love rather than their show factor.

We climbed a circular staircase of worn stone, a pilgrimage in bloodied bare feet. The women ushered us into a chamber at the very top, but the men stayed outside. They took their leave, faces scrubbed of humanity, and bolted the door with a heavy thud. I exchanged panicked glances with Leena.

The portly woman made a dour face. She waggled austere eyebrows painted black with kohl. "Never mind them. They look like a donkey's backside even when they are smiling. I'm Mahi. I'll look after you."

I shook my head. "My sister and I don't belong here."

Mahi's forehead crinkled as she frowned. "Are you so sure of that?" She turned to the younger woman, her manner brisk. "Aanya, look how they both shiver. Heat the water. Be quick about it."

The younger woman, called Aanya, nodded. She was in her early thirties, with soft eyes and a boyish figure. When she released Merlin, the hare squeezed under the stately bed.

"Don't worry about being missed in Boundless Bay. The general helpfully tacked up a sign to say you and your sisters had gone on holiday."

My legs went weak, my gaze glassy. I turned to look at the room, understanding why the general had called this the turquoise chamber. Bright blue paint and white bone carvings of fish, dolphins and turtles covered the walls. A thin duvet and medley of cushions in contrasting blues dressed the mahogany four-poster bed. A bowl of seashells sat atop a bulky dresser in dark wood. A small table and three chairs occupied one corner. A large circular bath decorated with tiny mosaic tiles and gleaming gold faucets stood in the centre of the chamber, surrounded by large potted plants. The roar of gushing water filled the room as Aanya opened the faucets. The reflection of the water on the ceiling created an almost ethereal glow. There was a small toilet and sink behind a dividing wall. Natural light flooded in through two large windows, framed by ivory silk drapes, on opposite sides of the turret. One provided a view over the kingdom; the other faced out towards Boundless Bay.

If we screamed, perhaps the wind might even carry our voices to our friends there.

The chamber did not resemble a prison cell, but we were prisoners all the same. Our bolted door, the turret, the guarded palace gates, the high kingdom walls: it all amounted to one thing. We were trapped. We were trapped, and Sitara was dead. I ran to the toilet, sank to my knees and vomited.

Leena followed and handed me a tissue, her face tight with grief. "Sitara…"

"We can't grieve now," I said, though we both reeled with it. "We've got to get out of here."

Leena bit her lip, her voice a whisper. "I've not seen one phone. Where the hell are we?"

I wiped my mouth and discarded the tissue. "It's locked down like a fortress."

Mahi approached, her voice gruff. She smelled of perfumed detergent, and her calloused fingers showed she was no stranger to hard work. "Have a bath, and then you'll be able to think better. When you get to my age, you learn not to fight the flow of life. Save that energy for when you can deal a knockout blow."

I balled my fists and pulled Leena behind me.

Aanya held up her hands in surrender, her sing-song voice like a comfort blanket. "Come now. Doesn't a bath always help?" She coaxed us as if we were skittish animals and not middle-aged women.

Neither of us had any fight left. So we let ourselves be led by them. Steam rose in the room, and droplets dotted the plants surrounding the bath. Mahi uncorked a vial of oil and tipped in half its contents, muttering indecipherable words. The scent of lavender and something earthier filled my nostrils.

Magic, said my mind again.

But it was easier not to think. My thoughts lost their sharpness. I gave into the hazy dream of nothingness as we stepped into the scalding water. Leena and I bathed together like we had as children before we reached double digits, and the shame of our pubescent bodies made us shy. The raja's staff scrubbed us with brushes as if they prepared horses for a gala. Mahi concentrated on me, cantankerous and grumbling but not unkind. Aanya washed Leena, taking care to set her at ease with soothing, undemanding cooing, a pitter-patter of words and song that required no answer. My sister didn't respond to Aanya's gentle ways; neither did she resist.

I drifted. It was always women who tended to me in grief. Always women who brought me blankets and water, who unravelled my knots, laid a hand on my forehead and murmured in my ear. Always women who shared their strength so I could replenish mine.

When the water cooled, our skin gleamed, and hair trailed down our backs in freshly washed and braided plaits. We stepped into plush towels, and they applied healing ointments and pastes to our feet. When Mahi brought us tall glasses of water and a plate of thin breads and cheeses, we ate small bites even though our stomachs churned. Aanya coaxed Merlin out from under the bed with a bowl of water, fresh hay and slices of strawberry, and soon, his gentle grizzling snores came from under the fluttering curtains of the turret.

My words were a wrench, like unjumbling thoughts and finding my voice after a deep sleep. "We won't be here for long, but in the meantime, he'll need a litter box. And outdoors time. He's used to that. But somewhere away from the tigers. And the elephants. I don't know how he'll react to them."

"Of course," said Aanya as though it was no trouble at all.

As though seeing to the needs of two female prisoners and a hare was a normal day in this sorry place.

The women provided us with fresh underwear and Indian garments that reminded me of our dead mother's moth-eaten finery packed in suitcases in our loft. Clothes that had always seemed too fancy to have been found in everyday shops. Mahi fussed over our appearance, poking and prodding. Her own informal faded Bollywood T-shirt contrasted deeply with what had been chosen for me: no sequins, silks or embroidery. Even her necklace was an afterthought, its pendant forgotten beneath her T-shirt. Her only concern was my presentation.

She prised open the ribbons of a corset and slid it over my rib cage. "It's made from whalebone."

I winced as she tugged at the ribbons, moulding me into an unnatural silhouette. "This is ludicrous."

"No," said Mahi, face grim. "It is necessary. You want the raja to like you."

Small pearl droplet earrings glittered on Leena's earlobes. "We couldn't give a fig what he thinks."

"In time, you will learn our ways," said slight, meek Aanya, as if she had no power at all.

Mahi added a peacock brooch to keep the scarf on my

shoulder in place, sweeping her hands over the fabric so it sat just so. "Be sure to make a good impression."

My voice was urgent as they clad our feet in sandals. "Please, let us have a pen and paper. Just get a message out for us. Whatever hold they have over you here, we can help you both."

An impatient frown knitted Mahi's kohl brows. "It is you who needs our help."

Then the iron bolt against the door shifted, and boots marched in. Clenching my fists, I scanned their faces, landing on only one I recognised: the general. He had changed his clothes. His cotton shirt with fancy embroidered cuffs was unbuttoned at the nape, revealing a muscular physique. He wore the same dagger belt from this morning's mission, and the knives gleamed like he had tended to them anew. His coal-black eyes drifted across the room without hurry, lingering on the basket of our dirty clothes and the sodden heap of towels. Then he assessed the outcome of our ablutions: how we had been dressed like dolls in fancy clothing and our hair teased into braids.

When he inclined his head in approval, my cheeks burned hot with shame.

"Very well done, Mahi," he said with insufferable arrogance.

Then he met my eyes, and the turquoise chamber shrank so that only he and I existed there. I imagined taking hold of the potted plants and knocking him senseless, wrapping the silk drapes around his neck and pulling tight until he gasped for air, or stealing a dagger from his belt and twisting it into his heart. How with his death, this would all be over. Sitara, Leena and I would all be together again.

But I had seen Sitara's lifeless body. I knew that could never be.

My sadness was a void that could never be filled.

"It is time. The raja awaits." The general pointed at me

like I was cattle. "He will speak to the older one first." With that, he turned on his heel.

"Kiya, don't let them–" said Leena.

It didn't matter what I said. It didn't matter how we shouted out using curses that had never crossed my lips before: curses that I had vowed were too coarse for me but now came flinging out like arrows.

Useless arrows.

They ignored our cries. The soldiers' steel crossed before us, keeping us apart.

"All these daggers and swords. It's not legal, you know," I said.

The general sighed. "Haven't you realised yet? Your laws are not ours."

I set my jaw, holding onto the shreds of my courage, though I had already endured one separation from a beloved sister, and my heart was a sore welt. "I'll find a way out of this. I promise, Leena."

I felt the uncertainty of it on my tongue: a promise I wasn't sure I could keep.

They shepherded me out in the general's wake.

CHAPTER 5

The sun sank into the horizon as we descended from the turret. As we moved as one through the halls of the palace, the rhythm of the soldier's boots meshed with the pounding of my heartbeat. Mahi accompanied me, fending off the soldiers, scolding them until they gave me a little room to walk at my own pace, though their drawn swords still harried at my back.

I couldn't tell if she was friend or foe.

Outside the carved doors to the throne room, she took a deep breath and smoothed down her clothes, though it made no difference to the unkempt impression she made. Then she dug ragged nails into my arm. "Dip your head when you meet him."

Anger flared in me. This wasn't my kingdom. The raja wasn't my king.

The need for revenge left acid on my tongue. I would rather starve than show him subservience.

A horn sounded, and the doors swung open. A pair of drummers started up a relentless rhythm. Torches flickered in a vast room flanked by marble columns. Members of the court tittered in small groups and sipped from goblets of wine or crystal tumblers of sherbet that left a sickly sweet scent in the air. I shrank under their searching stares as we made our way deeper into the room, past murals that depicted epic battles and scenes of courtly life. A thick wool carpet muffled my footfalls as I approached a raised dais at the far end, each step of my progression marked by a thud of the drums. The whalebone corset crushed my ribcage, heightening my horror. My breathing quickened.

How could such a place exist in such close proximity to our home?

Who were these people? Why had they taken Sitara's life so casually?

In the middle of the dais, on a throne encrusted with rubies and emeralds, sat the raja. I'd expected a stout, stern man of grandfatherly age. Instead, he was in his late forties with strikingly blue eyes contrasting his rich robes of purple hue. Slim, bejewelled fingers tapped the intricately carved armrests of his throne. He wore a thick moustache and beard, artfully shaped to show his defined cheekbones. Dark hair fell to his shoulders and was topped by a simple crown of gold. No advisors circled him, save for the general, who stood at the edge of the dais, his hand resting on a dagger.

At the general's signal, the drummers gave a last bash of their instruments, and the soldiers manoeuvred themselves into arrow formation around me.

"Go on." Mahi placed her hand on the small of my back and shoved me to the point of the arrow.

I stumbled forward, my voluminous skirt swishing against my legs, and looked up at the raja. Though Mahi had warned me to dip my head, I was stubborn.

A warm smile pulled at the corners of the raja's mouth. His voice was deep and sonorous, befitting a king. "Welcome to Jalapashu, Kiya Marlowe."

Jalapashu. The name sounded like a gong in my head. I

lifted my chin and addressed the raja with barely restrained anger. "You know my name. I have yet to learn yours."

"I am Prem, once a prince of Jalapashu, now seven years into my reign as its king. I've waited a long time to meet you." His cobalt eyes were shrewd. The muscles in his neck corded. "You are as beautiful as the painting of your mother that still hangs in a dark corner of the palace library."

His tightly coiled energy reminded me of the tiger in the gardens.

This was a man built for the battlefield, not the legal wrangling of kingdoms.

The court hung onto his every syllable.

I corked my anger, though it corroded my insides. "You speak as though you know my family."

"Oh, but I do. Long ago, your mother was a princess of Jalapashu—the child of one of five ruling families. There was great sorrow in this kingdom when your mother ran away with your father. Alas, how slight twists of history impact us all." His eyes flashed with mirth.

The court responded with muted chuckles.

My stomach clenched. "You're mistaken. My mother was born in Boundless Bay. She came from an ordinary family."

A deathly quiet fell over the court. All shuffling and sniffing stopped as if those present held their breath.

The raja's mouth twitched. "You are vexed at me."

The court tittered as if being vexed at the raja was a foolish thing to do.

My voice was small but fierce in the throne room. "Your men killed my sister. You kidnapped Leena and me. I demand you let us go."

He looked up at the court. "Her mother deserted this kingdom to marry a British man and never looked back. Her sister Sitara stole from us. She was killed in an act of misadventure when our soldiers were defending themselves. Despite this, we have shown the sisters impeccable hospitality. Yet Kiya Marlowe is aggrieved at *me*." He chuckled, but there was a tightness to his face.

Mahi shuffled forward, tempering her brusque tones in the presence of the king. "Forgive her impudence, Prem-ji. She does not know our customs."

The raja raised a well-groomed eyebrow. "Mahi, must you insist on dressing that way at court? You already enjoy unusual privileges." Before she could respond, the raja's voice echoed across the columned throne room, commanding attention. "Kiya Marlowe believes she can punish *me*. She thinks British law applies to us. She thinks we would let ourselves be colonised again. We don't *obey* British laws. We scoff at them." He beat a fist against his heart space. "We are governed solely by the laws of Jalapashu."

"That's absurd. We're in England," I said with a sinking feeling, although the general had also pointed it out. It didn't make sense for them to exist like this. None of it made any sense.

I flushed, anger building as I looked around the court. Mahi's lips formed a thin line of disappointment, her posture hunched as though my failure to impress was her fault. The members of the court and soldiers took their cues from the raja, the rhythm of their laughter mirroring his. Only the general stood expressionless, his face angled away from me. His sole focus was protecting the raja rather than the theatre of court.

The raja raised his strong, bejewelled hand.

Silence fell like a curtain.

"Mahi is right. I should not be too harsh. I want us to be friends, Kiya." His blue eyes shone with warmth. "Tell me, why didn't you and Leena use your magic against my troops?"

I shook my head, suppressing the images of Sitara at the washing-up bowl. "We have no magic."

He gave a benign smile as he shifted his robes. "Is this not a daughter of Hansa Malini and Jack Marlowe, whose eldest daughter could raise tempests? What wonderful magical talents might she be hiding? I can scarcely wait to find out."

My insides churned. I didn't care about this strange place and its strange customs. I didn't care about the lies he told about our mother. The raja was obviously caught up in a fantasy. I'd find a way to get revenge. For now, Leena and I needed to get out of his clutches and grieve our sister. I drew in a shaky breath and blocked out everyone else. My hazel eyes locked onto the raja's blue ones. "Will you free us?"

The raja arched an eyebrow. "No, I won't. I'm known to be a fair and responsible leader, Kiya Marlowe. It would be neither fair nor responsible of me to let loose witches on our doorstep—particularly the daughters of the gifted witch Hansa Malini, who turned her back on us. Treachery runs in their blood. We have guarded the secret of this hidden kingdom and its magic for too long to let Hansa's daughters jeopardise our safety."

The whalebone corset grew tighter around my middle, making me dizzy and my hands clammy. "We aren't witches." But even as I spoke, I remembered the tempest Sitara had called from the washing-up bowl and the icy arrows that had flown across the kitchen.

A beat of stillness before the raja's handsome face broke into a cool smile. "That you will have to prove."

I swallowed hard, panic rising. How had we ended up subject to a raja's whims? "What do you want with us?"

"Come now; it demeans you to speak to me as though I'm a monster. Have you not bathed in our waters? Are you not dressed in our silken garments? Have you not eaten our bread?"

My eyes locked onto his. "We want to go home."

"A reasonable request, some might say. As your mother's history shows, Jalapashu can be merciful." He leaned back on his throne, musing, and steepled his fingers. "We have it within our means to bind your powers. A binding. A blurring of memories. It will be tricky, but it can be done. Perhaps we can come to an arrangement and allow you to leave." A topaz ring gleamed on his finger, much like the one worn by the general, but this one had a showier cut and setting. Its hue was more orange than amber brown. "But you must answer one question."

Next to me, Mahi stiffened.

"Anything," I said.

The raja's cobalt eyes gleamed. "The jewel your sister stole and subsequently destroyed is of immeasurable value to this kingdom. Can you replace it?"

My knees threatened to buckle. "No."

He addressed the court. "See how easily lies drop like pearls from her lips? She expects me to believe her eldest sister, a mother to them, did not share her bounty." He turned to me. "You leave me no choice, Kiya Marlowe. At sundown, you will carry out funeral rites for your eldest sister. You and your remaining sister will stay in Jalapashu until you prove you are not witches." His smile was kind, seductive even. "Who knows, you might even wish to stay."

Heat rose behind my eyelids. I backed away, but Mahi's hand found the small of my back and soldiers started forward, ready with their steel. "We can't bury Sitara. The police will need to see her body."

"Then your sister's soul will be waiting a long time for release," said the raja quietly.

My body grew leaden. This king of his own backyard was telling me that my mother had been a magical princess and she might have ruled this place if it hadn't been for love. That Sitara had been a witch, and Leena and I were, too. That we would hold a funeral for our sister at sunset even though we hadn't touched her yet or even said goodbye. I pulled at my corset, gasping.

My world and all the knowledge underpinning it had spiralled out of control in the space of a day.

The raja sighed. "I see I have tired you out. You need not worry. You will be fed and clothed. You will have a roof over your head. If you are good, you may remain in the turquoise chamber with the hare." He waved a hand. "Tomorrow, my seer will begin his work. We will see whether you are witches or merely yourselves. You have met my general, Deven? He will see to the arrangements."

The general inclined his head. "As you wish, Prem-ji."

If you're good, the raja had said. How dare he? I opened my mouth and shut it like a fish.

The raja averted his gaze. "Bring in the elephants. Let us see their new tricks."

Around me, courtly life whirred with bowls of sugared almonds and skewers of cheese and grapes.

My gaze clouded. No one was coming to save us. We had to save ourselves.

CHAPTER 6

Twilight had fallen by the time Mahi and I trudged up the winding staircase to the turquoise chamber. The ground swayed beneath my feet as I shuffled after her grumbling form. Glowing lanterns lit our way, casting menacing shadows that twisted and reached for me. The braids from my audience with the raja made my scalp sore. I pulled at them, making myself into a scarecrow. Mahi pressed on, oblivious to the thinness of my breath and how I pressed my hand against my breastbone to regulate my breathing. When I couldn't take another step, I doubled over and laid my forehead against the cool stone of the stairwell.

"Well, that couldn't have gone any worse." She swatted my arm. "What are you doing stopping there? You'll fall to your death. Even if you survive, we'll struggle to do CPR with that whalebone around you. It's not like I carry scissors with me."

I lifted my head, my breath coming in small gasps. "Get it off me."

Mahi rubbed her brow as if to ward off a headache. "You can't take it off here. This isn't a nude colony, you know. Just a few more steps to your chamber."

TO SAVE A SISTER

My vision swam with hazy white dots. "Now, Mahi."

"Okay, okay." She steadied me against the wall and lifted her right knee to keep me from tumbling sidewards. Then she loosened the corset, there in the stairwell in the hidden kingdom, though the swell of the court, trumpeting of elephants and the march of boots still floated our way.

When Mahi lifted the corset over my head, I slumped with relief against her. "Thank you."

Her tone was crotchety as she stooped to retrieve the clothing. "In all my time coming and going through the halls of this palace, I've never known anyone to throw off their clothes outside their chamber. Apart from the orgie in the summer of 1969, when I was a spritely young thing with slender thighs, buoyant breasts and a forest between my legs. These days, I'm lucky to be able to grow the hair on my head." She sighed. "If you want to beat him, this will never do. You played your hand all wrong."

I fought to keep the heaviness in my body at bay. "How? How else could I have acted?"

Mahi supported me up the stairs with a sidelong glance. "I'm not one to judge, but you were like a turtle on your back in there. There you were, making outbursts, pleading for your freedom, demanding justice and appealing to the raja's humanity. You'll have to be cleverer than that."

Was she a friend or a trap? I searched her eyes and was none the wiser. "What do you suggest?"

Though a mere whisper, her voice echoed in the stairwell. "Nothing too difficult. Start with a little scheming, finding allies and understanding your power. Maybe some fireworks." She grinned. "He's right about one thing. You and your sisters are witches. Genealogy never lies. You can hide from history all you like, but mark my words, no child of Hansa Malini could be born ordinary. It's a shame you're too pigheaded or lily-livered to see it."

I gritted my teeth. "I'm not a coward."

Mahi's eyes narrowed. "Then, for the sake of your remaining sister, you should wake up from this deathly slumber of yours because Jalapashu has a habit of devouring those who shirk the truth." She pressed her lips together, clam tight, as sharp footsteps ascended the stairs behind us.

I looked over my shoulder and flinched at the sight of the general.

He stiffened in the tight stairwell, dark eyes drifting to my lacy bra and then to Mahi clutching the whalebone corset. "Funeral rites for your older sister will take place in one hour. Perhaps when you are dressed, Mahi could escort you and Leena there."

I blinked away the floating dots in my eyes and thrust my chest out, although every cell told me to shield it. "My sister's name was Sitara."

"Yes, indeed. We will await your arrival before we light the flames." He paused, shadows dancing across the hard lines of his face.

For a moment, I imagined him softening and showing his humanity. Perhaps he would express his condolences or tell me how sorry he was for the ill-fated mission under his command, or how terrible a blow it was to lose a sister, or how the raja had changed his mind, and we could go home.

But he didn't say that. He didn't say anything at all.

He simply spun on his heel and descended from the turret—an unthinking, unfeeling man in uniform.

He would light my sister's funeral pyre and let us all burn.

HALF AN HOUR LATER, LEENA AND I STOOD AT THE TURRET window dressed in funereal white. She stood a little taller than me, a willow to my oak. Behind us, Mahi and Aanya tidied the room, patting down cushions and rearranging ornaments as though their busy hands could give us a little privacy. In a palace courtyard, silent men stacked piles of wood into a pyre.

Leena turned her wan face to mine. "I never thought that we'd be without her." Her face twisted in grief. "I don't want to hold her funeral here. Sitara doesn't belong here. Neither do we." She whispered to prevent eavesdropping. "We can't stay."

"We have no choice but to go along with it for now." I gestured out the window to the guards at the palace gates and the impossibly high walls surrounding the settlement. "Just look. Escaping is impossible."

She studied the curtains. "We'll wait until we're alone, and then we'll fashion a rope from the curtains and bedding, Rapunzel-style."

I maintained an even tone, my expression carefully blank, in case Mahi and Aanya suspected our plans. "It's too high. We've got the upper body strength of gnats. We'll crack our skulls."

"We have to try. We'll wait until the guards get distracted, then run like hell." She pointed to the silent streets of single-storey houses with their eerie roof sculptures. "Someone will smuggle us back. There has to be at least one person who'll risk it. Who knows this is wrong."

I frowned. "Those gates are locked. I haven't seen one vehicle leave since we got here."

"This place can't exist cut off from everything else. They must go somewhere for groceries and schooling. They must have medical needs. They can't treat everything here." She wrung her hands together and darted a glance over her shoulder. "I think I can persuade Aanya to help. She has a kind heart. I can tell."

Frustration surged through me. "You're not listening, Leena. You'll meet the raja, and then you'll see. He isn't going to allow us to leave. Not until we prove we're not a threat."

She stared studiously out to where the funeral pyre had reached waist height. "You can't seriously believe what he said. You can't believe we're witches."

I forced a lacklustre smile, sensing the stillness of Mahi and Aanya behind us and how they wanted to decode our interaction. The hare suddenly launched into a frenzy of scuttling back and forth, making Mahi grumble and Aanya laugh. His noise cloaked our conversation. "You saw what Sitara could do. She raised a *tempest* from the washing-up bowl. What if she wasn't the only one?"

Leena sucked in her cheeks. "It was all so fast. I don't know what we saw. We've been through a lot today. Grief does funny things, but magic? I believe in science, not magic. In logic, not make-believe."

My voice was a hiss in her ear. "Don't do that. Don't make me question my own sanity. It wasn't just Sitara. I told you the tyre marks disappeared from the green on the way here. Those bath oils that Mahi used dissolved our resistance. I know you felt it, too. Our fight just drained away. We let them wash and preen us like we were mannequins."

"We're emotionally exhausted. Nothing more. Hallucinations can be a part of grief."

"Fine. But think about it. We haven't imagined Jalapashu. We haven't imagined *all this*. We both see it. How can this kingdom on the coast of England have remained hidden from prying eyes all this time? We live a few miles away, for goodness' sake. We've hiked up here, driven past a million times, and didn't notice it. With all the instruments of surveillance this country has–the drones, satellites, mobile and internet networks, police, the secret service, hell, bloody Neighbourhood Watch–how can a place like this still exist?" My voice trailed away, but the word in my head was no longer a whisper. It was an insistent bellow I couldn't ignore: *magic.*

"Stop it. You're scaring me." Leena shuddered. "Maybe we need sleep to soothe our frazzled hearts and nerves. Maybe someone at home has already raised the alarm, and the police will come and find us, and we can mourn Sitara and start to heal from this nightmare."

My gaze ping-ponged from her to the dusky kingdom. The sight of the funeral pyre clawed at me. I blinked away the thought of Sitara's body being prepared somewhere in the palace. I understood Leena's desire for the oblivion of sleep and to hope for rescue or help. I just didn't think that was coming.

My voice was barely a whisper. "Leena, I think we have a history in Jalapashu. I think Sitara knew about it. The raja mentioned our mother. Doesn't that pique your curiosity?"

"He probably read her name from the council website. All those complaints she made about late bin collections and those human poos on our doorstep."

I grimaced. We'd never gotten to the bottom of it.

Leena's face was still as she looked out onto the kingdom, and if someone watched us from afar, they might have thought we were holidaymakers admiring the view. She'd never been good at poker, though. Up close, I could see all the telltale twitches that revealed her pain. "Don't you get it? This *raja* is some sort of cult leader, not an anointed king. The stories he told you are the unhinged rantings of a madman. This kingdom isn't hidden by magic. Maybe it's been here all along, and nobody looked properly. You know what it's like. Nowadays, we're all too busy looking at our phones or simply surviving to really perceive what's under our noses. What's real is that Sitara made a mistake. A horrible mistake. Stealing that jewel got her killed."

I jerked my head back, an involuntary movement that I feared Mahi and Aanya could decipher. "Sitara fought so hard because she was protecting us." I breathed at her ear. "She wasn't a thief. She spent her career looking for hidden objects and sharing those findings with museums around the world."

Leena bit her trembling lip. "I loved Sitara. She gave up so much to look out for us. But she wasn't a saint. It is possible she stole from the raja. I remember the joyride in Barcelona. When she jump-started that moped, and how she liked to steal those mini shampoos and conditioners from hotels we stayed at."

I swallowed hard at the lanterns being lit in the courtyard with the pyre. "Everyone does that."

A kaleidoscope of emotions flitted over Leena's face. A film of tears covered her brown eyes. "I don't want it to be the end of her story either. If her doctor had listened to how bloody difficult she was finding the changes rather than telling her to put up with the temperature surges and the sleepless nights, things would be different. We should have done more. We should have forced her to open up to us." Her voice crackled with emotion. "We should have told her how much we appreciated and loved her."

"We were too busy fighting about who forgot to replenish the loo roll."

A moment of silence. "It's like we didn't even know her."

My stomach hardened. "None of us can know every thought and motive of the people we love. Sitara had secrets, but we knew her. We *know* that she fought for us with every breath in her body. She just didn't think it would end up this way, with her leaving us alone."

Leena's face crumpled. "I want her back so badly."

Glass shards in my throat. "Me too."

Mahi and Aanya drew nearer, signalling our time for discussion had ended.

"It's time," said Mahi.

"The hare can accompany us." Aanya scooped him up. "It will do you good to stretch your legs, won't it?"

Mahi hesitated, her eyes on mine. "You will survive this moment, I promise." Then she gave a sharp knock on the chamber door.

I reached for Leena's hand as it swung open.

CHAPTER 7

As the last rays of light withered from the sky, Mahi, Aanya, Leena, and I descended from the turret, our heads covered with white scarves. The hare hopped after us, weaving between our legs. He kept close as if he had caught our sombre mood.

Compared to the opulence elsewhere in the palace, the west courtyard was a simple space with smooth marble walls, elegant stone benches and palm trees. Oil lamps and incense burners filled the air with a sweet aroma. The soft chirping of birds and the distant sound of temple bells added to the sense of serenity.

Serenity was impossible when Sitara lay on her funeral pyre.

We weren't alone. A handful of foot soldiers joined us. High above the courtyard, the raja overlooked us from a palace balcony trailing with roses. The general stood to one side, stoic and unmoved in his uniform.

He raised an eyebrow at Merlin's presence. "You brought the hare to your sister's funeral?"

"There would be trouble if we kept him cooped up all

day. He meant a lot to Sitara." I frowned. "Not that I have to explain anything to *you.*"

His jaw tightened, but whether out of pity or disinterest, he didn't take my bait.

My scalp prickled, my stomach tight with grief as I wrapped my arms around Leena. In front of us–so close I could have reached out and touched her–Sitara's body lay on a neat stack of wood piled two metres high. There was no sign of her violent death. She wore a white cotton *Punjabi suit* when in life she had draped herself in colour. Her toenails had been scrubbed of varnish, her dark hair brushed until it shone, and her eyelashes rested gently against her cheeks. She looked peaceful, beautiful even.

I wished fervently that she had lived until she was a hundred years old, and I had seen her hair turn all grey, her lines deepen and her body curve with age.

"You may say goodbye if you wish," said the general.

I hated him. I hated him for the breath in his body when Sitara's lungs had emptied. I hated him for his part in her death, for bringing us to Jalapashu, and for the arrogant curl of his lip and unlined forehead.

But when I looked at my older sister, all hate drained away, and an aching, tender love came over me.

Time stood still. I wanted to steal Sitara away, but our mother had taught us that there was nothing to fear in letting go. That sometimes, goodbyes came sooner than you expected, but love remained. So, Leena and I stepped towards the pyre and placed warm kisses on Sitara's forehead and told her we loved her. Then I placed a cloth over her still face, and Aanya sang a hymn I didn't know but somehow remembered. Its notes trickled over us and into the air, mingling with the evening birdsong.

Somehow, more voices joined in from further afield: from palace balconies and at the palace gates, as if passersby had stopped and joined us in the common language of grief.

When the hymn ended, the general's inky eyes lingered on us. Then he lit a torch and held it to the funeral pyre.

Flames engulfed Sitara so quickly that they stole my breath.

I turned my head away, unable to watch, the pressure in my chest unbearable.

The hare trained his honey-hued eyes on the moon, his limbs quivering.

Wails ripped from Leena's body. "I can't. I can't let her go."

I held her close as tears streamed down my cheeks. "We'll be okay."

"We should have saved her," said Leena.

"How?" I asked although the same thought haunted me.

The pyre burned, and our sister with it. Leena and I rocked together under the dark starless night. The hare quivered against our cold feet. Twice, he hopped closer to the flames as if he needed a farewell of his own, but Aanya shooed him to safety. High above the west courtyard, the raja was no longer on his balcony. The general retreated to the shadows under the palm trees, and soon, even the evening song of the birds dwindled to nothing. To the citizens of Jalapashu, we seemed cowed and broken in our grief. But with every swirl of smoke into the sky, resolve settled into my bones and made a home there: we would resist.

Through it all, Mahi stood vigil over us, her dour face turned away from our intensely personal moment. She raged at the footmen, swatting them with her slipper. "Stop gawping, you buffoons. Have you no shame? Is it not enough that they lost their sister? That's right. Stare at your own hairy feet."

Her grumbling washed over us, strangely comforting despite her waspishness.

At last, the funeral pyre burnt itself out, and the ashes cooled. And I wondered whether the voices joining Aayna's as she sang her hymn meant we had friends in the kingdom, just as Leena had hoped.

Mahi scooped up Sitara's ashes into an urn and offered it to me. "It is over. You must be strong." Her kohl-smudged eyes flickered to the general standing under the palm trees.

I accepted the ashes, unease spiking in my belly. They were planning something. I tugged Leena's arm. "Grab Merlin. Run."

She picked up the hare, face grim.

"Don't be stupid. You won't get far," said Mahi.

I ignored her. "Scream out what they've done to us. The people out there. Maybe they'll listen."

Mahi scoffed. "It's a monarchy, not a bloody commune."

We ran. We ran through the west courtyard, our sandals slapping against lamplit paths, orienting ourselves to where the singing had come from. Our breath came in pants, and my face was sticky from dried tears. I held the urn like a rugby ball. It rattled dangerously in my arms. It would be the worst for Sitara's ashes to blow into my mouth.

I bellowed over and over. "The raja's men killed our sister."

Leena's shout was breathless. "They kidnapped us. We don't belong here."

No voices came in response. No help came from strangers. It was as if the night swallowed our voices whole, and the only sound was our footsteps and those behind us.

The soldiers captured us with insulting ease. I rued how often I'd spurned the treadmill at the gym, how often I'd chosen cake over Zumba classes. A short, squat man lifted Leena bodily off her feet. A rush of air behind me, and then strong arms closed around my waist. I kicked backwards, clasping the lid onto the urn as we tangled together. We fell to the earth with a thud and a grunt, slotting together like spoons.

Some people would pay for a tumble in the dark with a

man like that. Washboard stomach, a panther's energy, power rolling off him in waves, a knowing glance in his eye like he'd know what to do to you in bed. Pity he played a central role in this nightmare. The arsehole.

The general slid his legs out from mine with a sigh and raked a hand through the wayward curl of his hair. "You could have spared us both that." He stood up and offered me a hand.

I looked down at the urn, relief flooding through me that I'd managed to keep it upright. Then I staggered to my feet without his help. Anxiety surged at the sound of my sister calling for me.

"Kiya? Kiya!" shouted Leena in desperation. She screamed as they pulled away, away from the stairwell leading up to the turquoise chamber, away into the dark night, though the hare sprang from her hands, thumped his hind feet and did his best to trip up the soldiers.

I tried to reach her, but this time, his stony-faced men were ready.

My mind snagged. "Is it because we tried to run? The raja promised we could stay in the turquoise chamber together." I said his name because I remembered it from court, and somehow, it had been burned into my brain. Maybe, if I used it, he might feel connected to us and take pity. "Deven, please help us."

The general flinched. "The raja issued an order for you to be separated. Even before you ran."

I didn't expect the unthinkable cruelty of them separating us on the eve of Sitara's funeral. But that is what they did. "No." My voice crescendoed through the night. "Please, no."

The general's obsidian eyes glinted in the lamplight. "He said you can stay with the hare. It was his little joke."

I recoiled, thinking back to the raja's words. *If you are good, you may remain in the turquoise chamber with the hare.* Bile rose in my throat. The soldiers' vice-like grip dug into my skin. I jerked from their grasp. "He said you weren't monsters."

"Sometimes that's all we are. You have my word she will be safe," said the general.

I shook with anger. "Your word is worth nothing."

Though Mahi had melted into the night–a bitter sign that she hadn't been our friend at all–Aayna was there, following Merlin towards us. Worry filled her doe-like eyes. "Should I go with her?" she asked as if that was any consolation.

It was better than Leena being alone, so I nodded.

The General pressed his lips together and didn't intervene.

Then it was my turn. We retraced our steps. The general led the way, with me at his side, and the foot soldiers mirrored every step. Somewhere along the route, I had lost my scarf. The general picked it up and didn't offer it back to me. He simply tucked it into his waistband as if it were a trophy. I angled my head away from him and wrapped my arms around the urn: one sister gone, the other wrenched away from me. My body was a rigid vessel that carried only rage and pain. I didn't even have the softness left to carry Merlin up the stairs. He sprang after me, his large feet slapping against the winding stone steps to the turquoise chamber.

At the door to the chamber, the general stopped. "Good night."

My scarf still hung from his waistband. I ripped it out. "Rot in hell."

When the footmen bolted the door behind me, I leaned against it and shut my eyes, breathing hard. All was quiet apart from the shuffling of footmen outside the door and Merlin scuttling under the bed. I dropped the scarf and allowed the warmth of the urn to seep through my skin. A steaming plate of potato curry and naan bread waited for me on the table, but I ignored it. Instead, I sank onto the bed, placed the urn next to the lamp on the bedside table and kicked off my shoes before face-planting into the pillow.

My heart thudded dully in my chest. I let myself cry. The world spun.

I would scheme. I would find allies. I would ferret out the truth of my mother's history with this godforsaken place. I would peel away all the layers of deception that had led to this moment.

We would escape from Jalapashu. I would make the raja and his men pay.

Goosebumps chased up my arms at a sudden chill. I heaved myself up to check the turret windows were shut. They were. Outside, the moon glimmered over the west courtyard, where embers still glowed.

A crash came from behind me, followed by a bossy, exasperated, and oh-so-achingly familiar voice. "You really need to pull yourself together if you're going to get out of here."

My thoughts scrambled. I spun around, jaw slack.

The heavy-bottomed bedside lamp lay in a mess of ceramic and wires on the floor, though I had been nowhere near it. Mercifully, it hadn't taken Sitara's urn with it. The voice concerned me most of all. I searched the chamber, certain my imagination had conjured it. Clearly, my longings had made me susceptible to fantasy. Grief really did turn a person inside out. If Leena had been with me, I could have measured my reaction against hers. A failsafe to make sure I wasn't going mad.

But she wasn't with me.

She was holed up somewhere in the kingdom, grieving all alone.

I watched the shifting darkness, pale with fear. My voice was mouse quiet. "Is someone there?"

"I mean, honestly," said the familiar voice. "You could have spilt all the ashes left of me in that chase across the palace grounds. And I can't believe you two thought I gave my life for the jewel. I gave it for you, you idiot."

Then I saw her. A chill ran down my spine at an unnatural play of light near the dresser. It was my sister and not my sister. Not human, but a shimmering, translucent figure comprised of mist and shadow. The figure rippled and shifted, so much so that a photograph would have been impossible. My heartbeat thundered as I studied it. The figure had my father's heart-shaped face and a mass of midnight hair, and it wore the same linen shift dress in faded orange that Sitara had worn only that morning. A faint scent of orange and magnolia filled the air that had not been there before, the exact tang of Sitara's favourite perfume. A perfume she had worn since her twenties and remained loyal to despite our teasing.

I closed my eyes. "I'll count to five. When I open my eyes, you won't be there anymore. One, two, three…" As I counted, the icy air made my body tingle despite the summer's night and closed windows. On five, I opened my eyes, but it was still there.

The figure smiled. "Isn't magic wonderful?"

CHAPTER 8

Merlin hopped out from under the bed, bouncing with happiness for the first time since Sitara's death.

A giddiness overcame me. Only a day had passed, but I had missed Sitara like it had been a lifetime. "Is that really you?"

Her voice was thinner than I remembered, lacking depth. It ebbed and flowed like a radio station that wasn't quite on the right frequency. "Who else could it be? I died, you cremated me, and now you need me, so I'm haunting you. You didn't really think I'd just die and toddle off into the afterlife?"

I stepped towards her as my awareness stretched to include the new possibilities. "So you're a ghost?"

Sitara stared straight through me into the depths of my soul, her green eyes impatient. "Do I look like a banshee? Of course, I'm a ghost. I've seen your reaction to discovering magic before, you know. In the cave. Your brain is wildly recalibrating now, but let's cut to the part where we make a plan to get you and Leena out of Jalapashu."

Previously, I'd written off ghosts, witches and hidden

kingdoms as the fabric of fairy tales, fantasy books or horror movies. I had so many questions, but most of all, I wanted to hug Sitara. Leena, with her scientific leanings, would have been wary, but I threw restraint out of the window. For all the terror of my ghost sister appearing, it was heart-wrenchingly miraculous to see her again. When my arms closed around her, a glacial coldness hit my core. There was no warm flesh to embrace because Sitara's body was gone.

"Oh!" I cried out.

"Serves you right. I've been gone all of two seconds, and you can't stay united." The ghost flickered and disappeared.

"Leena's headstrong," I retorted, so used to the sibling dynamic of defence and attack. My eyes darted, searching for her. Though the cold persisted in the chamber, I worried she wouldn't reappear. That she had left me again.

But Merlin wasn't fooled. He hopped to the dresser, ears erect and alert.

Shadowy Sitara reappeared there. This time, she was a mere outline of my sister's curvy body, a flash of faded orange and sea-green eyes. She flung her arm out, and the bowl of shells rocketed off the dresser and scattered in shards across the floor. "Stop fooling around and listen."

I bit my lip. On her best days, human Sitara had been exacting, protective and full of empathy and warmth. This Sitara was different. Somehow, during her transition, ghost Sitara had become all business and no pleasure. The round edges of her maternal qualities had been filed away, leaving sharp edges. Not to mention her carelessness with beautiful objects, in contrast to her care of objects as an archaeologist. She was a distant echo of herself.

I strained to hear her fluctuating voice and to find the features in the shadows that I loved so much.

"I don't know how long I can hold on," said Sitara. "The raja won't let you go. To free yourselves, you'll have to find the jewel." The flickering grew ever more erratic. "You need to find a way to anchor me here. Bind me to an object. Merlin knows–" She faded away, leaving only the faintest traces of mist and the scent of magnolia in her wake.

The black and tan hare cavorted in circles where Sitara's ghost had been only moments before.

I crouched down to him and coaxed him to stillness. "What do you know, Merlin?"

When he didn't answer, I drew the drapes, stripped off my funeral clothes and tossed aside the scatter cushions from the four-poster bed. The mattress dipped as I crawled, bone weary, onto it. The weight of my body was nothing compared to the weight of my sorrow and confusion. Though I didn't fear ghost Sitara, my mind churned, and I doubted I would get a wink of sleep.

I wondered where Leena slept, whether she had the wisps of Aanya's songs to comfort her or whether she cried herself to sleep. Perhaps Sitara had appeared to her too. Missing them, I thought of how the three of us had slept entwined in the long days after our parents had died. Only when the sharp pangs of grief dulled did we reluctantly walk our own paths again. I didn't want to sleep alone, so instead, I fetched Merlin and climbed back into bed. The hare nudged closer to me, black and tan fur moulting over the silken covers.

Although my mind reeled, somehow, it seemed the bed in the turquoise chamber became a boat or a cradle that rocked me to sleep. *Magic, magic, magic,* went the wild chant that circled like starlings in my head. My breathing grew deeper, and my eyelids drooped with fatigue. When I could no longer hold onto the threads of my thoughts, I let myself slip away into a dreamless sleep.

I WOKE IN A TANGLE OF SHEETS AS THE SUN ROSE. MY THROAT scratched from unshed tears. Merlin gnawed at the intricate carvings of the headboard, his pungent butt bouncing against the crown of my head. Confusion clouded my brain as I took in my surroundings. When I saw Sitara's urn on the bedside table and the crashed lamp on the floor, yesterday's memories came flooding back.

I wanted so desperately to check to make sure Leena was okay. I needed to tell her about Sitara's ghostly visit.

If they had harmed even a hair on her head, I would raze Jalapashu to the ground.

Groaning, I heaved myself into a sitting position and reached for the hare. "Put a sock in it, will you?" I set him down in the middle of the bed, away from mischief. Then I padded across the room in my underwear to inch the drapes aside and peek out across Jalapashu. The kingdom slept. Then I put a careful ear to the locked door of my chamber. All was quiet in the palace. No boots marched through the marbled halls. No foot soldiers or staff hurried back and forth. No painted elephants trumpeted in the court of the raja. There was nothing to do in my locked chamber, so I downed a glass of water and returned to bed to plot my next steps. When Merlin nestled between my legs like a roosting chicken, I tangled my fingers in his soft fur.

"I wish it had been a dream. I wish I had woken in my own bed, and all I had to worry about was Sitara's grumpiness and fulfilling an order of teacups."

The hare snivelled in sympathy, and I almost felt a kinship with him.

"I've let Leena down. What if she's hurt and struggling to cope without me? If Sitara weren't already dead, I'd murder her myself. I really would. How could she get us tangled up in all this?" Even as I spoke, I worried her ghost would reappear to scold me. I worried that I would never see her again. I swallowed hard as dawn rays spiralled across the turquoise chamber. "But we can't turn back the clock, can we?"

The hare's honey-hued eyes didn't leave my face. He was a good listener as conversation partners went.

I pulled absentmindedly at his long ears, trying to bring order to the battlefield of my thoughts. "They're a well-trained operation. The guard has changed. They're alert and armed. Even if you were an attack dog or a territorial swan, we wouldn't stand a chance against them, Merlin." My heart raced as I tried to recall every detail of our conversation. "Sitara said to find the jewel, which would unlock our magic, but I can't get my head around it. How is that possible? We saw it shatter when she fought those attackers. Sitara spoke of *binding* and *anchoring* and *magic* as if being a witch was as natural to her as breathing. She said she had seen my reaction to finding out about magic in the cave. What cave?"

Merlin, until now uncharacteristically relaxed in my lap, pounded me with his forelegs and snorted.

The poor thing was as unsettled as me. A few days ago, I would have unceremoniously dumped him on the floor and prodded Sitara about housing him in a hutch. With my sisters gone, I'd developed a strange attachment to him. Not only because Sitara had loved him but because he brought the familiarity of home to the strangeness of Jalapashu. Because he was family. To give him his credit, though he was cooped up in the turquoise chamber with me, he had tempered his destructive habits. He had used the litter tray Aanya had brought, and apart from the headboard and a slight ravaging of the bed cushions, he had behaved.

I held his bulk against my chest. "I know you miss them, too. I'll look after you." My brows knitted. *Magic, magic, magic* went the chant in my head, not allowing me to forget. This time I didn't deny it, suppress it, or try to wrangle the idea into something more palatable. "Merlin, they brought Sitara's books here. The jewel is gone, but what if I can find the books?" I recalled Sitara's icy arrows and how the tempest had torn through the air at her command. My pulse sped as I imagined what I might be capable of myself. "What if they help with my magical awakening?"

I quietened the small voice inside me that told me not to stand out. That it would be better to be agreeable and follow the rules. The voice that said the raja wouldn't hurt us if we were ordinary. The truth was women had been told all their lives to fit in and to please others. We had been told we would be safe if we didn't challenge power. Where had that ever got us?

A frisson of anticipation raced through me. If I were powerful, it would be impossible for the raja to hold us against our will. I could control my fate.

I smoothed my hand over the hare's skull and followed his ears to their velvet tips. "I'll play the raja's game. I'll smile and build allies. But every chance I get, I'll glean information about the kingdom and the magic here. And when they least expect it, Leena and I will break free."

Merlin shifted in the dawn light. Then he emitted a noxious gas.

I retched. "No need for that. I wasn't leaving you out of the equation. Despite your issues, you're part of the family." My chest tightened. "Imagine that we succeed, Merlin. Imagine our escape leads to a raid on this kingdom, and a judge throws the book at them."

But that's not what I imagined. I imagined unspeakable things happening to every single brute who had stolen Sitara's future and laid a hand on us. Every person who had commanded or contributed to our suffering had to pay. I wanted justice, but I also wanted revenge, and the poison of that need snuck into my soul. How could I ever be at peace at the potter's wheel again with feral rage and enduring grief inside me?

Merlin's assessing golden gaze unnerved me.

It was ridiculous to be talking to him as if he were human. My mind flashed back to Sitara, how she had barricaded herself in her bedroom and talked to him, too. He obviously had that impact on people, or maybe all pets did. I gave him a sharp tap. "You're no help. Sitara said *you know* something, but it's not like you can show me with us stuck here. Or tell me, given you're a semi-incontinent hare."

The hare's black and tan body stiffened. Then he unleashed an earsplitting scream. His jaw gaped as he unleashed another–a shrill, high-pitched whistle that cut through the air like a knife–and another one after that.

"What's going on? Are you hurt? They're going to send armies to get to the bottom of this racket." My toes curled at the sound. I turned him over to check for injuries, though he struggled to stay upright.

Nothing. He was soft and smooth, with no wound or physical trauma in sight. At this rate, he'd wake the whole palace. My heart fluttered like a trapped bird in a cage. I needed this crucial thinking time.

"Merlin, stop that," I hissed, with none too gentle a shake.

The hare, who had never done my bidding, stopped short.

But the footmen responded all the same. The bolt dragged across the door, and two bleary-eyed soldiers tumbled into the chamber. On their heels was the general, his dark curly hair mussed from sleep, his shirt rumpled, untucked and open to his chest.

He arched an eyebrow and barked at his men to stay outside.

I flushed, remembering I wore only underwear and wrapped myself like a tortilla in the covers. Merlin settled, tranquil and serene, on Leena's side of the bed—the utter monster.

"Will you ever be properly clothed when we meet?" said the general.

"Do you ever wait for an invitation before charging in?" I shot back.

TO SAVE A SISTER

"The men reported hearing voices, and then the hare unleashed ... whatever that was." He huffed and buttoned his shirt. "It is five in the morning. In case you hadn't noticed, the rest of the palace is sound asleep."

I gritted my teeth. "Where's my sister?"

His jaw clenched. "Sleeping in her quarters."

My hate surged like the tide. "I want to see her."

He shrugged. "Take it up with the raja." His gaze darted to the broken lamp on the floor. He seemed to give Merlin the blame for it, which suited me much better than him realising Sitara's ghost had been responsible. "I take it you can control the hare, or shall I have a sleeping draught sent up for him?"

Right on cue, as if to try the general's patience, Merlin's jaw opened.

I'd promised myself to build allies, but I couldn't help a touch of arrogance. *This had better work.* "Thank you for your concern, but I have it under control." I lifted my finger.

The hare's amber eyes glinted, but he clamped his mouth shut.

The general gave a curt nod. "You'll find spare clothes in the dresser. I will send Aanya with fresh towels and breakfast, and to deal with the hare's mess." He frowned. "It is a little unusual for you to allow him to sleep in your bed."

That got right up my nose. "From everything that has happened in the last twenty-four hours, you pick up on that?"

His dark eyes glimmered. "At eight o'clock, I will return to escort you to your appointment with the seer. I trust you find this satisfactory?"

The seer. Even the word sent a shiver up my spine. A tight smile pulled at my lips. Sarcasm punctuated every syllable. "Just dreamy."

If I offended him, he didn't show it. "Until then, Kiya."

He strode away, and the door thudded shut, reinforced by the bolt.

"These people aren't like us, Merlin." I glared at him. "Did you confuse being a hare with being an emergency siren?" I chewed my lip. "Don't take this the wrong way, but it was weird when Sitara insisted on getting you. When we were young, Leena and I used to beg Mum and Dad for a cat, but they always refused. Sitara never cared much for animals. Apart from dinosaurs, that is. Only because of their history and fossilized bones."

Merlin grunted. The look in his eye would have withered a lesser woman. If he could talk, he would have been an arsehole. There was no doubt about it.

"Adopting you coincided with Sitara's withdrawal from us. I wonder, all those children's stories about witches and black cats…" My voice trailed off. *Magic, magic, magic*, went the chant in my head. Understanding dawned. "Is that why she gave you a mythological name?"

The hare's full cheeks turned my way, his gilded eyes unclouded and clever.

I hated hares. They were stubborn and unpredictable: a whole heap of bother and bite wrapped in a fluffy package. But this one had grown on me. Maybe because Sitara had chosen him, maybe because he had chosen us. I caressed his soft back, allowing my hand to linger there, feather-light, sensing the rhythm of his breath and where he liked to be touched.

Laughter bubbled up inside me like a fountain. "You were Sitara's familiar. And now, you're mine."

As Merlin relaxed against my hand, intuition told me he wouldn't bite me again.

He was saving his bite for someone else.

CHAPTER 9

At last, the kingdom woke. I had a cursory wash and dressed in an embroidered tunic over leggings I found in the dresser. With nowhere safe to store Sitara's ashes, I placed a napkin underneath the urn at an odd angle to alert me to any tampering with it.

Then I stood at the turret window to witness the unfolding of a new day in Jalapashu. Labourers loaded vans, women hurried children along, bells tolled in the temples and groundsmen hosed flower beds in the palace gardens. I wasn't fooled by the sheen of normality.

A wail built inside me at the sight of two women in the west courtyard sweeping away the debris from Sitara's funeral pyre. There was nothing normal about a kingdom that cut itself off from the world. A kingdom that sent troops out to blunder into people's homes and shed blood. A kingdom that imprisoned strangers without due process.

When Aanya arrived, she brought breakfast with her, just as the general had promised. Neither had she forgotten Merlin. The hare bounded up to her, eager for fresh hay and water, carrot tops and basil leaves.

Her eyes were kind but wary. Her last glimpse of me had

been my distress when Leena had been taken. "I hope you managed some sleep." Her uniform was neatly pressed, and her black hair was tied back into a bun that revealed an undercut.

I nodded. "How is Leena? Were you with her?"

"She misses you, but she is unharmed."

I gulped. "Is that how it will remain? Does the raja harm his prisoners?"

"I am a maid. I have no experience of these matters." She gestured to my clothing. "Your own things should return from the laundry later today, but you won't need them here. The general says I should give your measurements to the palace tailor, and he can make whatever you desire."

My heart pounded at the assumption we would be here long term. Every cell in my body itched to flee, but she didn't have a key to leave the chamber. She, too, had to knock to be released.

"I thought Mahi might accompany you this morning," I said.

"Mahi is not like the rest of us. She has the raja's trust. She plays by her own rules, within reason." Aanya crossed the chamber to set out my breakfast at the corner table, together with gleaming cutlery. Chai slopped over the edge of a gold-rimmed teacup onto a saucer painted with coral flowers.

In other circumstances, I might have stopped to admire the handiwork. That version of me seemed a lifetime ago.

Aanya continued. "Other magicals of her strength must live in the palace, but Mahi is free to come and go as she pleases. It's easier that way. Trapping Mahi here would make their lives difficult. She doesn't care about appearances or saying things to keep the peace. We often work side by side. The raja finds it amusing to pair my sunny disposition with Mahi's crabby one."

Even in one day, I knew it was true. Sweet Aanya was a

foil for Mahi's permanent scowl. They were an incongruous pair: one old, grumpy and buxom, the other young, gentle and boyish. Though we were strangers, and our world had been turned upside down, I trusted them somewhat. But I was wary of mistaking their small kindnesses for friendship. I was wary about how Mahi had offered advice but turned into the night after the funeral without a second glance.

Other magicals of her strength must live in the palace. I took a deep breath. "Aanya, are you magical?"

She smiled. "We all have our own magic. You didn't think you were the only witches around here, did you? Sit. Eat. The cook has made you a masala omelette with chilli paratha and a side of mango chutney. I hope the tea isn't too strong for you. It's steaming hot with a dash of spices."

I sat down at the breakfast table, a thousand questions in my mind. "What magic do you practice?"

An undercurrent of anxiety threaded through her words. "I will satisfy your curiosity if you eat. The general is particular about timekeeping. He won't be late, and neither should you."

I tore a piece of chilli paratha and folded it into my mouth. An explosion of spice hit my taste buds. I doused my flaming mouth with hot tea.

Aanya pretended not to notice. A tiny row of hoop earrings on her cartilage glinted in the sun as she spoke. The top one had a tiny amber stone on it. "Not all witches are the same. A witch may be good at spells or potions. Or their strength may be energy rituals or scrying. Perhaps they can speak to spirits or befriend animals. They may foretell the future and be adept at tarot or crystal balls or tea leaves. They may be a kitchen witch and infuse their recipes with magic. They may be a hedge witch connected to the earth or a folk witch channelling ancestral and historical magic. There is no one size fits all with magic."

I nodded, soaking up every kernel of information, though logic still warred with belief in my head.

It was easier to scoff than to open my mind. Maybe that was why Jalapashu remained hidden. Our brains blipped when we saw strange things as if we'd rather forget than accept reality had shifted.

My pulse raced. Time had come to embrace our new reality. "What's your skill, Aanya?"

Her doe-like eyes softened. "I can sense the energy of broken things and respond. My singing eases anxiety in all who hear me."

I grew quiet inside. "Prove it. Wipe the grief from my heart."

Aanya shook her head. "I can't do that. I've been smoothing the raw edges of your grief, but doing more would dim your humanity. It would put a dent in your love for Sitara. Love without grief is love without sacrifice. That is no love at all."

Aayna's humming and singing *had* brought ease. I sensed the truth of it in my bones. Her hymn at Sitara's funeral had fused the broken pieces of me just enough to allow me to function.

"Did you sing to my sister last night?"

"I did." Her face softened. "I drew her a bath and added salts. I sang. When she slept, there were no nightmares."

It wasn't a small thing that she had brought my brokenhearted sister solace. It was everything.

I swallowed hard. Any minute now, the general would return. I toyed with my food, treading carefully. I needed to use my time with her wisely. By the bath, Merlin lapped his water and munched on a carrot top. "I haven't seen vehicles travel out of the kingdom. You can't produce everything here. You must have to travel for food and medicine. What about books and furniture?" A life without online deliveries seemed unimaginable, let alone one lived cut off from the outside world. "Surely Jalapashu doesn't exist like an island inside England's borders?"

She scanned the room, looking for what she could tidy, dust or replace. She clearly knew every nook and cranny of the turquoise chamber. "Jalapashu is self-sustaining. Our soils are fertile from England's rain, and our groundsmen have a vast bank of seeds. You will get used to our seasonal dishes and annual rotations. Some years, we have a surplus of courgettes and sweet peppers. Others, a glut of grapes and apples. Our cellars are always full. Our medicines are well stocked. As for books, they are catalogued and held in the vast palace library. We have no need to go beyond the walls of the settlement."

My fork hovered in the air. *All books are held in the palace library.* Now I knew where to find Sitara's books.

Aanya's attention lingered on the broken lamp and shards of glass and shell in the rubbish pail. "Oh, that's a shame. They were lovely pieces. I didn't think potters could be clumsy."

I instinctively protected the secret of Sitara's haunting. "Sorry." It niggled me that she knew about my profession when we'd never spoken of it.

Aanya's smile was soft and accepting as if she chalked up the mishap to an outburst of grief. But when she poked around in the shards, her brow furrowed. She flicked me a questioning glance. Too late, I remembered she could sense the magic of broken things. "You lie."

I held my breath for a beat. There was rot at the heart of this kingdom with its marvels and magic, its columned throne rooms and majestic fountains. But how far did it go? What if not everyone in this place was an enemy? "I don't know if I can trust you."

The maid met my eyes. "There are never any guarantees, especially in a place like Jalapashu where wild creatures roam amongst us, and there is never any surety that the water and wine you drink hasn't had an extra ingredient inserted into it or that as you turn your back at a party, a witch may cast a spell. It's up to you, Kiya. Will you trust me? Will you trust me when you are all alone?"

A dark cloud of foreboding mushroomed in my belly. Our fates balanced on a knife edge, but when my Merlin bounded over to Aanya and scampered between her trouser legs, I decided it was a sign. He could be an utterly ordinary hare and not my familiar at all. Either way, animals had an innate understanding of who to trust. Unless he was a cheap date and liked her because of a handful of hay.

So I asked simply, "How did you come to be here, in this palace, serving the raja?"

She crouched next to Merlin, smoothing her thumb and forefinger over his silken ear. Her memories gave her eyes a faraway look. "When I was a young girl, the old raja heard me singing at the market. My teacher often asked me to sing to calm my classmates down. The raja had an inkling I might be magical and that my magic would be amplified if I touched the crown jewel. He offered my parents a place for me at court if I went with him. They were poor then, before I could send them my earnings, so they said yes, and I've been here ever since. When the old raja died, he asked me to ease his passage out of this life. His wife disliked me for the intrusion, but the raja was grateful. After his death, she demoted me to a maid."

"I'm sorry." My skin crawled. I couldn't imagine not being able to determine my own life path.

"Don't be. It's not a bad life." She pushed herself up to her feet. "Let me help you with your hair before the general comes. It's customary in Jalapashu to brush long hair until it shines. A shining crown of hair is said to bring luck, regardless of gender."

My mind flashed to the raja's long hair and Mahi's pixie

cut. "I'll do that myself, but perhaps I can learn other customs from you."

"As you wish." She handed me a hairbrush made of polished sandalwood from a drawer.

I studied its slender handle, adorned with tiny jewels, then pulled it through my tangled tresses.

"I hope I have earned your trust another way, even if the story of my past wasn't enough." A shy smile pulled at the corners of her mouth. "What is a witch without spells and potions? The hare has eaten his grass that I boiled myself in sage water this morning. I have spoken the incantation."

Boots sounded in the stairwell outside the turquoise chamber.

My heart raced like a stallion across a green. "What incantation?"

"By the end of the day, he will have his voice returned to him." Her eyes shone. "Maybe then you'll begin to trust me and tell me what happened here last night."

I drew in a sharp breath as the thud of the bolt dragged against the door. "Why would you help us?"

Aayna sighed. "Because all that glitters is not gold."

The general, infuriatingly handsome in his uniform, stepped into the room. "Do you have anything to report?" he said to Aanya.

Her eyes darted to the rubbish pail. She shook her head. "All is as it should be."

"Good." The general looked down at me, cloaked in his self-righteous authority. "Are you ready?"

Game on. "Yes." Every minute took me closer to wiping the smug look off their faces. I glanced at the urn on the bedside table. Tonight, Merlin would unravel the spool of secrets Sitara had left us with.

I just had to get through the day.

CHAPTER 10

I rushed to keep pace with the general, senses reeling from the hustle and bustle of the kingdom. My sandals slapped against the sidewalk as I matched two strides to each of his. Grief and worry clung to me like a shadow. The arrogant swine didn't cuff me or drag me along or even cast me more than a glance. He just assumed I'd follow. After all, what choice did I have? Part of me wanted to scream for help, but I heeded Sitara's warning: I'd need to turn the tables of power to break free.

So, I tried to bring ease to my tense body. I willed myself to remember the route, store every detail in my memory and ferret out opportunities for escape.

From the centre of Jalapashu, the royal palace looked even more impressive. Its glistening white walls, domes, turrets and gardens were crassly opulent compared to the simplicity of the town itself. The wide streets were dusty but clean of litter. The raja's subjects went about their business wearing *saris*, *salwar kameez* or *kurtas* like me: tunics over leggings. Some cooked at the side of the street, others polished shoes or cut hair in small shop fronts. Many worked as labourers, lugging wheelbarrows of bricks, soil or plants along the pitted roads. I peeked into a temple, where a holy man draped in a dhoti–a piece of cloth draped around his waist and legs–performed a ritual with tea lights and garlands of flowers.

Merlin hopped after us, prompting surprise from passersby.

The general strode ahead, never slowing. "I can't believe you brought the hare."

Witches were supposed to keep their familiar close at hand, and I was determined to test the theory that he was mine. "I told you. He's destructive when left alone. He needs to stretch his legs."

"You let him accompany you to your sister's funeral and sleep in your bed. Perhaps next, you might ask the tailor to make him some clothes."

The smirk in his voice infuriated me. "Don't be ridiculous."

"The seer requires many fragile and precious objects for her art. I hope the hare will not be a nuisance."

"I'd quite like it if he bit your nose off." A pause. "What is a seer exactly?"

"Someone who sees glimpses of the future, of course."

"Right." My voice was tart. "Silly me."

We settled into an uneasy silence as we walked through a market where bearded men with dusky skin sold honeydew melons and ripe mangoes. The air was thick with the fruits' sweet scent. Stall after stall paraded their wares: exquisite pottery, jars of turmeric and saffron, handmade jewellery, instruments fashioned from hide and bark, colourful shawls and looms of woven art. Schoolgirls in sunshine yellow smocks and schoolboys in shorts darted through the stalls, scolded by the merchants for their carelessness. They gawped at Merlin and lunged for him, but he evaded them with ease.

The general urged me onwards through the market,

glowering as an old woman in a frayed *sari* beckoned me to her table. Notes of caramel and stewed milk hung in the air.

"Pretty stranger, come and taste my sweets." She had stacked her wares at the very front of the table to give the illusion of plenty, but her forlorn eyes and bony hands told a different story.

"Keep moving." His warm touch on the small of my back prevented me from slowing down.

Sarcasm rolled off my tongue. "Yes, sir."

I snuck a look at him. The early morning rays illuminated his profile. He had an angular jaw, now clenched with impatience. His cheekbones were high, regal even, and his forehead was broad. His nose had a bend on the bridge like it had been broken before. The silver scar on his eyebrow and the tattoo hidden today beneath the high collar of his jacket piqued my curiosity.

They also meant it would be easy to identify him to the police.

"Don't you have better things to do than babysit me?"

His tone was mildly mocking. "Spending the morning with a beautiful woman is always a pleasure. Besides, you and your sister are the raja's top priority."

I flushed. "He must have a short list of priorities, then."

He could have made this easy for me, but his silence was deafening.

We pressed on through the lantern-lined streets with eye-catching trees. Not the oaks and yew trees that belonged in English soil, but eucalyptus, banyan and mahogany trees that we sped past on our way into the kingdom. They reminded me that the laws of science and logic faded in Jalapashu.

It wasn't a comforting thought.

Up close, I realised the eerie stone sculptures on the red brick houses were gargoyles. They lined the roof of each property, two apiece, their faces twisted into fierce snarls. Heat roiled in my belly as I strained my neck to view them.

Each gargoyle had a unique variation. I spotted one that resembled a snarling lion, its mane flowing back in the wind. Beside it, a serpent with wings coiled tightly, ready to strike. On the next rooftop, a horned demon bared its sharp teeth in a menacing grin. Its partner was a misshapen fish head with bulging eyes and a lolling tongue. Together, they looked like an army or guardians of a dark secret.

Even Merlin seemed worried. He bounded closer to me just as the general swerved into an alleyway that stank of cow dung. At the end stood a narrow, grey, three-storey-high house, remarkable for its height compared to other housing in the kingdom. It leaned precariously as if it might topple over. Every storey had a small balcony filled with herbs and withered plants. Its windows, narrow and tall, reminded me of a chapel. The front door was riddled with woodworm and stood ajar.

The general made a beeline for it. "This way."

A beady-eyed parrot guarded the threshold. It rose into the air and squawked a greeting. "He's back. Welcome! She said you were coming."

"I hate that thing," said the general as he stepped into the house.

"How rude," said the parrot. "I'm not the one who brought a dirty hare." Then it spread its luminous green wings and took off inside the house.

I followed them, heart pummelling. Inside the house, the walls were a deep shade of burgundy. The air was stale as if windows were seldom opened. Everywhere I looked, there were lamps and shelves filled with all manner of fragile and mystical objects: crystals, decks of tarot cards, clicking pendulums, mirrors and scrolls. The kitchen was cluttered with pots and an array of mortar and pestles clogged with the residue of strange-smelling powders. Each step risked toppling something.

The parrot, perched on a gilded cage, seemed to be the

only living thing in the house. Its squalls echoed through the air. "Watch out. Watch out. Clumsy hare."

I scooped Merlin into my arms. Even though I had only just awakened to this new reality, the presence of magic was palpable in the air. I tasted it on my tongue and recognised it in the total silence.

The general raised his voice. "We do not have all day, seer."

Thudding footsteps descended from the second floor, making the mystical objects judder. "All in good time. These old bones can only move so fast."

My stomach plummeted as Mahi appeared on the stairs.

In the turquoise chamber, she had held herself humbly, but now there was pride in the glint of her eye and a take-me-as-I-am thrust to her chest. It suddenly hit me that I had judged her all wrong. I had pegged her as a palace maid when all the signs had been there from the start that she was more: her lack of uniform, the way she dressed as she pleased at court, how the raja sought her opinion, and she was free to come and go from the palace despite being magical.

I set down the hare. "You? You're the seer?" The betrayal hit me in my gut.

Mahi sucked in her lined cheeks as though she'd tasted a sour lemon. She wore her usual black harem trousers with a faded T-shirt, this time depicting Luther Vandross. She clearly had a love of the nineties era. She had gelled her silver pixie cut in an odd manner that gave her the look of a highland cow. "I'm sorry I didn't tell you everything. A seer learns quickly that there's an art to the truth. It has to come in drips, not a gush. The truth can drown us if we're not ready for it."

"A gush, a gush, a lovely little gush," sang the parrot.

A visceral urge to knock him from his perch came over

me. Next to me, Merlin squirmed as if his bladder threatened to respond to the ditty.

"Don't mind Babbu. I've trained him to speak his mind. He is very loyal and an excellent guard. I've not had to lock my front door in fifteen years," said Mahi.

"Presumably being a renowned seer helps keep all but the idiots away," said the General.

I blended him out and fixed my gaze on Mahi. "You knew we'd come?"

She nodded. "I did."

The general, the hare and the parrot followed our conversation like the to-and-fro in a tennis rally.

I chewed my inner cheek and tried to order my thoughts. "Did you know Sitara would die?"

"I did not see a future in which she would live."

I couldn't lose my head. Leena needed me. But the tide of my emotions was too strong. I choked back a sob. "You didn't even try to help."

The general cut in. "Enough. Mahi, the raja is impatient for your analysis on whether the sisters are witches. Perhaps you can make a start." He eyed the parrot. "I'll wait outside."

Mahi dusted her hands together. "Of course, Deven. It won't be long. Everything is prepared."

"Good." His expression was unreadable as he glanced at me. Then he threaded his way through the house into the sunshine, remarkably light on his feet for a large man.

My heart was a hollow ache in my chest when I turned back to Mahi. "One sister dead. The other locked up away from me. I wasn't foolish enough to think you were a friend yesterday, but I didn't think you had been playing a role in getting close to us."

Her hackles rose. "Nonsense. I have known you would be visiting for a long time. In every version of that future, you could only function if Aanya and I made the transition easier.

By middle age, it's no secret to you that life can be dark and uncertain. It's not always rainbows and unicorns. Sometimes, it's tempests and tigers. Having friends can help ease the path."

Magic, magic, magic, came the call from my soul, urging me to listen. I swept my gaze around Mahi's house: how glimmers of sun caught the dust motes in the air, how Babbu the parrot hopped from one foot to another like he knew what was coming. Only yesterday, I would have rubbished the suggestion that a seer could exist outside of Greek mythology. Even Nostradamus and Rasputin had been phoneys.

"So tell me, seer. What do you have planned? A crystal ball or poring over the shape of tea leaves?"

Mahi drew her kohl eyebrows to a sharp point. "No one likes a sceptic. But go ahead. I'm not the one who's floundering like a newborn baby learning how to suck a teat for the first time. I know yesterday was hard. I'm sorry about that. There will be many hard days ahead. But I have great hopes for you, Kiya, and your impact on Jalapashu. The question is, will you trust me?"

I didn't know whether I should give her another chance. What if all we had to do was hold out until the raja tired of us and let us go? I looked at Merlin for reassurance.

The hare stared straight back at me. In the silent language that had developed between us, I found myself able to read his slightest movements. In the twitch of his nose and the forward hop of his black and tan body, I found my answer. We were so far into this mess that I was prepared to forgive Mahi's deception. The raja had proven himself untrustworthy by separating Leena and me. How could I ever believe that we would satisfy his terms for release? There was no turning back; there was only moving forward.

My mind roared with the now-familiar refrain–*magic,*

magic, magic–as if being in Jalapashu had uncorked a bottle that could never again be sealed. "I'm ready."

"I was hoping you'd say that." Mahi smiled slowly. "Babbu, let's show Kiya where we'll be working."

The parrot's feathers shone a deep green in the low light as he took flight.

CHAPTER 11

The parrot flew deeper into the house, towards the back, where pale wood met natural light as if Mahi had unpeeled the layers of her womb-like home to suit me. Though small and cramped, there was a potter's wheel, a sink, shelving and an adequate kiln. Two small worktables overflowed with bags of clay, an array of tools, glazes and paintbrushes.

"Once, Jalapashu had a great pottery master that created marvellous and fearsome objects. We have never seen his like again, and perhaps we never will. His workshop was packed away many moons ago. This is all I could salvage." Mahi's eyes gleamed. "Is there anything missing?"

Whatever she provided, this workshop would still miss a thousand elements of what made Soul Pottery mine: the imprint of my fingers on my weathered tools, beloved projects lined on shelves, and the sense of freedom. Who could create in these circumstances?

I meant to be polite. My mouth had other ideas. "The raja wants me to make pottery? What a twisted bastard." If so, I would make him masterpieces to fill a thousand slop buckets.

She harrumphed. "This is not the raja's idea. It is mine. We all have innate talents, Kiya. For me, it was my natural willingness to face and speak the truth, however difficult. From there, it was a small step to becoming a seer. Although my talents have naturally grown since my humble beginnings." Her voice was unclouded by doubt as if the equation of whether I was a witch had already been solved. "For you, it's pottery. Leaning into your talents is where you will find your magic."

"I've made a thousand pots, Mahi. None of them were magical."

She snorted. "Pottery has been entwined with magic for centuries. In ancient Egypt, Khnum was said to have formed the first humans on a potter's wheel. But he was a god. Mere mortals like us must work hard to achieve less."

I stared at her, a headache forming. Jalapashu probably didn't have paracetamol. I'd have to swallow my pride and ask Aanya to sing me a lullaby.

"You're looking at me like I'm a flatpack instruction manual you can't figure out." She grouched. "Listen carefully. There are four keys to magic, and until yesterday, you didn't have any of them. The first key is an intellectual one, the acceptance of a new reality. It took your sister many months to accept that magic exists. It took you one day."

Merlin nudged me towards the potter's wheel, his nose in the back of my knee, single-minded and assertive. There, a tray of balled clay waited.

My belly fluttered as I sat on a stool that moulded perfectly to my bottom.

With no apron in sight, I rolled up my sleeves, picked up some clay and centred it on the wheel. I waited for instructions, out of sorts, as if this were my first time. As if I were a clay virgin when I'd been passionate about it for half my life. "And the second key?"

"The second key is emotional. Magic is not just an intellectual concept; it's a living, breathing force that flows through us and the world around us. It is seeded in us, abundant, waiting to grow."

I added a little water to the clay, hands quivering. My foot hovered above the pedal. It wasn't a big leap to understand the web of magic that connected the world. In a way, I'd always sensed it in skies wrapped in blue, the first bloom of daffodils, the sway of an elephant's trunk and the sound of a piano through an open window on a summer's day.

Mahi was on a roll. "The third key is ancestral, lineal, bound in your ties to this land. Sitara's death may have led you here, but you know in your gut that you would have ended up here eventually. You and Jalapashu are tied together like yin and yang, bread and butter, Tarzan and Jane."

My heart thrummed. "And the fourth?"

She shrugged. "Like anything else. Practice makes perfect. You can't expect to headline at Glastonbury if you sound like a chicken, can you? Well, it's the same with magic. Witches have harnessed the power of the natural world for centuries. Now it's your turn to tune into that power. Trust your intuition, Kiya. You'll find your way."

Babbu the parrot perched on the sink. "You can do it. You can do it. It's not nap time."

I gulped and pressed my foot to the wheel, but the familiar rhythms of making and shaping eluded me. Instead, I worked in a haze of uncertainty, my fingers clumsy, not knowing what to expect.

Mahi stood at my side, her voice washing over me. "Jalapashu is a magical place. Things happen here that are impossible elsewhere. Your sister Sitara knew that, and your mother before her. You must let go of your fear and explore your potential. It's as easy and as difficult as that."

Still, I stumbled. Tears pricked behind my eyes as I ruined my first attempt at a simple pot and attempted another.

Witnessing magic was one thing; it was quite another doing it myself. But Mahi was adamant.

"I've seen you do this in my visions. It's not a case of *if* you can do it. It's a case of *when*. Trust yourself." Mahi counselled me, her hand on my shoulder. "Focus on your breathing. As you inhale, imagine that you are drawing in the energy of the earth. As you exhale, imagine that you are releasing all of your fears and doubts. Put all your anxiety about the future into that vessel."

I let her words flow over me and regulated my breathing. There was power in the rise and fall of breath, the expansion and contraction of my ribcage. Within minutes, I lost myself to the rhythm of the spinning clay beneath my fingers. I'd always enjoyed the feeling of the cool, wet earth between my hands, but today it was different. It was effortless, unlike anything I'd experienced before. I made a hole at the centre of the clay, pulling it, trusting myself, trusting this place, trusting even Mahi and her parrot. A warmth spread through my body, an awakening of magic, as if the clay was alive and responded to my every thought and intention. The pot grew taller and rounder, its sides even and its base sturdy. I paused the wheel and picked a tool to make minor adjustments by hand.

"That's it," said Mahi. "Don't work with your hands. Work with your heart. Visualise yourself as a powerful witch, with magic flowing through your body like a river."

As I focused, my fingertips tingled. Energy flowed through me that I recognised as magic by the otherworldly light that glowed through the pot. I held steady as a strange sensation infused my chest, as if something were trying to escape. Driven by pure instinct, I said the word *tyāga* and exhaled in a whoosh. A rush of emotions flowed out of me and into the pot. For a moment, I floated, like all my burdens had been removed.

This is what Sitara had died for: this feeling of expansion, potential, self-knowledge and power.

Mahi's belly shook as she punched the air. "I knew it! I've been waiting for you for a long time, Kiya Marlowe. It worked, didn't it?"

Merlin spun in excited circles on the floor.

I nodded. My mouth was dry, and my hands were covered in clay. I looked down. The pot was exquisite: it was the size of a pumpkin, with rounded sides and an even lip around its tapered neck. Most staggering of all was how liberated I felt. Somehow, I'd made a container and siphoned my anxiety about the future into it. I was determined to get Leena back and to leave Jalapashu, but the futile worrying had simply evaporated.

The parrot looped the room, his wings carving lines through the dust motes. "Winner. Winner. Chicken dinner."

My breath hitched. "I don't understand. How did I know to speak the spell?"

"You have magic in your blood, Kiya. Spells come from books but can also be drawn from memories and intuition. It could be that you've even done magic before. Strange things that you explained away because the world pushes us to choose reason over a leap of faith. Perhaps a cracked pot suddenly mended itself. Or a vase grew taller than physically possible from a meagre lump of clay. You probably blinked and had a little laugh to yourself about how you were going mad, but that was *you*. Your magic."

"But this… the way I suddenly made a container for my emotions. How? How did I do that?" My mind raced with possibilities. This skill is what Sitara must have meant when she said I could anchor her to a vessel.

"I helped you along a little, dear." A flat, amber stone shone on a necklace through Mahi's threadbare T-shirt. She touched her hand to it. "This jewel is an antenna for magic. It's locked on me and bears the imprint of years of my magic.

But a powerful witch such as I can rechannel its power for a little while."

At the sight of the jewel, Merlin stood on his hind feet and hissed.

The lines around Mahi's mouth deepened. "I gave you a little boost. But I'm afraid your magic will only simmer unless you have a jewel of your own, and there are none."

If Aanya was a friend and her potion worked, I'd know soon enough what the hare was thinking. My brow furrowed as images reeled through my mind: Sitara holding up the coveted palm-sized jewel, the simple ring on the general's finger, the showier one the raja wore, the tiny stone on Aanya's ear, and Mahi's medallion necklace, all cleaved from a similar stone. I sucked in my breath. "It's all about the jewels and how they connect to the magic. That's why Sitara died."

Mahi scrubbed a hand over her face as though her efforts to help me had not been without cost. "Many things have happened, Kiya. Some avoidable, some not."

I stood, circling the pot, shadowed by the hare. "What happens if I break it?"

Mahi gave a wry smile. "I expect those captured emotions will flood out."

On impulse, I slammed my fist through the pot. A gut punch of emotion winded me.

"Not a good idea. Stupid is as stupid does," said Babbu the parrot.

"Hush, Babbu. Experimentation is good. She's learning." Mahi rubbed her hands together with glee. "This is just the beginning for you, Kiya. You are capable of so much more. Who knows what emotions and energy you can capture or for how long. I can teach you how to be a witch. I can teach you how to use crystals, herbs and sacred spaces to amplify your power."

My breath bottled in my chest. The raja had been right. I

was a witch with magic inside me all along. I just hadn't known it. "Are you going to tell the raja?"

Mahi pressed her thin lips together. "No, Kiya, I'm not." She closed her eyes for a long moment, longer than a blink, longer than was comfortable, and in the space between her eyebrows, something shifted.

"What the hell?" I shrieked, my chest constricting. "That isn't in any biology textbook I've ever seen."

Mahi took a series of deep breaths. A rush of energy coursed through her body, making her tremble. On her forehead, an eye opened, violet in colour. Her pronouncement had the dynamism of a priest at the pulpit. "If I tell the raja the nature of your powers, Jalapashu and its people will perish. If I don't, everything is still to play for."

I shook my head, hoping her third eye wasn't real, hoping to unsee it.

Mahi's third eye closed, and her brown eyes opened with renewed clarity. She glowed with new vibrant energy and patted my hand. "The sight of it made me queasy for years. You'll get used to it."

Her narrow house, with its dusty rooms and unfathomable magic, was too much to process, and my brain short-circuited like a fuse. My legs buckled, and I slid to the floor. Though I could still hear voices, shadows folded in from the periphery of my eyes.

Somewhere, the hare grumbled with worry and laid his soft head against my cheek.

Somewhere, the parrot squawked a warning. "He's coming! The general is coming."

"Will that bird ever shut up?" Hurried footsteps stopped next to me. He cursed. "What happened? Will she be all right?"

"Calm yourself, Deven. Nothing that some lavender sprigs and valerian root won't fix."

A sigh of relief. "Did you come to a verdict? Is she a witch?"

"I didn't find anything conclusive."

"He won't be pleased, Mahi."

"She has a part to play in shaping Jalapashu. Whether it's for good or bad, I can't say. It is best we keep her close." A damp cloth dabbed half-heartedly at my clay-covered hands. "The future is a fickle thing, always changing. You know that, Deven."

A harsh laugh. "Yes, I know that more than most."

"That avenue has not yet closed. You could still be king."

His voice cracked like a whip. "Your prophecy was useless. I will never harm my kin."

"We can't know what we will do until we are faced with the choice." A pregnant pause hung in the air before Mahi sighed. "Tell the raja I did my best. Maybe I'll have better luck with the youngest sister… Now bring Kiya out into the sunshine, will you? My house needs a hoover, and perhaps she has sensitive lungs. I'll be right behind you. Now where's my mortar and pestle? I need to whip up a remedy."

Strong arms scooped me up. A grunt. "Come along, hare." His breath fanned my cheek.

I couldn't fight the retreating tide of my consciousness anymore. I let myself fall into the darkness, lulled by the beat of his heart.

CHAPTER 12

Mahi's concoction roused me as she promised it would, leaving a pungent bitterness on my tastebuds. I came to my senses on her doorstep, where someone had shoved my knees between my legs.

"She looks wan." The general towered above me, his expression pinched. "Perhaps some food?"

Mahi baulked. "Don't look at me. I've been too busy to go shopping. Perhaps a quick stop at Biryani Junction?"

The General checked his clock. "Although we are already late. I could ask the palace staff to bring out a platter. Is she well enough to see the raja?"

His arrogance got under my skin. "Hello. I'm here. You could ask me."

Mahi's grin revealed a row of uneven teeth. "Never mind him, dear. Men in power have a habit of not seeing what's right under their noses."

"My apologies." He gave a long-suffering sigh. "The raja wants to see you, Kiya."

I heaved myself off the floor to even the power balance. "Do I have a choice?"

His body blocked out the light. "Not really, no."

"Well, we'd better get on with it then." I turned to Mahi on unsteady feet, willing her with my eyes not to stay true to her word. "You will make sure Leena is okay?"

A jolt of understanding passed between us. "Of course."

I dared to hope she wouldn't betray me.

Mahi's austere kohl-painted eyebrows rose to a peak. "Deven, perhaps you can arrange for Vikram-ji's pottery equipment to be delivered to the palace turret so Kiya may have access. Now my little experiment is over, they are only cluttering up my house. It's better she has them as a creative outlet. Unless Prem-ji would like to drive our guests mad with boredom as well as grief."

The general straightened his jacket. "Of course. I will see to it."

With one last look at us, Mahi returned to the shadowy innards of her house.

The parrot flew after her, cawing with glee. "A cluttered home is a cluttered mind. Oops. Too late."

"Should I send for a car?" The general's black eyes glimmered. "It is a twenty-minute walk back to the palace, and despite the smell of dung in this alley, Mahi doesn't even have a donkey to lend us."

I shook my head. "The fresh air will do me good. And I don't think Merlin would enjoy riding a donkey."

His mouth twitched. He took my elbow, presumably to keep me steady, and chaperoned me through the streets of Jalapashu. Above us, seagulls soared in dark cutouts against the sky. Hours could have passed in Mahi's house, but by the height of the sun in the sky, it can't have been later than eleven in the morning. This time, the general slowed his pace to suit me, but it didn't come naturally to him. His rhythm jerked as if I put him off kilter. Though my head was woozy, my thoughts were resolute. The raja thought he controlled all the pieces on the board, but I didn't know everything.

Secrets held power. I locked mine up tightly inside me: I was a witch.

My head spun with the incredulity of it.

I sifted through the nuggets of information I had uncovered: Mahi's apparent willingness to deceive her king, her seer abilities, the power-enhancing nature of the jewels, and how the general served the raja, though he had a claim to the throne himself. I missed my sisters fiercely. We'd always faced our problems together until Sitara made a different choice. I blew out my cheeks and released the air, bitterly regretting how I had crushed the pot that had lifted my feelings of overwhelm.

The general darted me a glance. "Perhaps you need a rest after all. I can speak with Prem."

Some referred to the raja by his title. Others added *ji* to his name as a mark of respect. In contrast, the general used his unembellished first name. That had to mean something. Even so, now the foundations of my reason had been shaken, I added meaning to everything, even how the gargoyles leaned over the houses, watching our every move.

"No need. I'm fine." I wriggled my elbow out of his grip and checked Merlin followed us. "So, you're the raja's right-hand man?"

His lips pressed together in a slight grimace. "I'm a soldier."

"Don't soldiers have a say in who they serve?"

"They serve the kingdom." He flicked me a glance. "But let's talk about you. You're a potter. What kind of pottery do you make, Kiya Marlowe?"

My name sounded pretty in his deep voice. "All kinds. Vases, plates, mugs, saltshakers, pepper mills, planters." I cocked an eyebrow. "Sometimes effigies."

He had the grace to smile. "What is it that draws you to pottery?"

"I'm an introvert. Constant interaction drains me. I like

focusing on each piece individually. I like the flow of the clay. Every piece tells a story. Maybe I'm feeling frivolous and choose a summery glaze. Or maybe a customer has put in a special order. Or maybe an old mug I made at my first class now has a chip. And that small imperfection tells its own tale. Perhaps, the mug came off worse from a run-in with the dishwasher or fell off a crowded countertop. Or maybe it was wrapped up for Mother's Day by a clumsy child, and its chip gives it character because it is a reminder of that child's innocent joy. Pottery has a life of its own."

He listened attentively and without interrupting, even though my passions must have seemed boring to many. "Perhaps I should try it sometime," he said like we were friends.

I lifted my chin. "Back at our house, when your troops attacked, you deliberately smashed a plate that was of great sentimental value to me. It had our family's handprints on it. All five of us together. Apart from the odd photograph of us, that's all I had."

He fiddled with the sleeves of his jacket. "I'm sorry. That was insufferable of me. Part of the general's guise is to rattle a few bones. It's expected."

Silence stretched between us. I didn't accept his apology.

A pause. "My research told me you also have a sideline in rude ceramics."

"So I've run a couple of raucous hen parties." I shrugged, but my chest grew leaden at the reminder he was my enemy. He had researched us. He had planned his mission and executed it without mercy.

The general slowed for a moment, coal-black eyes glinting. "I'm not judging. It's a little quirky, perhaps."

"I like quirky. It's why I run a pottery shop in Boundless Bay rather than taking an office job in the city." Running Soul Pottery seemed a world away now.

He steered me back towards the bustling market, where

weary stallholders still peddled their wares under the summer sun. "I'm not made to sit behind a desk either."

I side-eyed him while pretending to look at a table of harps and drums. His butt was a dead giveaway that he led a more active lifestyle. At the general's impatient glance, I shooed Merlin onwards from where he dawdled at my feet.

He waited for me to catch up with him. "The website for your business says something about cathartic creativity. What is that exactly?"

I thought back to the clay penis I had encouraged Sitara to make in my studio after a relationship went horribly wrong. We fired it in the kiln, and she smashed it, bringing closure of sorts to her relationship with a man who promised her the world, then walked away. Sitara's tears had turned to laughter as we swept up the debris and put it in the bin. We'd opened a bottle of gin and talked about how our parents had spoiled us, how after witnessing their love story, nothing quite measured up.

I told him straight, knowing full well how badly this activity landed with some men. "I sometimes help broken-hearted women make monuments of their exes' private parts and shatter them to help them heal."

He suppressed a grin. "Do they have a good likeness? I suppose it's a novel way of seeing a wide variety of–"

"Of course not. They are symbolic. Most of the mock-ups look like dented courgettes."

His mouth twitched. "I see."

At the next corner, a young boy of about six, cute as a button, threw plump arms around the general's legs. "Uncle Dev, the teacher said we could have rice kheer with a dollop of jam for break time because we did well in our arithmetic."

The general bent down and wiped a smear of jam from his mouth. His aloofness morphed into loving familiarity. It was clear they had a rapport. "Then you must have done well, Ishaan. I am proud of you."

Merlin whizzed around the boy, sniffing to check for food or assess whether he was a predator. He stilled, satisfied.

The little boy giggled and eyed me and the hare with curiosity. "Can I play with the bunny?"

"We are on our way to a very important meeting. And you have very important things to learn," said his uncle.

The boy gave a great sigh of disappointment, then perked up. "Maa said you are coming to play cricket with me tomorrow."

"Yes, Ishaan. I will see you tomorrow. Run along, or your teacher will scold you."

"Okay." The boy hugged his uncle's knees and skipped off to his classmates.

The General pushed me onwards towards the palace, his face flushed as if showing his softer side in front of me had somehow embarrassed him. I ground my teeth. The interaction might have humanised him if he hadn't clammed up. Not that I would allow myself to like a man who had been central to my pain.

At the palace gates, a mere glimpse of him propelled the guards into action. They levered the gates open, barely glancing at me. The pristine environment made me conscious of the remnants of clay on my skin, the beads of sweat on my nape, and the frizz of my long hair.

"Should I freshen up before I meet him?"

"He's already waiting. You look fine." His jaw clenched as he searched the gardens.

I followed his dark eyes across the endless courtyards, spraying fountains and fragrant bushes, to the shade of a banyan tree where the raja waited. He wore an elegant silk *kurta* in mauve and a regal grey turban instead of his crown, but it wasn't his outfit that stopped me in my tracks. It was the leashed leopard that lay at his feet. The leopard showed no interest in the roaming peacocks or the pair of painted elephants in the distance. Its frame was lean. It cowered from the raja, stretching its body as far away from him as the leash would allow.

I sucked in my breath as we approached. "Is leashing big cats normal in Jalapashu?"

"Hush. It does you no favours to criticise him," said the general. "You would be wiser to court favour if you want to leave this place."

I told myself that now wasn't the time to lecture him on how to deal with bullies or murderers, for that matter. "Will it try to eat me?"

"That particular leopard does not feast on human flesh unless Prem commands it."

"Oh, then there's nothing to worry about." I grimaced. "I'm not letting Merlin get anywhere near those jaws." With everything I had experienced in the past few days, my doubts that the hare was my familiar disappeared like mist in the morning sun. I bent down and murmured in his ear. "Go inside. Find the palace library. Try and locate Sitara's books."

Merlin's golden eyes sparked with cunning, and he sprinted off.

I wiped the wariness off my face when we reached the final few steps.

The raja crossed the last few steps of the manicured lawn to greet us, tugging the leopard with him. He reached for my hand, a smile breaking out on his handsome bearded face, his penetrating blue eyes eager. "Good morning, Kiya." His smile deepened when I edged back from the leopard. "I have been excited to hear about your accomplishments since dawn. What news do you and my general have for me?"

"The seer did her best. Unfortunately, there is nothing to report," said the general.

The raja's face tightened, and he studied my face. "Never mind. It is early days yet. Perhaps you are still recovering from your time on English soil. Rest assured, the magic of Jalapashu will seep into you eventually."

It sounded like a threat. The lie tripped easily off my tongue. "I'm not a witch, and neither is Leena."

The raja jerked the leopard's leash with the air of a man who always got his way. "Come Kiya, walk with me. Perhaps my persuasiveness will edge you in the right direction. Deven, you may walk behind us."

"I must ask the chef to send out a platter of food." The general hesitated. "It has been a long morning, and I am sure you could both do with nourishment. A glass of *mango lassi*, at least."

The raja waved a dismissive hand. "Nonsense. We can wait."

We strolled through the lush gardens, through winding paths fragrant with jasmine, under arches trailing with roses, past benches trailing with honeysuckle and marble sculptures that glinted in the sun. My heart raced at my proximity to the leopard, and though I hated the general, I was glad he stayed close. My mouth twisted wryly at the irony of being in a cage with two predators and preferring the one who was slightly cuddlier.

The raja's voice was low and smooth. "I want to apologise for my behaviour the other day. I didn't mean to upset you by separating you from your sister. But you must understand that I have to put the needs of this kingdom first, and it is much more prudent to keep two potential witches apart. Who knows what dangers your powers might pose to us." His lip curled. "As you said yourself, your allegiance is to the British, not Jalapashu or its sovereign."

I clenched my fists. "My allegiance is to myself and my sister. I don't give a damn about this place or the British. I just want to live my life in peace, but you destroyed that."

His face darkened. "Be careful. Nobody raises their voice to me. Nobody uses language like that."

"Perhaps you surround yourself with the wrong people."

Just like that, his mood changed. "See, you understand. I

knew we just had to spend a little time together, and you would. I marvelled when I learned that Hansa and Jack Marlowe's family had stayed so close to Jalapashu. There are no good matches for me here, Kiya. Powerful men such as I must be careful about who they let into their inner circle. Who they let into their bed."

I bit my lip in disbelief to stop the laughter that bubbled up in my throat. He was making a move. Despite everything, he thought I could warm to him. Maybe I could close my eyes and blend into this life. Maybe Sitara's death had been an accident, as he said. If I scrubbed my memory of Sitara's death, our kidnapping and how he had separated me from Leena, perhaps I could warm to him. Maybe I would be seduced by the strange magic of this place, his electric blue eyes, his rugged jawline and his wealth. Maybe he could be a gateway to hidden knowledge about my past and a new me. Maybe if he wooed me, I could unearth kindness behind his cold eyes, and I would find that under his casual cruelty was a wounded heart that I could mend.

The only problem was that our mother had given us sage advice: when someone shows you who they are, believe them the first time. I wouldn't invite the raja to a dinner party, let alone into my bed.

Still, I was curious. "You longed for my family to return to Jalapashu?"

He trailed a finger down the leopard's coat. "Well, of course. I had to be firm with you at court, but I was devastated when I learned your eldest sister had been killed. That's not how the mission was supposed to unfold." He twisted to face me in a secluded seating area. Only inches separated us. "I'm sorry for your grief. You deserve better."

The scent of lemon soap crept up my nostrils. My skin crawled. I cast a quick eye at the general, who looked studiously in the other direction, then dropped my eyes. I kept my voice steady, not wanting to risk his ire. Spurned men were hard enough to deal with. How would a spurned raja react? Besides, I wanted more insight into his motives. "I appreciate you saying that."

"You're so beautiful." His eyes searched mine. "We could be so good together. Two old dynasties of Jalapashu joined together. There's power threading through your veins; I know it. I can't help but feel drawn to you."

The blush that crept up my neck was from anger, not attraction, but I kept my voice gentle lest I drew his wrath. "Dozens of women in this town would be flattered by your attention–"

Before I could finish, he leaned in and pressed his lips to mine.

The soft, gentle kiss sent shockwaves through my body. I pulled back, stomach heaving, wishing I had a witch's powers at my fingertips. That I could access some dark magic and send him to oblivion. I remembered the spell *tyāga* and wondered if I could make his soul leave his body and trap it in a vessel if I wished it.

The raja didn't notice my revulsion. His eyes twinkled. "There is so much I can show you. There is so much about Jalapashu you still haven't discovered. So much you haven't experienced." He made a sweeping gesture to the leopard. "How many times have you walked with a jungle beast? Have you ever held the leash of one before?" He unpeeled my fingers and put the leash in it.

I shook my head. "I couldn't possibly."

"Nonsense." The raja wrapped the leash firmly around my wrist. "Only fools turn their noses up at new experiences."

I swallowed hard and accepted it, and we meandered on through a garden of tall pink thorny roses tipped with white. My hand trembled, sensing the leopard's taut muscles through the lead as he padded next to me, the way its tail swished with resentment at the control I held over it. A small amber stone glowed on its leather neck collar.

"See," said the raja. "There's nothing to it. Look how calm and content he is under your care, Kiya. That's what it's like ruling this kingdom. Once the rules are in place, life just merrily ticks along."

My hands were clammy. Instead of powerful, I felt utterly vulnerable. I gave him a weak smile of apology as I fiddled with the leash around my wrist. "Actually, I think I'd rather you–"

Out of nowhere, the leopard took off. Shouting in horror, I braced myself against the ground, but my wrapped wrist and the leopard's strength and speed meant I was at its mercy. It dragged me across a lawn, jerking me like a rag doll. With no chance of convincing it to stop and let me free myself, I had no choice but to speed up after it, running at a pace I never knew I was capable of. A pace that should have qualified me for an amateur Olympics. Somewhere, the raja hooted with laughter, but I drowned it out, focused on survival. I fought to keep my balance, but the leopard surged faster than I could manage. I lost my footing, my left arm freewheeling, then flew through the air superwoman-style.

Suddenly, the general was there, and a dagger slashed through the air, freeing me.

I crashed to the ground, landing on my front, winded, with a burn on my wrist, my sandals broken, and my cheeks burning with humiliation. For the second time that day, I was grateful for the mid-length tunic over sturdy leggings that had somehow preserved my modesty.

I looked up, breathing hard. In the distance, a large cat–a tiger perhaps–felled the leopard before I lost sight of them.

The general replaced the dagger in his belt and crouched next to me, concern etched on his face. "He does these things from time to time. I'm sorry." He inspected my hands. "That will need ice. You broke a fingernail." Then he removed my sandals and turned my feet over in his calloused hands. "You need more of Aanya's salve for your feet. They still haven't healed from that day."

I held back my tears. "Thank you, general."

He gave a brisk nod before placing my foot on the cool grass. "I use your first name, Kiya. Perhaps you can use mine. Call me Deven."

"Thank you, Deven," I said quietly.

A shadow fell over us. The raja clutched his belly, laughing still. "Well done, general. I didn't expect to see my leopard take Kiya for a ride." His mouth twitched. "I trust you are okay?"

I nodded, shaken but otherwise okay. Clearly, I was just another pawn for his amusement.

Deven stood up and retreated from my side. "Perhaps Kiya should go back to her chambers to recuperate."

I stood with difficulty and picked up my wrecked sandals from the lawn.

"An excellent idea, general." The raja skimmed his fingers over his beard. "But tell me, how can I make up for this inauspicious start to our friendship?"

I hesitated. "I would very much like to choose a book from the palace library. Without my sister and confined to my chambers, there are precious little ways to whittle away the time."

Deven interjected. "The seer has suggested you might allow Kiya to have a small pottery studio in her chambers."

The raja's topaz ring glinted as he waved a benevolent hand. "Of course. Kiya will have her little pottery studio in the turret, and I will show her the library." He cupped my chin and searched my face for cuts and bruises. Although my hands and feet had taken the brunt of my escapade, he'd had a ringside seat. "Unless you do need to rest first?"

Deven shot me a look of warning. "That sounds sensible."

My heart clamoured in my chest. Being alone with the

raja was ideal, but what choice did I have? "That's kind, but for me, the best way to relax is with a book. I would very much like to see your library."

"Then it shall be done." He offered me his arm.

I smoothed my hair and clothes, clamped my broken sandals under one elbow, and accepted his arm.

The raja grinned at Deven. "She likes her taste of royalty. She behaves as a queen already."

Thoughts spun through my head as we turned towards the cool marble of the palace, making a web of their own: I was a witch, Sitara's books were within reach, and the raja coveted me like he coveted the amber jewels. I stilled my nervous heart. Moreover, if every person in this kingdom who wore a topaz stone channelled magic, then what was the raja's power? And what was Deven's?

CHAPTER 13

Deven took his leave from us, his manner haughty. "I have all manner of tasks to attend to." His inky eyes lingered a moment on my face.

"Then, of course, you must go, general," said the raja. "Kiya and I will get on just fine without you."

Deven gave a curt nod and turned back towards the kingdom, beckoning men as he went.

The raja patted my hand. "You're safe with me."

We made our way towards the palace, where warm sunshine turned to cool shadow, and scurrying staff bowed and curtsied to their passing king. The library occupied an entire floor on the ground floor of the east wing, with heavy doors of polished wood that were locked overnight. A wispy-haired librarian sat at a vast desk at its opening, its surface cluttered with reading glasses, ornate globes and dusty books. Two gleaming swords lay within easy reach on the wall behind her as if she might cut down trespassers despite her demure appearance.

She peered over crescent-shaped glasses at us, her papery skin creased into a smile. Her eyes flicked to my bare feet.

"Welcome, Prem-ji. I see you have brought a guest with you today."

"Nothing gets past you, Chandani." The raja chuckled and gestured to a row of tall cabinets in mango wood adjacent to the librarian's desk. "She has records on every book and reader in the kingdom and catalogues their tastes and what they borrow."

I gulped, ears pricking to listen for the sounds of Merlin, but a heavy quietness blanketed the library.

The librarian's eagle eyes assessed me. She was well-spoken with soft vowels, but there was a fierce edge to her stillness. "You will be filling out a log card presently, Kiya. What is it you are after?"

My eyes flicked to the topaz jewel at the centre of her watch, and I remembered what Aanya had told me about magicals working in the palace. "A novel. A mystery novel, perhaps."

"Prem-ji knows every inch of this palace like the back of his hand. He can show you the way." She reached for her wastepaper bin and offered it to me with a curious look. "I will dispose of your broken sandals. You will need two hands to find the right book."

"Thank you." I dropped my sandals into her bin with a dull thud.

The raja patted my hand, hooked into the arm of his silken *kurta*. "We'll begin with Agatha Christie then or Sherlock Holmes. Don't look so surprised. I don't have to like the English to appreciate aspects of English culture. And I admire Arthur Conan Doyle for his moustache alone." His cold blue eyes sought mine. "I can show you the painting of your mother, too, if you like."

My heart drummed in my chest. "I'd like that."

He stepped into the library, keeping my hand tucked into his arm, alert to the changes in my expression, as if he needed the validation of my awe. He needn't have worried:

the library filled me with wonder. The rich scent of old books and the faint fragrance of sandalwood incense drifted over us. Double-height ceilings had been filled with bookcases, each lit by lamps and fitted with a railed ladder of its own. Reams of manuscripts and tomes lined the towering shelves, their leather-bound spines and parchment pages aged by the passage of time.

"This way," said the raja, taking me deeper into the aisles.

I found reference books on nature, geography and world history, as well as fiction classics and chart toppers from recent years. This wasn't a library stuck in time. It was a living, breathing organism that the raja kept updated though he fiercely guarded the kingdom's access to everything outside its walls.

"How is it that you learn about the outside world? Is it through books in this vast library?" I asked. "I have seen nothing here to suggest you have telephones or internet."

"The kingdom is small enough that telephones aren't necessary, and my messengers are quite happy to relay my memorandums on foot," said the raja. "As for keeping abreast of news in the rest of the world, I have a man who goes to an internet café in the city to bring me printouts. He is very thorough. You see, it would be foolish for us to have that technology here. It would make us traceable, and we guard our privacy like a lioness guards her cubs."

I shook my head in disbelief. So that's how they stayed closed off from the world. However unique and different Jalapashu was, to me, it seemed too big a sacrifice–maniacal even–to miss out on all the culture and promise the world had to offer. But I was convinced that there were hidden layers to Jalapashu I had yet to witness.

I allowed myself to be led, scouring every corner for a glimpse of Merlin, my mouth dry with worry. We passed desks and leather armchairs, where the quiet hum of scholars engrossed in reading was punctuated by the turning of pages. Vast windows provided natural light to offset the heaviness of the room. Under each one, a reading nook nestled, complete with a plush mattress, piles of velvet cushions and draped with sumptuous silks. I imagined being a noblewoman in this kingdom, whiling away my time on those beds with my nose deep in a book. Still, I couldn't believe that had been my mother's life. I couldn't imagine that this had been her life.

Suddenly, we found ourselves in a circular walled opening under a chandelier, a gallery of silence, where dozens of paintings hung. I gasped at a portrait of my mother and slipped away from the raja to get a closer look. She was younger than I had seen her before but recognisable nonetheless with her oval face, amber-brown eyes and golden hair. She wore an Indian ensemble of glittering pink, and the rose tucked behind one ear was unmistakably plucked from the gardens of Jalapashu. White spots swam in my eyes as I read the tiny gold plaque next to the portrait: *Hansa Malini*. The engraver had used her maiden name Malini, not her married name Marlowe, corroborating all the raja had told me. The air was thin around me as I wrestled with my thoughts. Why hadn't she shared this part of her history with us? What could have driven her to build our lives on a lie?

The raja murmured in my ear, his breath ruffling my hair. "I told you. Beautiful, isn't she? You have her bone structure and fire, if not her colouring."

The vivid pigments and finely rendered details of the portrait made me want to reach out and touch the brushstrokes. I shook with a visceral need to touch her. *Long ago, your mother was a princess of Jalapashu. The child of one of five ruling families*, the raja had said at court. I turned to face him. The wall of his chest at my nose, his beard brushing the top of my head. At that moment, I was so alone. I could have tucked my head under his chin, wrapped my arms around his waist and asked for protection.

The way he looked at me–intensity sparking from his blue eyes–I think maybe he might have given it.

His voice was quiet. "Is it true Hansa died in a car accident?"

"They both did. They were away for their wedding anniversary. Sitara was twenty-four. I was twenty. Leena was barely eighteen." I caught my lip between my teeth. "We don't know what happened. There was no other car involved. But in a weird way, it comforted us that they had died together. I don't think they could have lived without each other."

He trailed a light finger down the arm of my tunic. "You know, it was hoped Hansa would marry my father and that they would rule here together. When she ran away, it broke my father's heart. Though perhaps fate has another union in mind."

I ignored his implication, heat rising in my cheeks. "Were they dating?"

He sighed. "No, nothing like that. In fact, she had refused him, but it made him even more determined. He protected her honour at court when it was rumoured she was enamoured with an Englishman. He never got over it."

I made a noncommittal sympathetic noise, though his father had clearly nursed a wounded ego rather than a broken heart.

His eyes darkened like a storm. "When he married a few months later, my own mother was second best."

"Your poor mother." I took a deep breath and spun in a slow circle.

A vase of white roses, snapdragons and asters brought warmth to a quartz-topped table under the central chandelier. A mixture of grand canvases and miniature portraits depicted past members of Jalapashu's ruling families. I read their family names from the plaques: Malini, like my mother, but also Reddy, Banerjee, Trivedi and Kumar. The raja's chest puffed with pride when I noticed an entire wall devoted to a painting of his coronation, complete with trumpeting elephants and adoring subjects. I lingered at an oval miniature of Deven hung in a shadowy corner, his inky eyes proud under the soft curl of his hair. Its presence there confirmed his place amongst the ruling families.

The raja's footsteps stalked me around the room. "Tell me, Kiya, has there ever been someone special in your life? Someone you would have given it all up for?"

I kept my body language loose, although inside, I was wound as tightly as a coil. "Maybe once. A boy I went to school with and dated through my teens, but I didn't let myself fall hard. I had my sisters. I didn't need anyone else." I met his eyes and hoped he could read all the hidden meanings I couldn't yet risk putting into words. "Actually, it was Sitara who taught us that."

He skirted over her death as if it were just a bump in the road, not a deep wound that would always stay with me. "There was never anyone else?"

It was hard to be satisfied with lukewarm love when our parents' devotion to each other had burned red hot until the end of their days, despite cultural opposition. "I've dated plenty of men, but only Tommy could have been something more." As soon as I spoke Tommy's name, I knew it was a mistake. My goal was to glean information, not give it away.

The raja caught my hand and pulled me closer. "It is good to learn more about you. I hope this pattern will continue. Perhaps the next time we meet, you will present me with a pottery gift made with the studio the general is arranging for you."

A sixth sense made me turn my head. A flash of black caught my eye at the entrance to the galleried enclave of the library. My pulse leapt to a frantic rhythm. *Merlin.* The hare dragged a book with him. His body strained with effort; jaw clamped around his prize, his bottom bouncing in the air as he lugged the tatty red tome, stopping every few minutes to glance over his shoulder. Though the marble floor made it an easier task than across a carpet, the noise he made would attract attention.

My heart soared that he had understood my request, but I had put him in peril. Were he to be discovered, the raja would know at once that I had no intention of blindly jumping through the hoops he had set out for us. He would know that I had teeth and claws like any other cornered creature, and I meant to use them.

I kept the raja focused on me and raised my voice to help the hare. "Of course, I will make you a gift." I looked up at him from under my lashes, using my femininity to distract him as women had done for centuries when their bodies were all they had as a weapon. "But you know so much about me, Prem. May I call you that?" It was bold of me to spurn a mark of respect. I didn't know what this handsome, vainglorious man was capable of or what boundaries he set in stone.

The raja sidled closer, and the silk of his *kurta* rustled against the soft cotton of my tunic. "Yes. I think you may." He kissed me, harder than our kiss in the garden. Strong arms closed around me.

I let the kiss linger, hoping to give Merlin time to escape. Then I pressed my palms flat to his chest and pushed him away gently. "We can't be friends when you're not being entirely truthful with me, Prem. Jalapashu is more than you've told me. You're not telling me the truth about this place." Over his shoulder, the hare soldiered on.

A cloud of irritation drifted across his face. "I accept I've not told you the entire truth. I can remedy that tomorrow. I can peel back the layers of what Jalapashu really is." He pursed his lips before they stretched into a slow smile. "I'll put on a show you will never forget. It has been a long time since I have transformed the south courtyard into an eye-popping spectacle. You will be my guest, Kiya."

My stomach churned with anxiety, ears alert to any commotion Merlin might cause. "And my sister?"

The raja searched my face and considered it for a long moment. "Very well. She may join us too."

Relief washed over me at the thought of seeing Leena. "That's gracious of you."

He ran a hand over his beard. "See to it that you both visit with the palace tailor in the morning. It will be a grand occasion."

I nodded and, with one last look at my mother's portrait, moved away from the galleried enclave, away from where Merlin had stolen away Sitara's book. "Now for that mystery novel you promised me. I think I deserve a quiet evening after all the excitement of today."

The raja chuckled and led me towards the classic mysteries section of his library. Ten minutes later, we took Agatha Christie's *Murder on the Orient Express* to Chandani, the librarian. I knew it well enough to answer questions about it should anyone quiz me on its contents, though I had no intention of reading that particular book. As Chandani catalogued my borrow, the shadow of my beautiful, industrious familiar loped along the adjoining palace hallway, his hard-won treasure in his mouth.

Chandani stiffened, and for a moment, her hands flexed as if she might reach for her swords, but a stack of dusty books fell from her desk, distracting her.

Prem arched an eyebrow. "Don't look at me."

My scalp pricked. I hadn't been near them either, but I was glad Merlin had been able to make his escape.

The marble floor was cool under my bare feet, and my stomach rumbled as the raja walked me back to the turret. There was no sign of the hare, though I searched for him.

Aanya waited for me at the bottom of the winding stairwell up to the turquoise chamber.

The raja passed me my novel and kissed the back of my hand. "Until tomorrow, Kiya." His eyes bored a hole in my back as we ascended the stairs.

For once in my life, I considered that I may have bitten off more than I could chew.

Aanya hurried me past the guards, speaking soft words about sunflowers growing as tall as balconies.

The layout inside the turquoise chamber had changed to allow for a rudimentary setup of a pottery studio, complete with bags of clay, a potter's wheel and a small kiln vented outside of the window in the furthest corner of the room. No doubt, the backbreaking work had been carried out by lowly servants, but the general's speed was nonetheless impressive. Still, the chambers remained a prison, and my worried heart could only think of Merlin.

Aanya allowed me to catch my breath and the door to bolt behind us before lowering her voice. "It was risky to send your clever hare through the palace alone, though he has a knack for speed and stealth and remained unnoticed. I suspected Merlin was more than a mere hare when I first laid eyes upon him."

My chest tightened. "You found him?"

Her eyes shone. "It's quite something to find a hare hiding beneath a stairwell guarding a book. I put the book in my waistband and lugged them both past the guards and up to your chamber." She pointed at Merlin curled up sound asleep amongst mountainous cushions on the bed. The worn red book poked out underneath him.

The mattress dipped as I sat next to him and stroked his back. "Thank you, Aanya." On the bedside table, Sitara's urn was unharmed, with the square of tissue underneath it, just as when I had left that morning.

She drew the curtains. "He's tired himself out. Let him

sleep while you replenish yourself. The general insisted I apply more ointment to your feet, and what is this I hear about the leopard hauling you across the palace lawn? It's all the groundsmen are talking of."

Her lilting songs rejuvenated me as I unpeeled my clothes, sank into a bath of swirling oils and washed the grime from my body. I sat on the floor in fresh clothes while she tended to my feet and brushed my hair. This time, I didn't resist. Instead, I ate from a plate of fresh breads and chutney and sipped hot chai.

"Did you see Leena?" I asked her when I felt more like myself.

Aanya nodded. "I think you will be pleased with the progress Mahi made with her."

My stomach fluttered. "Does she have magic, too?"

"She does. The sunflowers were of her making."

"Tell me more. Tell me everything," I said, hungry for every morsel of information about my sister.

Aanya tucked an errant strand of hair behind one ear. "Wouldn't you rather speak to the hare?"

A shuffling and a bounding sounded behind her. Merlin hopped towards me. He sat erect, a few feet away, his whiskers twitching in the twilight. He looked like he had always done, mischievous and unpredictable, but today, there was triumph in his honey-hued eyes.

When his jaw opened, I flinched, expecting the siren noise, not words.

"I've been waiting for this moment for a long time, Kiya. Now that I have a voice, I plan to use it," said Merlin. His low, rumbling voice reminded me of lost forests and wandering beasts.

Aanya laughed in delight and set aside the brush. "My potion worked. Now do you trust me?"

My heart pummelled in my chest. I only had eyes for the hare.

CHAPTER 14

Aanya left us with a promise to return. "The seer has told me I must leave you to talk alone. Much rides on the sacred bond between witch and familiar." She knocked for the guards to release her.

When she was gone, Merlin hopped onto his hind legs so we were eye to eye. He tilted his head to one side, sizing me up. "Well, this is a change in fortune. In Boundless Bay, you had no time for me at all."

I couldn't deny it. At home, I'd considered the hare to be a nuisance. I had rarely fed or stroked him and cursed him often for the messes he left around the house. But since Sitara's death, I had become fond of him. His presence comforted me, but it was more than that. Even without words, I'd understood his body language. I'd worried about him this afternoon, not because Sitara had once cared for him but because I did. I didn't need Sitara or the seer to tell me he was my familiar. The sudden blooming of our connection made me sure of it myself.

I picked my words carefully to wash away the residue of my previous rejection of him. "I'm happy you're here. It's nice to finally meet you properly."

The hare's rumbling voice filled my ears. "I shall expect a lifetime of fresh hay, herbs, clovers and strawberry slices to make up for the past."

I quirked an eyebrow. "That sounds very reasonable."

He continued to air his grievances. "Your insults of my digestive tract were hurtful. It's quite clear from looking at me that I am the Einstein of hares. I mastered toilet training at four days old. My mother took great pride in my achievement. My siblings weren't so tidy. The only reason I evacuated my bowels indoors was to protest how Sitara had spelled me into silence."

I bit back a bark of laughter. "You defiled our house on purpose?"

Merlin slumped. "How else was I supposed to make my feelings known when Sitara had taken my voice? Except it added insult to injury when she allowed you and Leena to believe I was a pet. Downgraded even from a common field hare." He blew out a warm puff of air. "I warned her that a witch can't survive without a coven. But she disagreed. She wanted to be the protective older sister. She stopped me from telling you what you needed to hear." He paused dramatically.

Encouraging drama queens wasn't my style. "Spit it out."

His ears drooped. "Your sister was much more polite."

My lips curved in a ghost of a smile. "Get used to it. I'm not Sitara."

His gilded eyes gave him a canny look. "Then maybe we have a chance of getting out of this unstewed. I loved your sister, but keeping secrets from you is what got her killed. Jalapashu is full of secrets. We need to be a team."

"What is it you wanted to say?"

"I've been building up to this announcement for so long. I was sorry the raja got there first. But he didn't do it like I would have." He tap-danced a few steps, then threw his paws apart. "Tada, you're a witch."

I gawped. "You tap dance?"

"Of course. I am not only an Einstein amongst hares but also a Fred Astaire."

Quirky little thing. My skin tingled, knowing he was a telescope into my history. "I have so many questions, Merlin."

The hare shifted position, but one cautious ear remained turned towards the door. The weight of decades hung in his words. "Let me start at the beginning. I knew your mother as a child. Field hares don't tend to live more than five years, but the Malini family loved Hansa so dearly that they used enchantments to give me a supernaturally long life. I was her confidant. The first person she told about your father."

"My maternal grandparents sound loving."

"Indeed they were. They taught her to be kind and strong, and in time, she developed formidable magic. She was a silver witch. Wise, sensitive, with great skill in time magic and warding. But parental love is no match for young love. She gave it all up for your father. She met him on a trip to the seaside. Back then, the kingdom hadn't entirely closed itself off. When children came of age, they celebrated by dressing in ordinary clothes and taking a trip to the world of men. That first fateful trip to the beach, she fell in love with your father. After that, she would beg and plead to be allowed to venture into Boundless Bay. Her parents thought it was the ocean she longed for. They never fathomed she had set her heart on ordinary Jack."

"Maybe if she had confessed, her parents would have accepted their relationship."

The hare sniffed. "No. They would have thrown her out and cut her out of their lives unless she had promised to give him up. Hansa knew she could give up anyone but him. So she hid and lied and plotted how she could start her new life with Jack."

I gulped. "And my father? Did she tell him her secrets?"

"She told him everything. She warded the house, but she knew the danger he was in by marrying her. Marrying outside of Jalapashu was forbidden. For a princess to do so was unthinkable. If her wardings failed, she wanted him to be prepared. But she never could have kept anything from him. They were so close you couldn't slip a piece of paper between them. Like Romeo and Suzette."

"You mean Romeo and Juliette."

"Yes. That's what I said." His nose twitched. "When Hansa ran away from Jalapashu to be with Jack, she took me with her. I was glad because I would have withered without her. Being with Hansa nourished my soul, just like hay nourishes my body. But magic has a way of dwindling when you pay no attention to it. Away from Jalapashu, Hansa was free to invent another identity. Loving me was a reminder of all she had left behind: parents who loved her, a beloved brother, friends like sisters, and magic beyond compare. She wanted to look forward, but I kept her stuck in the past. So I said goodbye."

His words resonated deep in my bones. "Didn't she beg you to stay?"

Merlin's body quivered. "Yes, but her heart wasn't in it. I promised her I'd return once a year so she knew I was safe and wasn't far. I kept my promise. But it bothered me that her eyes shone with happiness when I wasn't there, and she could focus on this new life of hers with Jack and three young children. When I returned, the old sadness would turn her amber eyes muddy, and the frown lines of her ageing face would grow even deeper."

"I'm sure she missed you." I hugged myself, forlorn for them both, remembering the faraway look in my mother's eyes that I had never entirely understood. She'd left Jalapashu for love but had never been altogether whole again. I went quiet inside. "Do you know what happened the day they died? The police never gave us an answer that made any sense... Our father lost control of the car, they said. But he was so good behind the wheel. He was too careful with our lives to speed. So proud of his classic cars. We couldn't work it out."

The hare sighed. "I tried to warn her that night that she shouldn't go. She was packing the boot of the car and shooed me away. She said she just wanted an adventure. A simple road trip with her love." He placed a soft paw on my hand, the briefest caress. "Do you know why your mother never tried to raise you far away from here?"

I leaned forward, my throat tight, painfully aware of the turret curtains dancing in the wind.

"Magic is more than a skill. It is life itself. Hansa longed to see shores away from Boundless Bay, but at her core, she was a witch, and her magic and her life were tied to this land. But your mother had forgotten the havoc magic can wreak. She'd forgotten that what we take from the earth, we have to give back. She thought herself free, but in fact, her chains were simply longer. I don't know what happened in that car. But I can guess your mother became unwell the further they travelled from Boundless Bay. She left her topaz bracelet in Jalapashu when she fled. She didn't even have me as a conduit to the earth. So I imagine she weakened quickly, alarming your father at the wheel. What happened next is anyone's guess. Each passing mile sealed her fate and your father's with it."

Deven's words echoed in my head. *This backwater place is the root of our magic.* I squeezed my eyes shut. All these years, I'd yearned to fill in the gaps, but the truth was worse than I could have imagined. They would have been safe if they'd stayed in the bay and celebrated their anniversary over a home-cooked dinner with a bottle of bubbly. Yet, I was fiercely proud of them for the love they shared until the very end and how they had risked it all to follow their hearts. There was bravery in that. It had been a good life.

I took a deep breath and scooted closer to Merlin, needing his warmth. He smelt of wildflower meadows and damp earth. "So that was then. What happened all that time in between? Where were you when we were at university, getting our first jobs and falling out of pubs? Where were you when we moved back in together, when Leena introduced her first girlfriend to us and Sitara had her heart broken? What were you doing, Merlin?"

His amber eyes glimmered. "I kept my promise to your mother. I visited each year like I said I would. I noted all the changes. Each year that you grew fatter, sadder, or finally found your way. Each year that you chose to spend alone. The year Julia Roberts inspired you to grow your armpit hair. The year you wore too much plaid. The year you took up power walking. The year you first discovered pottery and the light that sparked in you. I saw it all. The pretty bits and the not-so-pretty bits. It gladdened me to see Hansa's children living, if not thriving."

I winced. "But I never saw you."

He blew out his cheeks. "Hansa didn't want you to have a magical life. I could hardly bound up in April and pretend to be the Easter Bunny. Besides, I prefer to live surrounded by whispering woods, burrowing moles and the soft chirping of birds than the jarring noise of man, with construction clangs, roaring engines and warring voices."

My brow furrowed. "But you *did* return one day. Or am I supposed to believe that Sitara found an advertisement for you in a local paper?"

The hare's chest puffed with pride. "Sitara didn't find me. I found her."

I jumped as a plant pot toppled off the side of the mosaic bath. "What the–"

The hare grizzled. "Stop that, Sitara. I will tell her exactly what I want to."

My jaw went slack. I eyed the broken plant pot suspiciously. "She's here?"

"Where do you think her spirit has been these past few days? She's here, just unable to speak to us until your anchoring work is done. She still thinks she can boss us around, even as a ghost. I'll continue *if* you keep your peace, Sitara. I will not be silenced again." He grunted. "Just as I noticed the changes in you, I grew suspicious of changes in Sitara. Except I wasn't stupid enough to think they were down to menopause."

I shot him a dark look. "I was hardly going to guess that there was magic involved. How did Sitara first make the leap?"

"Through her archaeology research." He sprang into action, leaping onto the bed, nosed the book onto the ground and manoeuvred it in front of me. "She came across this book by chance. Once she discovered your mother's maiden name in it, she was like a skeleton with a bone–"

"A dog with a bone."

"That's what I said. A skeleton with a bone. She pieced together the hidden Malini history and your witch ancestors bit by bit. The curiosity that had driven her to succeed in her career became a millstone around her neck. Everything else fell away. Professional pride. Sisterhood. Hygiene. She abandoned it all and was consumed by a ravenous hunger to know more about your past."

I turned the book over in my hands. It was a hardback wrapped in a layer of weathered crimson cloth and moist where Merlin had it in his jaw. Faded gold lettering on its spine spelt out its title: *A History of Jalapashu*. I leafed through its yellowed pages. They were filled with flowing ink and hand-drawn illustrations, some of which had been stained with primary colours. I paused at a drawing of a jewel shaded in swirling saffron, but Merlin was impatient.

He turned the pages, piecing together a past I had no idea

existed. "Jalapashu was set up at the height of the British Raj when five families who served as household staff for British families found the first magical jewel and set up a secret pact. These men and women decided to disappear overnight from their households. With their new powers, they would set up a hidden kingdom and take turns to rule. At first, they were all friends, excited by the possibilities ahead of them. The kingdom grew, and each person from the bloodlines of the founders had their own jewel to amplify their magic, but the rajas and ranis had been hasty. The Amber Hollows didn't provide an endless supply of topaz jewels. The jewels were tricky. They fused with their person and couldn't be used again. So the rajas made arbitrary decisions about who could access the magic. So a divide grew. Those with magic lived in the palace. The rest lived normal lives without access to the kingdom's real bounty—its magic. As for the original five families, their friendships waxed and waned, dependent on marriage or petty grievances, or in the case of your mother, the bending of established rules."

I held my breath, drinking up every detail. "Where are the Amber Hollows?"

His gold eyes glimmered. "Locals in Boundless Bay know them as the Crypts."

I frowned. "The Crypts?" That was the name local parents gave to the network of winding caves to prevent their children from taking the treacherous hike down the steep cliffs or swimming out to where choppy ocean currents met the dark cave mouth. Our parents had forbidden it too, but all the children in Boundless Bay ventured down there at some point. "There's nothing down there but a musty scent and the flutter of bat wings."

"No jewel has been mined there for centuries until your sister's magic allowed her to mine one." The hare shuddered. "Sitara was a blue witch at the start of her journey. She had learned basic spells. She had powers of divination and finding lost items. Her books told her the jewel would amplify her magic, and she didn't stop looking. Exactly a year ago, she discovered the location of a jewel with her divination magic. She brought you along for the ride."

My chest was tight. "My god."

"She was going to tell you everything. In that cave, she told you it would be possible to have magic and asked whether you wanted to take that step. You and Leena thought she was crazy, so she went first. And when she touched the jewel, her magic blossomed. She could manipulate water."

I curled and uncurled my fingers in his soft fur. "That's how she managed to fend off our attackers initially in the kitchen."

"That's right. In that cave, you and Leena watched in awe, and you said yes. You wanted to experience it too. You held that jewel, and your dormant magic brimmed. She told me it was everything she had imagined and more."

Sitara's ghost had alluded to my experience of magic in a cave. This is what she had meant. "But why did she take it away?"

"I warned her that for centuries, a soldier from Jalapashu has been assigned that watch. A sleepy watch that never usually amounts to anything but boredom. But Sitara poohpoohed me. It was hard for her to imagine the kingdom still existed. To her, it was almost a story. Her archaeology background, given to the study of fallen empires, fooled her into thinking Jalapashu was gone. A toothless beast from the past."

I nodded, understanding Sitara's stubbornness. How being the eldest made her convinced she was always right. "But the raja had been hoping to get his hands on another jewel."

The hare arched his back against my hand. "The magic in the kingdom can't be replenished without it. It trickles like a reservoir run dry, and his subjects notice. Why should they put up with the raja's rules when the magic is all but spent? So he sent his troops to that cave to retrieve what Sitara had found. The three of you only just escaped. Afterwards, she decided to wipe your memories of that incident. She decided to bear the burden alone, despite my counsel."

An image came to me unbidden from the deep burrows of my mind. In it, three naked women in their seventies sat on a shore, utterly at ease with themselves. They finished their vinegary chips, exhilarated with what they had accomplished. The oldest of the women's expressions changed to sorrow. She chanted a simple spell.

The women were us.

My chest ached. "That wasn't her choice to make."

"Sitara's research told her that when you touched the jewel in the cave, your cells changed. The magic acted like moorings to this land. She suspected what had happened to your mother and didn't want history to repeat itself. She began furiously researching a new plan for you all to keep your magic but leave Boundless Bay. With every passing day, she inched closer to her goal. She thought she had more time. Time to find a safe way to leave with your magic intact. But when the three of you painted the outside of your house, the last of your mother's warding fell away. Then the general and his men came." His body trembled under my fingers. "I kicked myself for not telling you about your history all those years ago. Before another Malini woman died on my watch."

I pulled him into my lap, and energy flowed between us. Witch and familiar. "It's not your fault."

He settled against me. "Now, do you see what we are up against?"

I buried my nose in his earthy, grassy smell. "Yes, Merlin. I do."

"Sitara was right about one thing. This time, there will be no escape from Jalapashu without a show of strength. If you want to free yourself and Leena, you'll need to work on your magic. I really want us to succeed. It would be an ignoble end to a hare's long life to end up in a casserole."

"But I don't have a jewel, Merlin."

"You have me. It's enough to make a start."

I eased him from my lap and took tentative steps to the makeshift pottery studio Deven had arranged in the corner of my chamber. A deep resolve and peace filled my bones as I began work. My fingers didn't need thought to power them. As I fell into the rhythms of the clay, it grew quickly and evenly, even in the half-light of evening.

The potter's wheel whirled. The hare sat at my side, a conduit for my magic in the absence of a jewel of my own. As I worked, I slipped into a trance-like state, thinking of Sitara and magic, and a new urn to hold her ashes took shape beneath my fingertips. Whether through Merlin or my subconscious, lost spells, incantations, and ancient rituals flowed through my mind to the tip of my tongue. There wasn't just *tyāga*. There was *āgaccha* and *bhava*. There was *gṛham* and *vāpas āo*.

If Sitara's urn was to anchor her, I had to imbue each speck of clay with magic. My shoulders ached, but my mind sang. With each passing hour, Merlin weakened, but he insisted I continue. I fed him handfuls of hay from my palm and brought him sips of water between bouts of creativity. Finally, he slept, and I had only the moon for company.

When I was finished, a gentle glow bathed the urn that could have been moonlight or magic. On impulse, I made an additional small vase for the raja and used a needle tool to dot a delicate column down its length. I had my bond with Merlin to thank for my intuitive spell-casting, and though ripples of fear edged closer, I leaned into the newness of my learning. I kept the cycle of my breath even, feeling my way around the letters and vowels that formed in my mind, testing them out on my tongue before I spoke them aloud. I called the raja's face to mind. A spell drifted through my subconscious like a paper boat on a stream. A rush of energy left my body when I uttered the phrase *hamen bhūl jāo*.

Eventually, I placed both pots in the kiln and sent a silent prayer to the kiln gods to keep them safe. Once I had washed the clay from my skin and tidied everything away, I picked up the hare as a mother picks up her sleeping child and brought him to bed with me. Somehow, he had buoyed my resilience and my magic. His stories had opened up horizons beyond compare. My body curled around him, and sleep came readily, accompanied by the low humming, crackling and hissing of the kiln.

At dawn, I crept out of bed while the hare snored beside me and crossed to the furthest corner of the chamber where the silent kiln waited with its bellyful of my creations. Sliding my hands into heat-resistant gloves, I opened the kiln door, mindful of escaping hot air. My heart soared at the fruits of my labour. Both pots had survived the process uncracked. The urn was an elegant vessel, fired to a warm, earthy brown, with subtle variations in shade and texture that gave it an organic feel. Its base was bulbous, with plenty of room to hold Sitara's ashes, but its neck was slender and encircled with an ornate carving. On it, I'd etched swirls of water in homage to Sitara's love of the ocean and her blue witch magic. The vase was tall and thin and had blackened in the furnace. The column of dots glistened, blacker still.

I transferred the urn with care to the work table as it cooled. Early rays rippled across the room, illuminating the urn. With quiet blanketing the world, I decided to hold my own personal funeral for Sitara. I sat cross-legged on a stool and allowed myself to drift into my memories, jumping from year to year: Sitara pushing Leena and me on a basket swing; her beckoning us into a musty wardrobe to find Narnia; beach walks with three sisters arm in arm; Sitara keeping up the tradition of making mother's bean curry and chapatis dish; how she never complained about having to be mum when she was in mourning too.

I found grace in those moments. The cracks in my heart fused.

When I was ready, I poured her ashes from the old vessel into the new one. A whisper wound itself out of me. "I forgive you for the secrets you kept. I love you. Please haunt me again."

Then, I sat back and found peace in the stillness of dawn.

Somehow, I dared to believe we could turn the tides of our fortune.

CHAPTER 15

Before I'd eaten a morsel for breakfast–perhaps deliberately so–guards marched me to my early morning appointment with the royal tailor in his atelier. They stood vigil at the door as I entered alone, blinking as my eyes adjusted from the shadowy interior of the palace to the light-flooded atelier.

Inside, magnificent windows and colourful fabrics vied for attention. An array of Indian clothing–*saris*, *Punjabi suits*, *ghagra cholis* and *anarkalis*–hung from gleaming clothing racks. Shelves of rich silks, satins and brocades lined the walls. Rows of sequinned shoes and Indian jewellery glittered on display tables next to two chaise lounges in puckered velvet. Mannequins draped in the latest fashions, each more beautiful than the last, caught my eye.

The display of wealth unnerved me. After all, I was happiest in clay-splattered overalls. I searched for the tailor, taking soft steps across the creaking oak flooring. The scent of roses from the palace gardens carried on a gentle breeze that flowed through the open balcony doors.

That's when I saw her.

Leena turned, towards me, astonishingly beautiful in a

traditional *ghagra choli* in teal blue. The skirt was crafted from layers of flowing fabric, with each layer adorned with delicate beads. Her fitted blouse had a modest beaded neckline, and a matching scarf skimmed her bare stomach. The bangles around the wrists clinked with every movement, and her fingers were entwined loosely with Aanya's. Her golden hair had been blow-dried to perfection, its blunt asymmetric style skimming her shoulders.

Exhilaration jolted through my body. "Leena!"

Her face, when she turned towards me, was free of makeup and pained. Her worry fell away as she ran towards me, fabric swishing around her. "I didn't believe it when the raja said I'd see you today."

My hug must have squeezed the breath out of her body. A sob escaped me. "Thank god."

She searched my face. "Are you okay? Two nights apart felt like forever."

I nodded and sucked in my breath. "They didn't treat you badly?"

"No, nothing like that. I kept telling myself not to trust their kindnesses." Leena cast a furtive glance over her shoulder and cupped her hands together between us. Heat radiated between us, and when she opened them, a stemless bluebell lay there. Her eyes shone. "I could do more with the help of Mahi's jewel. Can you believe it? Her kitchen was bursting with blooms. I wonder if Sitara knew. I wonder if she knew this was possible."

I plucked the flower from her palm and crushed it in my own. My whisper was a hiss. "Leena, we have to be careful. The raja can't know what we are."

"I know." Bangles jangled on her clenched fists. "He said it was an accident. That he didn't mean for Sitara to die."

Anger, hot and raw, pulsed through me. "We can't trust him."

"No, we can't. But not everyone in Jalapashu is bad.

Aanya said we can change things here." She looked at the flower in her palm. "This world is scary, but it's shown me things beyond my wildest dreams. I don't know what to think." Leena glanced at Aanya, and her brown eyes softened.

My eyes widened. I liked Aanya. She had been kind to us. Her potion had returned Merlin's voice to him. But there was a time for romance, and it wasn't when our lives were in jeopardy. "You've fallen for her, haven't you? Of *all* the places for you to get embroiled."

Leena stiffened. "That's not fair. I'm crushed that Sitara is gone. I cried until I was empty, and then I cried again. And you know what? Aanya sang me to sleep. She told me stories about this place. She told me about how the people here suffer."

I frowned, knowing how Leena had never been able to stand suffering. How she jumped in with two feet, without any thought for herself. "The strangers here aren't my concern. You are." Even as I said it, the notion rang hollow.

"The people here have the same worries and dreams as anyone else."

"We've been over this. The raja is dangerous."

"Yes," said Leena. "His orders led to Sitara's death, but that doesn't mean he intended it to turn out that way. It doesn't mean we must turn our backs on all we have found here."

I pleaded with her to understand. "We wanted revenge."

Leena shook her head. "We wanted justice. All leaders make bad decisions. Maybe one day, Prem will have the grace to apologise and make amends."

Prem. My belly knotted. She was on first-name terms with him, too. But in her case, it wasn't a manipulation. My little sister, who always wanted to see the best in people, was being taken for a fool.

"You'd never say this to Sitara," I said. "You wouldn't dare."

"Sitara would never have listened. She would have pushed us into doing what she wanted."

"They *killed* her." I couldn't know for sure that murder had been their intention, but they had ended her life, and they hadn't grieved her, turned themselves in to the police, or even beaten themselves up about it. They had simply gone on with their lives, and to me, it sounded like Leena wanted to do the same.

"Don't look at me like that," said Leena. "We've discovered magic here. Don't we owe it to ourselves to learn just a little more about it?"

I tried to keep the scathing note out of my voice and failed. "What happened to *I believe in science*?"

"I was hasty. I needed to see it. To experience it. Aanya's been telling me all about how witchcraft is a deep and ancient tradition with a rich history and meaning. It's not like it's depicted in pop culture at all. Although apparently, parts of *The Craft*, the new *Sabrina* and *Practical Magic* are accurate."

I briefly closed my eyes, not wanting to drive Leena away. Being the oldest sister came with responsibilities. That was my role now. We had to hold together. "Don't you want to get back to Boundless Bay?"

"Yes." She hesitated. "But not right away. I want to explore my magic. Don't you?"

"Of course I do." I couldn't help feeling that we were spiralling away from each other when we needed each other most. That even when we could escape, Leena wouldn't want to, and that terrified me.

She reached for my hands. "Then tell me everything."

So I did. I bent my head to her ear and spilt the secrets of my soul to her, leaving no detail untold. Just as I wished Sitara had spilt her soul to us and our mother before that. I spoke of Sitara's ghost. I spoke of the raja and how he had tried to woo me. I spoke of my bond with Merlin and how clever he had been. I told her of our parents' history, the dark secrets of Jalapashu and the jewels. I told her of my magic and how the general had carried me out from Mahi's house. The whispers of sisters don't require elaboration because sisters know each other's yearnings and values. They need three words when strangers need ten.

But when we drew apart, I could tell Leena hadn't changed her mind by the shy glances she gave Aanya and how her grief had turned to wonder. I knew I had to find out what lurked beneath the golden silks and exotic colours of Jalapashu before I lost another sister to this perilous, new world.

The raja had promised a spectacle. Leena wanted to learn about the culture of Jalapashu. I wanted to poke at its dark underbelly, even if I had to play the part of a meek guest to do so. When the palace tailor finally appeared, I allowed myself to be swept along by his prodding.

The royal tailor was in his sixties and accompanied by a nervous assistant. He glided swan-like across the oak floors without a creak, his walking stick making no contact with the ground. He wore a grey *kurta* suit paired with a bright yellow turban and a long pearl necklace. Bright feathers covered the midsection of his walking stick.

Shrewd eyes assessed my figure before he offered me his smooth hand. He clearly knew how to moisturise. "My name is Lokesh. You may call me Lokesh Saheb."

Aanya stepped forward, her manner mild. "Leena looks exquisite as you promised, Lokesh Saheb, but Kiya must also be ready at the appointed hour."

"I make no apologies for being late. It is not long until the Maharaja's Summer Soiree, and it is my busiest season yet. I woke at the crack of dawn, pausing only for my morning ablutions and prayers before developing looks for the newcomers with only a few hours' notice! My work cannot be rushed. Tell me, young maid, have I ever left a client wanting?" The tailor pressed his lips together. "Even you shall not leave my atelier without finery to wear."

First, Lokesh Saheb turned laser attention on me. He poked and prodded me, his eyes lingering on the slight curve of my stomach and the love handles at my waist. His assistant brought me underwear, glittering sandals and armfuls of garments, each personally crafted by the tailor. Gold lettering spelt out *Lokesh* on internal labels.

It didn't take long for the tailor to decide on the right garment and shoes. Lokesh Saheb's firm guidance was preferable to choosing fancy clothing myself. Having gravitated towards comfort rather than beauty all my life, I didn't have a clue. He laid out his final choice on a chaise lounge and disappeared with his assistant, the tap-tap of his feathered walking stick urging me to hurry.

Together, Leena and Aanya helped me dress. They hoisted up my breasts, pulled tight the ribbons of my blouse and hooked my skirt while I breathed in. Aanya teased my dark hair into ringlets that rested across my shoulders. She applied translucent powder to my skin and blush to my cheeks, then added a sweep of kohl to my eyes and the barest hint of pink to my lips. Lokesh Saheb returned, fussing over the exact height of my skirt, pinch of my blouse and fall of my *dupatta*. When all was done, he turned me to my reflection in a cheval glass mirror framed in dark wood.

Leena stood behind me, sadness in her still frame. "Imagine if Mum could see us now."

I swallowed hard. Mother would have wondered what the hell we were doing.

The woman in my reflection didn't look like me. The dusky orange of my *lehenga* flowed down to my ankles in countless pleats, a beautiful sense of movement with every breath. Silver embroidery in swirling floral patterns, inspired by the traditional art of *mehndi*, extended all the way up to the waistband. The matching chiffon blouse had sheer sleeves and added a touch of lightness to the look. A row of silver sequins adorned the edges of the low neckline. A simple *dupatta* covered one shoulder, its ends tucked into my waist.

The hint of a smile played on Lokesh Saheb's lips. "My work here is done. You're a marvel."

I ran my hands over the soft sway of my skirt, heart pounding. "It's time for the raja's spectacle."

THE SOUTH COURTYARD WAS CIRCULAR, ENCLOSED BY SANDSTONE pillars that stretched up to a summer sky scattered with cumulous clouds. Overnight, groundsmen had erected tiered seating around a vast open arena, where a thick layer of sawdust covered the smooth paving stones. Our skirts swished as Aanya ushered us to our seats in the royal box close to the action, next to an ornate high-backed chair reserved for the raja. I slid his gift underneath my seat for safekeeping, then straightened.

My pulse sped at the sound of horns and flutes that filled the air. Families dressed in colourful garments drank exotic juices from tall glasses. Children bounced in their seats, munched on sweets or waved crested flags. A number of other boxes for court dignitaries were situated at intervals around the arena.

Leena nudged me. "Well, this is awkward. Everyone's looking at us."

Hundreds of eyes had indeed turned our way. I tried to act normally, but a flush crept up my cheeks. "It's one thing appearing briefly at court, quite another being dressed by the palace tailor and sitting in the royal box. I'm guessing the rumour mill is in overdrive."

"We don't have newspapers in Jalapashu. Rumours are how news spreads," said Aanya.

Lokesh Saheb had loaned her an embroidered tunic with gauze sleeves and slim trousers that lent femininity to her boyish frame. She made adjustments to a table of sweet treats tucked into the corner of the royal box. Their aroma drifted to us on the breeze: warm orange spirals of *jalebi*, a tangy pastry soaked in sweet syrup; and *gulab jamun*, spongy dough balls soaked in a sweet sauce flavoured with cardamom and rose water. I shook my head when she offered me one. It was impossible to relax.

The secret of this spectacle had been guarded so closely that it set my teeth on edge.

The minutes stretched. Eventually, Prem entered the royal box to a lengthy drumroll and the tooting of a horn. He played the raja for all he was worth, with a golden outfit, long gleaming hair, his crown low on his forehead and a regal wave. The crowd leapt up and cheered for all they were worth. Leena and I stood, too, involuntarily, as if by some pre-programmed subservience. Her smile was uncertain; mine was fixed, a pretence.

At the raja's left was Mahi. She had swapped her misshapen T-shirt for an equally misshapen scarfless *Punjabi suit*. Her pixie hair was a grey cloud about her head, and her kohl eyebrows had been drawn with more ferocity than usual. She pursed her lips at the pomp. At the raja's right stood Deven in his general's uniform. Daggers gleamed on his belt. His glowering expression was enough to set my heart racing.

Four of us took our seats: the raja in his throne-like chair, with Mahi at one side and Leena and I at the other. We sat in one fell swoop as if we had rehearsed it. Pangs of shame infused my stomach at being part of the charade, but Leena looked around with interest. Deven took up guard behind us.

His eyes bored a hole in my back, where the neckline of my blouse scooped low.

The crowd's fervour settled into an expectant hum, but the raja stole a moment to murmur in my ear. "Lokesh's work is exquisite. I'll be sure to give him my compliments." He took my hand, blue eyes like chipped ice. "You wear glamour as easily as I hoped you would."

Mahi leaned forward. "Be sure to stay in your seat once the festivities begin."

When the raja raised his arm, goosebumps chased up my arm despite the sun's warmth.

His arm fell like an axe. A hush descended over the courtyard, and the arena nestled within it. He peered over the edge of the balcony. Even the fidgeting children in the crowd seemed to hold their breath. A few hundred yards away from the royal box, two men entered the ring in simple tunics and bare feet. Drums pounded out a rhythm as the men trod across the sawdust towards us. My brow furrowed, unsure whether to expect a serenade, a Laurel and Hardy comic act, acrobatics, or a two-man theatre show. But the men had neither props nor microphones, and their faces were more serious than smiling.

They drew to a halt directly in front of us and bowed low while Prem held his hand to his heart.

My breath bottled in my chest at the sight of a tiny amber jewel embedded in a leather strap at the skinnier man's neck. The more muscular man wore a jewel embedded in an armband. My muscles tightened as I recognised Sitara's killer, Mustachio. I pulled my hand from Prem's grip. "What is this?"

A glimmer of a smile passed over his lips. "A chance for justice, perhaps."

Next to me, Leena's knuckles were white on her seat. "It's that bastard."

I laid my warm hand on her cool one. "Stay calm."

TO SAVE A SISTER

Though Prem was sandwiched between us, I tried to catch Mahi's eye. I hoped for an explanation, a word, a show of solidarity that would set my mind at ease. Her averted eyes and the studied stillness of her body sent a message to me and the raja. She was playing the role of loyal court seer, or perhaps her allegiance was merely to herself.

Hysteria bubbled up my throat. The joke was on me: a seer who chose to be blind to my overtures.

Leena shot me a worried glance as the men sprinted to opposite sides of the sawdust-strewn ring.

The sense of anticipation in the arena reached a fever pitch. My intuition whispered: this is what I had been waiting for. This was the last secret of Jalapashu, the one I had sensed in my bones was coming.

A gong sounded, and the two men in the arena suddenly convulsed. Their skin rippled and shifted as if something were moving just beneath the surface. In a shortening of their legs, lengthening of arms and brutal growth of their rib cages, their tunics split, but their jewels remained in place. Fur grew where there had been smooth skin. Bones cracked. The men let out primal screams, and their eyes glinted with a feral intensity. They transformed into beasts: the leopard I recognised for his thin frame and my near miss in the palace gardens when he had dragged me across the lawn and a sleek panther with bright yellow eyes.

I suppressed a cry of surprise and gripped the railing of the box, transfixed. My heartbeat thundered in my ears. Their ferocity wasn't directed at us. It was directed at each other.

Prem's shout of ecstasy reverberated in my ear. "Fight!"

The crowd roared in approval; kind faces transformed into braying ghouls. Their feet pounded the ground to thunderous effect. I recognised the churn in my gut. The sudden awareness when a crowd was turning, when civility hung in the balance. Even if I had been able to leave, I was rooted to the spot as the beasts circled each other. Both were skilled fighters. The leopard was sharp-clawed, lithe and quick, able to dodge and weave around the panther's attacks. The panther was larger and stronger, tenacious and clever, with powerful muscles. It seemed wrong to take a side, but I did. Was this where we achieved justice for Sitara? Even as I pushed down my dark emotions, I lied to myself.

The truth was, I wanted her killer to lose.

I might even have wanted him to die.

Leopard and panther tested each other's defences as the crowd's excitement grew. The leopard was resourceful. He moved in quick, darting movements, striking with quick swipes of his claws before retreating. But the panther was methodical and confident. He snarled, baring his teeth as he prowled. He waited for the right moment to strike, then lunged forward with a powerful pounce.

Suddenly, the testing phase was over. A new intensity filled the arena. Even the raja leaned forward. The leopard crouched low, its muscles tensed and ready to spring. The panther lunged, claws extended, but the leopard darted out of the way, its agile body moving with lightning-fast speed. The panther spun and charged again, but the leopard leapt onto its back. It dug its claws into the panther's fur.

Their roars sent shivers down my spine. My mouth went dry. I wasn't sure what I had envisaged, but not this. Spectacles such as these–bearbaiting, beheadings, hangings, floggings and gladiator fights–were how barbaric rulers gave their people an outlet for violent impulses.

This wasn't justice. It was control.

Cheers and jeers filled the air, and the crowd vocalised their support or disdain for the fighters. The noise was deafening. The sweet scent of the treats mingled with the tang of sweat and blood made me nauseous. I winced as the sound of flesh thudding against flesh echoed through the arena. The surreality of experiencing this in England, where laws and norms had long driven such spectacles out of practice, made me light-headed.

The panther twisted and turned, trying to dislodge the leopard, but the smaller cat held on, his sharp teeth sinking into the panther's flesh. Blood flowed freely from the panther's wounds. But Mustachio had a stubborn resilience that allowed him to weather the leopard's attacks and continue fighting. He was in the raja's guard for a reason, and it showed. He tumbled to the ground, loosening the leopard's grip, and suddenly the tables turned. He leapt up, and with a twist and a ferocious lunge, he drove his powerful teeth and claws into the leopard. The crowd jeered, urging Mustachio to deliver the final blow.

Prem leaned over, and this time I heard the challenge in his tone. "Exhilarating, isn't it?"

Bile rose in my throat as blood dripped onto sawdust.

The panther bent his powerful jaw to the leopard and ripped out chunks of flesh.

"No!" cried Leena next to me.

My heart became a stone.

The leopard collapsed, its body limp and still.

I flinched as the crowd bellowed; the leopard transformed back into a man, his body battered and bloodied from the fight. A rib poked out, and the rise and fall of his breathing was nonexistent. Sitara's assailant was already back in his human form, panting heavily as he stared down at the body of his fallen opponent.

The fight had been a closely contested battle of wills, but it was clear who had been stronger and better nourished at the start of the fight. It was clear in the tensing of the raja's body that he was rooting for the panther. For Sitara's killer.

Mustachio lifted his arms in victory to wild applause.

A dull ache pervaded my chest. I was aghast that I'd done nothing. I'd sat next to the raja in my finery while a man bled to death. It took me a moment to realise how pale Leena had become next to me, how she kicked off her sandals and leapt into the ring. My nurse sister, primed to heal. Leena, who had always intervened as a young child, though there was no hope for a crushed beetle or a snail whose home had cracked or the broken bird in a cat's mouth.

Leena leapt into the ring without hesitation or considering how she herself could be mauled. She had no stethoscope, bandages or oxygen, no defibrillator or even a simple first aid kit.

"Stop," I called out. But my pleading fell on deaf ears. I kicked off my own shoes as Leena skirted around Mustachio and knelt in the bloodied sawdust, tearing off her scarf. She bound the dying man's wounds though the crowd booed, and Mustachio strode towards her.

Mahi sprang up, her neutrality punctured. "Don't be a plum. Come back, you two."

I evaded Deven's grasp and tumbled into the ring myself with an inelegant thud.

On the balcony, Prem issued a calm command. "Let them go."

Winded, I ran for my sister, putting myself between her and Mustachio. His short, powerful neck had been sliced in the fight, and he bled from his back and his thigh, but he was uncowed. His blood thirst had not abated, driven to a frenzy by the crowd. His expression twisted. He wanted to finish the job. He sprang for Leena, naked, his nether regions slapping against his thigh.

I let out a shout of fury and kneed him right in his pickle, ripping Lokesh Saheb's beautiful skirt. With no weapons in the ring, I picked up sawdust and threw it in his eyes. Energy rushed through me as the sawdust clumped unnaturally, hitting him with force and provoking a shout of surprise from the crowd.

Leena sought the fallen man's pulse. She looked over her shoulder. Mustachio barrelled forward despite reddened eyes and clutching his bruised bits. She flung out a defensive hand. Maybe it was instinctive. Maybe it was planned, and she expected to shoot darts of thorns his way or to grow a wall of vines to shield us. Instead, a spray of delicate flowers blossomed from Leena's palm: tiny, fragile blooms with pale pink and lavender flowers. Flowers that added a sweet fragrance to the musty scent of death.

Mustachio stopped in his tracks, jaw slack with surprise.

The crowd's anger turned to laughter.

And the fallen man gave a final moan as his life ebbed into the ground.

I wrapped my arms around my sister, heart thudding. "Oh, darling. I'm so sorry."

Leena's voice shook. "I couldn't just sit there and watch him die. That's not me. Kiya, that's not me."

The raja stood in his royal box, and silence descended over the arena. "I commend the fighters for their efforts. It has been a good show, has it not? With an extra pizzazz at the end, thanks to our esteemed guests."

The crowd cheered and waved their flags as Mustachio ripped the bejewelled collar from the dead man's neck. In one quadrant of the arena, the chant of *raja, our raja,* started that caught on around the arena.

He knew. He knew Leena was a witch. I thought I had the upper hand, but it had been him all along. He had planned this gladiatorial spectacle, knowing that bloodlust was alien to us, knowing how our emotions would flare when we witnessed the shifters. Mustachio's involvement was a *fait accompli*. How could Leena and I remain in control when faced with Sitara's killer?

The noise, smells and images would linger in my mind for an age. Would Leena finally understand?

Jalapashu wasn't the place of dreams.

Jalapashu was blood, gore and secrets lurking in the dark.

CHAPTER 16

Leena and I watched from the floor of the arena as the raja gave a benevolent smile and waved to his subjects. At his bidding, the crowd dispersed, still munching on their sweets and giddy with excitement, as if the body lying in the dust was mere litter and not somebody's son.

When Prem called out to us, the ground swayed beneath my feet. We returned to the royal box with Mustachio's hot breath at our necks. My thoughts scrambled. I had one more play to make. I hadn't come to the spectacle empty-handed; I had come with a gift.

"Do you trust me?" I whispered to Leena.

She stared at her blood-soaked hands. "I messed it all up."

"You did what you are trained to do. Follow my lead, okay?" I leant my forehead against hers, though Mustachio's rank smell made me retch and willed my strength to buoy hers.

Mustachio shoved us forward. His growl was a stark reminder of the beast inside. "Keep moving."

In the royal box, the raja turned his concentration to Mustachio. "You did well." He pressed a coin into Mustachio's hand in exchange for the bejewelled collar. "The kingdom will not forget your service."

Mustachio thumped a hand against his chest. "My raja."

Aanya wheezed with fear, helpless though her magic was made to soothe. Having kept the secret of Merlin's relationship to me, she was as much on the line as anyone. Mahi's body was tense, her prickles up. I felt her censure from a few feet away. We shouldn't have been so careless. But then she was accustomed to Jalapashu's brutality. In Boundless Bay, even a dead pigeon or seagull caused a stir.

Deven bent to my ear, face grim. "You didn't really think he'd let the leopard live after he ran away, did you? There was only ever going to be one winner today."

I balled my fists as hatred surged in my breast. Then Mustachio was gone, and Prem turned his attention to us, cobalt eyes assessing our blood-stained, ripped garments, the tears that streaked down Leena's face and the dirt on mine. The departing crowd still hummed and craned their necks to see what fate awaited us. But my world shrank to the royal box: the sweets and strangers, the sister I needed to protect, and the wildness of this kingdom and its raja.

The raja's voice was calm, but there was the promise of a storm in his stillness. Cool eyes rested on Leena. "We have a witch among us, after all. Your gift is…palm flowers?" He turned his steely gaze on Mahi. "I am affronted, my seer. With all your powers of vision, did you keep secrets from me?"

Mahi's all-seeing eyes shuttered, and her voice remained steady. "No, Prem-ji. I have been with you for a lifetime. I would never do that."

Hooded eyes swept across the blood-splattered arena. Raw anger laced his voice. "You know what happens to traitors in Jalapashu."

"I do." Mahi bowed her silver head, her *Punjabi suit* hanging off hunched shoulders.

She could have been a grandmother knitting in a rocking chair, razing hell in a bingo hall, diving into a lifetime's library of books, or the intrepid leader of a scout group teaching a new generation how to survive in the wild. Instead, she was here, bound by the raja's rules and desires, when she had such power. Yet, she had kept the secret of my magic at great personal risk.

I could win favour with the raja by telling him about the betrayals in his inner circle.

Only my sense of loyalty and fairness made that impossible.

Prem flicked his gaze to me. "You and your sister have not been forthright with me. That was not the first time she has done that." He gave a disappointed sigh. "You asked me to reveal the secrets of Jalapashu, Kiya. Have I not delivered? Or perhaps I am misremembering our intimacies in the library?"

In my peripheral vision, Deven stiffened.

I stepped forward. "I remember our conversation well, Prem. You fulfilled your side of the bargain. Now let me fulfil mine. You suggested I make you a gift, and I worked through the night to do so."

A slow smile spread across Prem's lips. "It's not often that a beautiful albeit *dirty* woman makes me a gift. My father said Hansa was an enigma. In a similar fashion, you have a way of alleviating my boredom, Kiya. Well, where is it? I want to see it."

I pointed under my seat to where the gift lay wrapped in a simple scarf next to our abandoned shoes. "May I?" At his nod, I scooped it up. Merlin wasn't here, but the work had already been done. My magic was sealed inside the vessel. I handed it to him with care, letting the spell fill my mind once more: *hamen bhūl jāo*. Forget us.

Prem accepted the gift and unwrapped it, smiling at us all in the round like a precocious child at a birthday party. Even so, a vein throbbed in his neck. He admired the tall, charred vase and its column of dots as our destiny teetered in the balance. "This would look well in my chambers, holding a single pink rose. But it doesn't make up for your lack of decorum today. You may be accustomed to other norms, but it Jalapashu, subjects—and yes, guests—ask the raja's permission before undertaking anything. Even pissing in a pot." He held up the vase to the light, and as he did, confusion washed over his face. His expression went slack as he glanced around the royal box, looking for answers. His gaze snagged on me and Leena. "General, who are these women?" he asked Deven with a shake of his head.

I held my breath and reached for Leena's hand, euphoria sparking in me. The spell had worked. If the raja had no use for us, we wouldn't have to stay. We could grab Merlin and walk away from Jalapashu. We could disassociate from these memories. Like mother had done. We could grieve Sitara and start again somehow.

Deven's jet-black eyes ping-ponged from the raja to us and back again. His brows pulled, gaze dropping to the vase. With a curse, he snatched it from the raja's hands. He threw the vase against the wall of the royal box. It smashed, raining down shards on the table of sweet treats.

I looked at Prem in horror, my heartbeat sluggish, a rush of cold trailing goosebumps up my nape.

Leena's blood-caked fingernails dug into the back of my hand.

Prem's confusion melted away, leaving quiet satisfaction. He clasped Deven on the shoulder. "I can always count on you, general. It seems we have our answer. The Marlowe sisters are indeed witches, like their sister and mother before them. Remarkable. Three sisters with different eyes—green, hazel and brown—each with their own type of magic. The eyes are always a giveaway." He gave a spontaneous burst of laughter. "Did you think you could hide it from me?"

I swallowed the lump in my throat. "You said at court that you have it within your means to bind our magic. You said we could come to an arrangement, and you'd let us leave." Even as I said it, resentment bloomed. Why should I have to give up *my* magic for *him*?

His jaw hardened. "You have much to learn about courtly life. I say all sorts of things all the time, Kiya." His icy eyes glinted. "I'm having far too much fun to let you leave. Only one matter remains to be seen, my virgin witches. Are you for me or against me?"

The door to the turquoise chamber slammed shut behind us. In fact, the raja judged us to be so little of a threat–scoffing at Leena's palm flowers and my quaint spell of forgetfulness– that he had allowed us back into the same room. Added to this, he reduced the number of guards outside.

Without a jewel to amplify our magic, he found our powers to be a sneeze rather than an earthquake.

I didn't know whether to be insulted or grateful.

At the sight of me and Leena, Merlin hopped out from behind the curtains, making soft chirps of pleasure. We slumped on the bed, thoughts reeling, as the hare nuzzled against us. On the bedside table, Sitara's new earthy brown urn with its etched swirls of water glowed.

Merlin's sonorous voice was the fabric of fairy tales. "So, the youngest returns to the fold. How does it feel knowing you treated me with less respect than a diseased goldfish bought at a funfair?"

Leena shook her head in chagrin. "You talking is going to take some getting used to." Awestruck, she listened to his rich, resonant tones.

The hare turned to me with a puff of air. The expansion

and contraction of his small body matched the tides of his emotions. "I heard the ruckus in the palace grounds, Kiya. I sensed your turmoil."

I raked my fingers through his satiny black fur as I told him of how the raja had outwitted us: separating us, wooing us, how Mustachio had fought in the ring, and we had unwittingly revealed our witch identities. "We can't underestimate his cleverness again. Without that bastard general, my spell might have worked."

Merlin sniffed. "That *bastard* must have suspected I was a familiar, given Sitara was a witch. And yet when you demanded I come with you, he agreed. He could have left me in Boundless Bay."

Leena chewed her lip. "What I don't understand is why you didn't tell us about the shifters, Merlin? You must have known, but you didn't prepare us."

I rubbed my forehead, eyes closed. My stomach churned at the memory of the leopard and panther. The cracking bones, the distorting ribcages, savage teeth and sharpened claws.

The hare shifted uneasily, nose twitching. "I told Sitara every last detail about this kingdom, but she thought I was telling tall tales to scare her. Would *you* have believed me?"

I gulped. "Maybe not."

Leena sighed. "No."

The hare made himself tall. His eyes glimmered. "I knew, sooner or later, you'd witness the brutality of the kingdom for yourself. When you saw Sitara die through that window, you understood nothing of Jalapashu. Sitara's blindness made her weak. But your eyes are wide open. I've lit a bonfire of knowledge in your minds."

Leena frowned. "Lit a candle of knowledge, you mean?"

Merlin huffed. "Yes, that's what I said."

"Wait, are the painted elephants shifters? And the

peacocks? How about Mahi's parrot?" I swallowed hard and edged backwards. "Are you?"

"Yes," he said. "I'm a ninety-year-old bald wizard with bad knees who likes to cosplay as a magical hare."

My heart thudded. "Really?"

The hare grunted. "No, not really."

I let out my breath in a whoosh and poked him with my forefinger. Merlin rolled over, playing the fool, but there was no doubt that it was me who had been foolish for the second time that day. I was an intelligent woman in my forties who believed I could think or drag myself out of any situation by sheer force of will. But my aching bones and flawed reasoning told another story. Our inner compasses had spun wildly since Sitara's death, but our survival depended on gathering our wits.

"And the raja? What is his magic?" I said.

Merlin scrambled up. "There are rumours from when he was a child when he was a prince of the kingdom and one of many who could have taken the throne. Some say he is a bear. Others swear they saw a wolverine or mountain lion. But the tussle for the throne culminates in a battle behind closed doors. There have been sightings, but when Prem Kumar won the throne, the secrets folded like shadows around him. He has no need to shift into his true form. His guard protects him, and the secrecy surrounding him made his legend grow wings. No one would dare challenge a king who might be a bear or wolverine."

Foreboding churned in the pit of my stomach. "There must be someone who knows."

"His general knows. Perhaps some of the guard," said the hare. "There are no law courts here. No judge or judiciary. Revealing the secret would be on pain of death."

A chill crept up my spine. Secrets were etched into the stones of this palace. They hung in portraits in the library and the jewellery adorning members of the court. They were hidden in the rooftop gargoyles and the padding footfalls of exotic creatures. Whispers were woven into the very fabric of Jalapashu, a reflection of the mysterious magic that lived here.

Goosebumps chased up my arms.

I smelt the orange and magnolia tang of her perfume and heard her before I saw her.

"Thank goodness I'm here to help." During our last meeting, Sitara's voice had ebbed and flowed like a radio station on the wrong frequency. This time, her voice was like a bell chime on a mountaintop: far away but clear all the same. She materialised in shimmering mist and dense shadow. "Your little ploy in the south courtyard might not have worked, but anchoring me to a new urn was impressive, Kiya. Well done."

A thrill of exhilaration rushed through my body. Sitara appearing went some way towards making up for the humiliation of my earlier failure. Judging by the raja's admissions about the lengths he went to be tech-free, we didn't have to fear listening devices. But I held my index finger to my lips just in case the guards heard one too many voices and decided to venture in. At my feet, the hare bounced with happiness, but Sitara paid him no heed. Her heart-shaped face turned by slow degrees to our younger sister.

A shudder ran through Leena. She pushed herself off the bed and inched closer to our sister, mouth gaping. "How is it possible?"

Our ghost sister smoothed her mass of silvery midnight hair. "Through death, unfinished business and residual energy of my earthly body, of course. Add a few electromagnetic waves and a splash of magic, *et voilà*."

Even though I'd told Leena what to expect, she trembled as she inched towards Sitara, taking in the strange flatness of her ghostly form, the spark of life that our sister had lost in death and could never return.

Sitara's matronly tone was achingly familiar from all the times she had played mother as the eldest sibling and after our parents' deaths. A faint aura of light surrounded her. "Now get out of those ruined clothes, will you? I don't know how anyone is supposed to think in that state of disarray."

Neither Leena nor I dared to mention how Sitara still wore the linen dress she had been killed in. We stripped, scrubbed ourselves clean and changed into simple clothing while Sitara and Merlin resumed a seesaw of affection and gentle chiding about paths taken and ignored. The sun had dipped in the horizon by the time we sat in a circle on the floor, with restless Sitara hovering beside us.

Though this Sitara was all sharp angles and no softness, her sea-green eyes were earnest. "By now, you know everything I hid from you. I have so many regrets about the last year of my life. Missed dinners. Lost chances to laugh together. Not throwing out grubby underwear before I carped it. The times I snapped or closed the door when I could have been honest. Merlin urged me to tell you our secrets a thousand times, but I was arrogant. I'm sorry."

My stomach quivered at being so close to her, but I forced myself to relax. "It's all in the past."

Leena snuck Sitara a sidelong glance. "It really isn't. We're locked up in a turret." She opened and closed her palm, releasing a clutch of daisies and carnations.

Merlin sniffed the flowers. His black and tan fur shimmered in the fading light. "As apologies go, that was a little meagre, Sitara. I always thought a good apology involves a *mea culpa* but also an effort to make amends."

"Hush, hare. I've already chastised myself enough." Sitara's ethereal form squirmed. "However, Merlin is right. I assumed I could control the situation. I was wrong. I've been trying to make up for my mistakes. That pile of books falling off the desk in the palace library as Merlin escaped? That was me."

I nodded, remembering the prickling of my scalp. "Let's focus on the here and now. We need an old-fashioned family conference. The raja knows we are witches but doesn't see us as a threat. For whatever reason, he has taken a shine to us. That puts us at an advantage."

Leena brushed the petals from her lap. "He's taken a shine to you, you mean. He must know by now I'm swinging from a different chandelier."

"So the raja wants a roll in the hay with Kiya," mused the hare. "We may yet find a use for that raw animal magnetism. After all, a man's blood supply can either go to his brain or his dong. Not both."

I frowned. "Did you learn that at hare school? I simply mean this is all a game to him. We can blindside him because he's not taking us seriously. Our goals are keeping our magic, escaping and justice."

Leena's posture went rigid. "Our goals are keeping our magic and staying. If Mum's story tells us anything, it's that our magic will wither in the ordinary world."

"You can't be serious. Don't you see?" Sitara's ghost form lit up like a bulb. "My story was a cautionary tale. Why would you want to repeat it? You need to give up magic and live out your lives to a grand old age, with leaking bladders, drooping bosoms and sticky-fingered grandchildren."

"I won't do that," said Leena quietly. "That's not my idea of happiness."

Sitara jutted out her chin. "I've roamed all over this kingdom as a ghost. I've mapped out this kingdom. I know where you can steal back the three broken segments of my jewel."

My breath hitched. "I thought the jewel had smashed to smithereens on our kitchen floor. The raja said it was destroyed. He told me at court we had to replace the one you stole. In lieu of that, we had to prove we were not witches."

Sitara shrugged. "He lied. He's had it all along. His general gave him the fragments."

Heat flushed through my body, and wild fantasies of violence surfaced in my mind. "How *dare* they?" Not only had these men stolen my sister from me, but they had also stolen my peace and had done it while telling bare-faced lies. I wanted a trapdoor to hell to swing open and swallow them up. No, that would be too good for them. I wanted a cannonball to appear from nowhere and take them out. Or them to be devoured by rabid squirrels. No, even that would be too good for them.

"It's not about either of them. Listen, both of you," said Sitara. "I know when the guards eat their meals and are distracted. I know how to navigate the secret passageways underneath the kingdom and escape undetected. I know the precise place where you can slip through the foliage back to Boundless Bay."

Leena's brown eyes widened. "If we find the jewel fragments, we'll find out what we're truly capable of."

Sitara fizzed with anger. "*That's* what you surmised from everything I said? I saw what you were capable of in the caves. You didn't just make palm flowers, Leena. In a blink, you grew sweeping vines from your hands. And you, Kiya, you created and collapsed entire cave walls, and that was just the beginning. But no amount of magic is worth your life."

"We did that?" Leena turned over her hands in wonder.

"You're not listening. All that time, I was stubborn as a mule, determined to keep our magic. It took losing my life for me to understand what a fool I'd been. There's a way to break your connection to the magic of this land. In death, I had access to all the answers in the palace library. That's what Mum didn't realise. If she had returned the topaz from her bracelet to the caves, she would have been free." Sitara pleaded with us, palms pressed together. "I asked you once if you would leave Boundless Bay. Surely you would consider it now?"

I opened and shut my mouth like a goldfish, unable to find words that felt true on my tongue. The thought of never setting foot in Boundless Bay again pained me, but her reasoning made sense. We had always trusted Sitara's judgement. She had spent a year learning about the kingdom, whereas we had been in Jalapashu for mere days. She had roamed the kingdom, free of her corporeal body. We were accustomed to her running roughshod over our judgement and calling the shots. It was how we had always functioned as a family unit.

Why, then, did I feel a seed of rebellion growing within me? *Magic, magic, magic,* went the old chant in my head. It made me giddy with excitement despite the dangers, despite all we had experienced.

The spells I had cast felt true, and the need for revenge grew like a thicket of thorny roses within me. "Don't you want justice for what happened to you? Don't you want us to expose the raja for what he is?" A shiver ran through me. "Don't you want us to kill him?"

Sitara's face was tight, her tone sharp. "Forget justice. Forget revenge. Forget this kingdom and its thorny magic."

Merlin had been unnaturally quiet at my feet. When he lifted his head, his long ears drooped, and his gilded eyes were molten pools of sadness. "Jalapashu wasn't always like this. Today you can smell the rot in the hungry bellies of the people, the way their dreams slip through their fingers while the raja turns a blind eye, the way his entertainment is more important than their life chances. But once, this kingdom brimmed with magic and hope. There are many like me who wish to see it succeed, though they hide in plain sight."

I listened, swayed by his arguments. Maybe we didn't have to give up all we had found. My mind circled back to the same thing. Deven might be an arsehole, but Mahi and

Aanya were different. They could have ratted us out, but they hadn't. We just had to figure out how far they were willing to go as they put themselves on the line. But when Sitara shook her head and her lips compressed, I kept my mouth shut. I'd been wrong about Deven. How did I know my radar was right about Mahi and Aanya?

"That's not up to us, Merlin," she said. "One day, Prem Kumar will die, and a new raja or rani will take his place. But my sisters will be gone by then. They will be just a chapter in Jalapashu's history. Their real stories will be written far away from this place."

I cast an eye at Leena, whose palm flowers had become an altar between us. I thought of my own magic: specks of clay imbued with power; earth growing beneath my hands, faster than possible within the laws of physics; spells weaving through my breath, parcelled up in my pots like little ticking clocks of possibility. I wondered how it would feel to crush and raise cave walls in one swoop. One day this would all seem like a dream. My breath caught in my chest as I met my sister's eyes. "If you're sure?"

"I am. There is no other way." The fire in Sitara's green eyes mellowed. "That's settled then. We have our plan. Steal the jewel fragments. Escape the kingdom. Return the jewels to their rightful place. You can grow old in London or Leeds or Liverpool. Or anywhere your heart desires. We start tomorrow. In a few days, you'll be on a train or plane speeding away from Jalapashu. You'll sprinkle my ashes from a hilltop or woodland strewn with bluebells. You'll be sad, but I'll have done my job as your big sister. Until then, will someone find a hiding place for my new urn before it comes to harm?"

Leena crushed her altar of flowers.

I buried my nose in Merlin's fur, a dull ache in my chest.

CHAPTER 17

Sitara paced and plotted, her brow furrowed, green eyes flashing with conviction. Though she wanted our encouragement, she didn't want our ideas. With the threat of losing our magic hanging over us, Leena chose to exhaust herself of magic rather than freely give it up. She created flowers in a wild frenzy at the pace of a machine gun. Soon, a spray of flowers covered the bed, and every corner of the chamber and even the bath was half full. I knew better than to reroute my sister's passions.

Without my studio as an escape route, I gravitated towards the potter's wheel with the hare at my side. The choppy sea of my thoughts calmed as I made a flurry of pots: a small, deep plate with a flat bottom in dark rich clay; a tiny cup designed to fit perfectly in the palm of my hand; and an oval casserole dish with two sturdy handles. With every turn of the wheel, the clay flowed, stretching towards the promise of its final self, and the river of my magic thrummed, aided by Merlin.

"Merlin, you seem to have abandoned me for Kiya," said Sitara. "I expect the warmth of her mortal hands has a lot to do with it. My ghostly hands are a poor comparison."

But my hands lay deep in the clay, and the hare didn't move from my side. Instead, he made low grunts of contentment. Spells unfurled in my head like ribbons. Jumbled-up letters became words that felt true and pure. They didn't come purely from me or Merlin but from our connection. I filled the pots with spells like little magical grenades. *Abhayam. Nidrāṃ dhāvatu. Tvamapaśya.* Then as the afternoon deepened into night and Sitara's scheming wound to its conclusion, I placed the pots into the kiln to seal in their magic.

Escape was an impossibility while locked in the turret, so the first step of the plan was to convince the raja to allow us to roam the kingdom freely. Fortunately, Sitara's ghostly roaming gave us an insight into the raja's mentality–and the taupe colour of his underpants. The crowd's adulation had boosted the raja's ego and convinced him of the need for more interaction with his subjects.

He had absorbed their cheers like an addict absorbs a drug. He demanded more of the same.

What is more, the raja had an antenna for the power of rumours at court and amongst the common folk. Our presence at court and in the royal box had ignited intrigue like never before. Hansa Malini's daughters had returned to Jalapashu. We had magic. A potential marriage match was in the cards. Sitara hovered in the raja's chambers as a maid combed out his hair and noted one thing above all else: Prem Kumar was powerful, but his love of being the centre of attention made him susceptible to manipulation.

With a little encouragement, Aanya agreed to deliver a message to him when she arrived with our dinner.

Kiya and Leena Marlowe
Request the pleasure of the raja's company
For lunch at Biryani Junction
Noon, tomorrow

Sitara's gleeful report of the raja's acceptance came before his formal response. In some ways, I welcomed this new side to her. It was an antidote to the rigid, glowering Sitara from the last year of her life. She revelled in the freedom of her ghostly form: the previously closed doors she whooshed through, the information she gleaned, the leading role she resumed in our relationship. She threw herself into this chance to save us and demanded only one thing: our circle of trust included only the three of us and the hare. No one else could know she had returned. No one else could know the particulars of our plan.

That was how we came to be part of a procession through the streets of the kingdom. Trumpets announced our departure from the palace. Dressed in a turban and his finest silks, the raja rode alone in an ornate, shaded *hathi howdah*—a carriage affixed to the back of an elephant. The bright colours of its painted face and trunk contrasted with the dull grey of its tough hide. Leena and I followed them on foot, swept up amongst a small clutch of court members that included Mahi. An elite group of *dhol* drummers accompanied us, with a substantial palace guard led by Deven, distinguished in his uniform—the jerk.

The sun shone on our heads, and thick dust clouded the air as we progressed. Soon, people lined the streets, drawn by the echo of the drums. I was grateful for the clothing rail Lokesh Saheb had sent to our chamber, and both irked and impressed that his sizing guesses–taking in my love handles and curves–were so accurate.

Mahi found her way to us, heavy-footed and dressed once more in pocketed harem trousers and a nineties T-shirt, this time featuring The Bangles. Her face remained impassive for the benefit of the crowd, but her words stung. "That was reckless of you yesterday."

I glowered. "We're reckless? We're not the ones playing with people's lives."

Mahi's frown deepened her wrinkles. "No need to be touchy. I have a little advice for you both. I know you are communing with your sister."

Leena rolled her eyes. "Yes. Although it is hard to pursue a green agenda or raise goats or our non-existent children together when we are *locked in a bloody turret*."

Mahi gave her the stink eye. She lowered her voice, and the din almost drowned her out. "Not a commune. I mean communing with your *other* sister… Close your mouths. You'll catch a fly. And yes, I know. I've seen her in my visions. Sometimes it's hard to distinguish past from present, but when Aanya sensed residual energy in your chambers, I knew we were dealing with a haunting."

The thunderous beats of the drums reverberated through my body, dark and foreboding, at odds with the crowd's palpable joy. I strained to hear her amongst the hullabaloo.

"Death is part of the natural cycle of life. Your sister's body returns to the earth. Her soul should be transitioning to a higher state of existence," said Mahi. "She has no business interfering down here anymore. You two still have living to do."

"What would you have us do?" said Leena.

"Lean into your destiny," said Mahi. "I'm an old woman now, but it took me a long time to learn how to live my truth. Midlife is about possibility. It's when you shake off your shackles. Your fear. Your protection mechanisms. The burdens you carry because other people said they were yours. You are on the cusp of possibility. You can shake everything up. Stop pretending. Claim your power and demand the space that is yours."

"Just as our mother before us, we don't belong here," I said.

Mahi sighed. "Nothing good can come of the dead interfering in mortal affairs. Don't let Sitara rule your decisions."

I blew out my cheeks. "Our decisions aren't your concern, Mahi."

"Oh, but they are." When she turned her face to mine, her forehead shifted.

My belly knotted. I turned away, not wanting to experience the horror of her third eye again. Mahi got the message, or perhaps she had delivered hers because she dropped back into the column of courtiers.

"Do you think she's right?" asked Leena.

My chest tightened. "I don't know. Either way, we stick to the plan."

We allowed ourselves to be swept along. Every step of the procession, faces lit up with happiness at the sight of the raja. Snatches of conversation came our way about how the raja had found a new love for his people since Hansa's daughters had returned. How this was just the start. There would be banquets and feasts and celebrations in the streets. They waved and showered the raja with long-stemmed roses and handfuls of soft petals. Their joy and frivolity bumped up against my dark mood. Mahi didn't know us. She didn't know what she was talking about.

Leena pressed my hand and gestured towards a group of children. "Look. Just as Sitara said."

Deven's nephew, Ishaan, threw a handful of sawdust at a girl. She threw a clutch of petals back at him. My heart jolted. They recreated our roles in the south courtyard when we faced up against Mustachio. Sitara had merrily told us to expect this. In fact, we had engineered our plan to ensure that the raja noticed. Up on his elephant, his gaze snagged on the horseplay too. The same pattern played out along the procession: boys and girls pretending to be us, a simple role play in a kingdom where they didn't have a myriad of toys or computer games, where their imaginations made us special.

I swallowed hard. All my life, I had taken our freedom for

granted. Now I had to barter and scheme for it. A dark cloud of foreboding hung over me. Dancing flags added to the frenzied atmosphere. Members of the court eyed us warily, weighing up if we were a threat or an opportunity. Gargoyles on nearby rooftops leered down at us, their stone faces twisted in sinister expressions. The beat of the drums sounded less a celebration, more a warning.

So much rode on this moment.

The elephant slowed outside Biryani Junction, a small, hidden gem of a restaurant nestled at the crossroads of two streets. The raja dismounted, his broad shoulders and slim hips showcased to perfection in a raw silk *kurta*. His slow and deliberate movements sent a clear message: he may have accepted our invitation, but a king hurried for no one. Once the elephant handler had coaxed the creature away, the raja beckoned Leena and me to his side.

He studied the worn restaurant sign. "So, you two like slumming it away from the palace. Is this a test to see if I can party with the common people? How amusing." He offered each of us the crook of his arm.

My stomach hardened. "Forget fine wines. You'll be drinking shots with us in no time."

His eyes dropped to my lips. "I hope so."

Leena shot me a look that read *creep* and accepted his arm.

At the general's command, the guards held back the crowds as we led the small column of court members through the unassuming entrance. Though I had only chosen Biryani Junction because Mahi had mentioned it, I was pleasantly surprised. A simple door opened up to a cosy room of tables made from mosaic tops and warm wood. The cool air inside was a welcome respite from the summer sun and the eagerness of the crowds. Polaroids of customers adorned the pockmarked walls. The palace guard had allowed a few tables of customers to stay to lend a feeling of authenticity. Tantalising aromas of spicy *samosas* and slow-cooked *dal* wafted through the air. The kitchen was in full view as if customers dined in a friend's kitchen rather than a formal restaurant. A man and woman in their fifties made haste, chopping vegetables and stirring large saucepans that bubbled over open flames. When they saw the raja, they washed their hands and hurried over to touch the raja's feet as a mark of respect.

Deven's soldierly stiffness melted into a smile. "Jilu and Radha have been married for over twenty years but spend most of their lives here. Biryani Junction is their calling."

I bristled. His clear affection for them hardly made up for how easily he'd thwarted my spell.

Jilu bowed his head. "We never imagined we would be your hosts, Prem-ji. We are honoured."

The raja had the snooty air of someone who had never known the joy of eating cold pizza for breakfast. "It remains to be seen how your creations compare to palace food."

His tactlessness provoked a nervous tick in Radha's face, which I rushed to compensate for. "You've built something special here." I didn't say it lightly. The sounds of sizzling pans mixed with the whispered chatter of locals. I could imagine the place on a Friday night, with no king to dampen the atmosphere. There would be clinking glasses, a raucous exchange of stories between locals and the occasional burst of laughter.

"That's kind of you," said Radha. "There's no menu here. Just point at what you want."

"How quaint," said the raja. "General, you do the choosing."

Deven nodded and headed to the counter while we took our seats at a makeshift setup with assorted tables and chairs, worn plates and dull cutlery. The clutch of other customers forgot their plates of food and stared at their king, who paid them no heed. The raja sat at the head of our table of twenty, with Leena and me on either side of him. His eyes scanned the room with a regal detachment and lingered on me for an uncomfortably long moment, taking in the cut of my simple *Punjabi suit* across my breast, the sweep of my hair across my shoulders, trying to read the expression in my eyes.

Jilu and Radha brought large platters of steaming hot biryani, tender curries, and freshly baked naan, making my mouth water. But no one relaxed. Everywhere the raja went, he held court, and his entourage didn't dare set the tone for fear of a misstep. No one dared to eat a morsel, with the exception of Mahi, who crunched on a *poppadom* dipped in mango chutney and mint sauce as if she had not fallen out of favour with the king. Across from me, Leena was still and pale.

The air was thick with tension until Prem spoke. "Why so serious, my courtiers? Have I not provided you with two spectacles this week?"

"This is most untoward," said a portly man towards the top of the table.

"Typical nonsense from a palace dweller." Mahi dragged a napkin across her mouth.

The raja's whiplash voice indicated she was still in his bad books. "May I remind you, seer, that I, too, am a palace dweller? In any case, let us feast. Perhaps you'll serve my food, Kiya?"

My anger flared, but a woman my age knew how to play dozens of roles: dutiful daughter, siren, ingenue, housemaid, hot girlfriend, and long-suffering wife. I took a serving spoon and heaped saffron rice, succulent lentil, and aubergine dal on his plate, with a helping of raita and naan stuffed with coconut. His full plate was the starting pistol for everyone else, and soon, mounds of curry, bread and pickled carrot filled the courtiers' plate. The smell of the spices and the sizzling dishes added to the ambience. While Leena and I used cutlery to eat, the rest of the court used their fingers.

Mahi was in her element, by far the least uptight at the table, the only one to suck hers with loud noises of appreciation. Despite the grandeur of palace cuisine, the honesty of the food shone through. Murmurs filled the room about Deven's wonderful choices and how perhaps Jilu and Radha could cook after all.

Diagonally opposite me, a vein throbbed in Deven's jaw as if he disapproved of the crude incivility of the courtiers. But that made no sense. After all, he was part of the court after all. He was the raja's number one protector. His eyes and ears. His sharpened blade.

I scowled at him. I'd almost fallen for his stern, dutiful general guff. He'd cut me free from the leopard's leash and worried about my feet. He had brought Merlin to Jalapashu and had a cute nephew who seemed to love him. He'd made it possible for me to do pottery in the turquoise chamber. A small part of me had enjoyed him picking me up when I fainted. I'd felt protected in his arms.

But Sitara's revelations had proved he was a duplicitous arsehole.

"Have you thought more about what I said?" At my frown, Mahi heaped more on her plate. "Since your mother did not bring you up in our culture, I imagine you are used to lunches of curdled baked beans on crusty toast, perhaps with a side of burnt sausages. I won't judge you if you can't handle the heat."

Right on cue, Leena took her first taste of the chilli *paneer*. She dropped her fork and flapped her hands.

Deven pushed a spare glass of water her way. Midnight eyes glinted with amusement as my sister scraped her tongue; table manners be damned. "I'm sure Kiya and Leena have experienced authentic Indian cuisine."

"Tikka masalas at an English curry house don't count," said the raja. "It's like they're afraid of flavour."

I ignored the intense stares of a birdlike lady in her

eighties with henna-coloured hair swept up in a beehive and concentrated on my food.

Mahi smacked her lips together. "Recipes like this are like my grandmother's, with ingredients crafted over generations. They are infinitely preferable to watering down dishes for the palettes of pale men."

The raja gave a nod of agreement and sipped from a glass of passion fruit juice. Though Leena sat next to him, he tilted his body in my direction. "It was sensible of you to smooth things over by inviting me here. I've not forgiven you for your naughtiness, although witnessing the birth of new magic is always a thrill. I had my seer look into your spell. It seems you wanted to win your freedom. I thought you were growing to like Jalapashu. I thought you were growing to like me."

I swallowed my mouthful of *biryani*. His vanity was insufferable, but this was our chance. I prayed I was a better liar than I gave myself credit for. I glanced up at him from under my lashes. "Jalapashu has its attractions."

Mahi slurped her *lassi*. "Not every woman welcomes the attention of a king. Some like it rough and ready," she said, winning smothered laughter from the courtiers around the table.

I threw her an irritated look. "I miss home. We're caged birds here."

"Even birds have more freedom in Jalapashu. I think of your gloriously clever parrot, seer." The raja's tone was dangerous. "Tell me, Marlowe sisters, do you think so badly of me?"

I fought the urge to pelt him with *samosas*. Had the moron really compared us to Babbu, the parrot?

Leena's voice rang out across the restaurant. "You said we're your guests, but we're your prisoners."

A curtain of silence descended. The conversation around

the table drew to a halt, and the clattering of the kitchen stopped as if every ear had turned our way.

Dark anger clouded the raja's face. "Clear the restaurant of everyone but the court."

The guards carried out his command. Chairs scraped against the floor, and plates of food went uneaten as the guards turfed out paying customers from Biryani Junction at the raja's request. Even Jilu and Radha found themselves on the street. But I wasn't scared. The unnatural fluttering of nets at a window told me that Sitara was here, willing us on and possibly mourning the death of her tastebuds. Her presence gave me strength.

When only his courtiers remained, the raja turned his reddened face to Leena. "Speak. Or was your only purpose to embarrass me in front of commoners?"

Leena met his steely gaze and did not waiver. "We want to learn more about Jalapashu. Free us from the turret."

As per our plan, the court didn't need to know that the raja had the fragments of the jewel in his possession. The court needed to know the mood of the people because, in a kingdom, power always rested with the peaks and troughs of public sentiment.

I took a deep breath. "Out there on the streets of your kingdom, children mimicked my and Leena's actions from the south courtyard. Won't the mood sour once they realise we are kept captive in the turret like Barbies in a dollhouse?"

The first silence had a slight fizz of anticipation. This silence was like the quiet in a tomb. Judging by the raja's taut expression and the stony faces around the table, I'd gone too far. No one chewed. No one spoke. Collectively, the courtiers held their breath–even Mahi–as we awaited the raja's outburst.

I cringed as the raja leaned back in his chair.

His laughter boomed. "The Marlowe sisters keep me on

my toes. Am I wrong to enjoy it? There is a perverse logic to that dollhouse analogy. I understand that previous rajas actually used the turret as a whorehouse. So it could be worse." He considered his bejewelled fingers for a moment and smiled. "Perhaps my courtiers would like to give their opinion. Should we let Kiya and Leena freely roam the kingdom?"

Twenty people were around the table, and only a handful dared to meet the raja's icy eyes. Poisonous anger sparked in my belly at his power over us.

This time, Mahi leapt fearlessly into the chasm. "Their trivial magic poses no threat to us. They are as harmless as rubber ducks in a bathtub."

Charming. If she was on our side, she made a damn good show of pretending to be otherwise. I made a promise to myself to surpass all their expectations of me.

"Then your visions have given you no reason for concern?" The raja's eyes shone at her nod. "Who else has the courage to speak?

"I disagree with the seer. We have your reputation to think of. Releasing the witch sisters shows weakness and a lack of control," said a giant of a man with a twiddly moustache and shrewd gaze.

Next, an ageing noblewoman wearing intricate *jhumka* earrings that jingled addressed the table. "Quite so, Bhavesh. Their mother and eldest sister could not be trusted. Why should they?"

Several courtiers murmured in agreement.

A bookish young man with a penchant for rhyming couplets stood up with a flourish: "Let's not be hasty, but take a pause. Should sisters pay for their family's flaws? We are better than that; it's plain to see. Let's not punish the innocent; let them go free."

The raja led a round of enthusiastic applause. "Bravo, Nitin."

Leena and I followed the conversation, lips tight. Underneath the table, I leaned my foot against hers. She trembled as much as I did.

"I cannot express myself as elegantly as Nitin, but I have read the tarot," said a thin man with a mystical air and a collection of talismans looped around his neck. "With the sisters' arrival, the endless dreary days are behind us. Jalapashu feels colourful once more. I, too, noticed children imitating the witch sisters. Our raja would gain popularity if he released them."

The raja's attention was rapt, his eyes bright. "Anyone else?"

A beautiful courtesan with a dancer's grace spoke with a small voice. A topaz jewel shone from the *tikka* on her forehead. "Hinduism teaches that we are all connected and deserve compassion. It teaches us about karma. Every action has consequences. Release the sisters. Let them prove their loyalty."

The raja turned his attention to Deven. "You have been quiet, my general. Don't be shy. What is your opinion?"

The general's neck corded. "Release them. Keep them in the turret. It is your decision. We can mitigate the risks by closely monitoring their movements."

Fury loosened my tongue. "Great. Just give us an ankle tag."

"They have not committed any crime. They should go free," said the birdlike lady with the beehive hair, who had stared at me so intently.

"Kavita, that cannot be. I will not leave us open to suggestions that we are putting the interests of our blood first." The portly man next to her pulled down his bushy brows. "The safety and security of the kingdom is our top priority. If there is even a chance that their magic could be used to harm us, they should remain in the turret and allowed out only under supervision."

White dots floated before my eyes. The penny dropped.

Yes, I could see it now. The old lady had my mother's oval face and her frame. The old man had her amber-brown eyes. How had I missed it? My breath bottled in my chest. How had I not realised Mum's family could still be in Jalapashu?

The colour drained from Leena's face. "*You're* our grandparents?"

"Oh yes? Didn't anyone tell you?" The raja's mouth twitched. "There you have it. Your maternal grandparents have opposing views. Your grandmother has a soft heart despite life's disappointments. Your grandfather, however, is made of iron and steel. Mere sentiment can't persuade him to risk this kingdom's future."

Every cell in my body screamed out to them to stick up for us, claim us as their family, and do what families should always do: protect and support their own.

Their faces remained impassive, despite the raja's taunting.

The raja steepled his fingers, contemplating his options. "I thank you for your sage advice, courtiers. After much consideration, I have decided to grant the witch sisters their freedom. They may leave the turret but not the kingdom. With one condition." He paused. "If either of you breaks my trust, you will spend a night alone with me, Kiya."

Leena started forward, her face pale. "No, that's insane. You can't demand that."

Somewhere, glasses full of gloopy juice crashed to the floor like Sitara, too, made her opinion clear.

The room circled around me. What else could I do? It seemed in Jalapashu, everything came with a price. "I accept," I said quietly. Better me than Leena.

Leena's shoulders curled over her chest. "I won't stand for it."

"It's okay," I said, though my stomach roiled. I thought of the men who had wanted something from me and how some had reacted when I said no. And I longed for Merlin and to fill my mind with spells of protection and rage.

"You should have listened to me. Freedom always comes with a price," said our grandfather.

"Indeed it does, Prakash." The raja signalled for Jilu and Radha to be allowed reentry into their restaurant and for wine and liquors to be brought to the table, and soon the air was full of joviality. "Biryani Junction is a marvel. See, someone has enchanted the alcohol. The shot glasses run towards us as if they have legs. Let us not disappoint them. Let us toast to your freedom."

I knew by the goosebumps chasing up my arms that the shot glasses didn't move of their own accord but of ghostly impetus.

The general clinked my glass, crescent shadows beneath his inky eyes. "Drink. It may give you courage."

Mahi gargled her drink and swallowed it with a grimace. "Oh, she has courage in spades."

I threw stinging pale liquid down my throat and wiped my mouth with the back of my hand.

Our grandparents sat solemn and still at the other end of the table. A hundred questions whirred in my mind. Did they regret their part in our mother's story? Did they wish they had welcomed our father into their family? Did they wonder what it would have been like to be a part of our childhoods? Why hadn't they insisted on being there for us, showing us the night sky, teaching us to bake, or reading us bedtime stories of kingdoms full of shining jewels and mystical beasts to prepare us for this day?

Neither Leena nor I reached across the divide.

As the night thickened in starless swirls around us and the raja and his court fell into a drunken stupor, Sitara's plan was well and truly in motion.

CHAPTER 18

The moon was a shining orb in velvet skies, and my feet were sore by the time we returned to the palace. The raja, wildly inebriated, passed out in the *hathi howdah* on his way back, lulled into dreamland by the sway of the exhausted elephant. When woken in the palace grounds, he grumbled and protested like the man-child he was and slid ingloriously down, losing both his turban and dignity. The guards he landed on top of didn't dare complain. He swatted at them with drunken lethargy as they hoisted him to his feet. They half carried, half dragged him through the palace halls as Deven accompanied us up the turret stairs. Eventually, the raja fell silent, save for the occasional groan or hiccup.

By now, Deven had undone the top button of his dress coat, revealing his toned upper chest. "I sent news ahead about your renegotiated stay in Jalapashu. My men no longer stand at your door. You will find no bolt there. You are free to explore the kingdom."

"Thank you, General." Leena took the steps quicker than us, eager for bed.

Deven cast me a sidelong look as her departing steps

echoed in the tight space. He wasn't drunk, but he'd had enough alcohol that his words ran into each other, a chipping away of formality that suited him. "I was unkind in the royal box. That must have been a shock, seeing Sitara's killer like that. It was unconscionable of Prem to parade him in front of you like that."

"It was cruel. But that is nothing new here." I bit my lip, hating myself for noticing he smelt like summer woods and worn leather. I'd never heard him criticise the raja. I wondered if it was as dangerous for him as for everyone else.

He gave a curt nod. "Kingdoms are shaped by their leaders."

Wasn't that the truth. So why did he put up with Prem?

Our hands brushed on the last turn of our ascent. I paused and spun towards him. We had spent so long sitting across from one another that I couldn't help pointing to the silvery scar through his right eyebrow and the slight bend on the bridge of his nose. "Where did you get those?"

His ring glinted as he touched them, suddenly self-conscious. "They're battle scars."

Warmth emanated from his body, leaving me giddy. Or maybe it was the alcohol. Not that I had consumed a lot. Drinking heartily in enemy territory was a no-no, especially for women. Regardless, in the narrowness of the turret, electricity sparked between us. I quashed it like a boot on a beetle. "I didn't think you'd cut yourself shaving."

His jaw tightened, and I pushed up the stairs ahead of him, seeing at once that the guards had melted away and the bolt had been removed outside our chamber, just as he had said. When I turned around to thank him, he had already gone. My pang of disappointment surprised me.

There was no time to dwell. Inside, my mortal and ghost sisters awaited, together with the hare.

He sprang high up in the air in celebration. "Freedom beckons. I can run through fields of grass. I can feel the warmth of the sun on my back. I can poo in the wild. I can make friends with the locals and make myself irresistible for strokes. This is a good day. Let us frolic under the moon. Let us dance like a leaf in the bin."

I frowned. "You mean leaf in the wind."

The hare nodded his silken head. "Yes, that's what I said."

Sitara's shimmering mist darkened into a dense shadow. "We can't afford to dillydally. I don't want you to stay in Jalapashu a minute longer than necessary."

The hare slumped. "Sometimes, Sitara, you really are the grapefruit in a fruit salad."

Leena grinned. "Huh. That kind of makes sense."

Sitara put her hands on her hips, glowering. "My priority is your wellbeing. Palace staff organised two events over the past few days. They are craving a rest. The guards have only just left. No one will expect anything untoward tonight. You'll need to push through your tiredness. We strike while the iron is hot. Besides, it is perfect that the raja is drunk."

She was right. There would be no better time to put step two of her plan into action. To undo the deep magic of the jewel we had touched in the Crypts and complete our escape, we had to return the trio of fragments to their point of origin. That meant first stealing them from the location Sitara's divination magic had pinpointed: the raja's bedside drawers.

My skin crawled just thinking about being in his chambers.

But I could do this with my sisters in tow. After all, hadn't Mahi said to us: *no child of Hansa Malini could be born ordinary.* If these past days had proved anything, it was that. We were not ordinary. We could outsmart the raja. With our family secrets finally out of the closet, we could achieve whatever we set our mind to. We had set our minds on escape. So why did my heart beat with terror? Why did I hear the old call in my head? *Magic, magic, magic.* I didn't matter. I wanted us to be safe. I wanted Leena to be safe.

This was the only way.

If our plan succeeded, we wouldn't return to the turquoise chamber. I scanned the room with its blue walls, white bone carvings of sea creatures, mosaic bath and potted plants, and picture frame windows, with the kiln vented from one of them. I wondered if the pots I had created would brim with magic once we were far away from Jalapashu, even once my own magic had faded. Whether I could keep the vessels on a shelf, like mere keepsakes, and only Leena and I would know the power they held. Perhaps I'd never want to think of this part of our lives again. All the same, when Merlin nudged me towards the kiln, I retrieved two magical pots and left the casserole dish behind, judging it to be too heavy. I wrapped them in a pillowcase and fashioned a crude handbag from another pillowcase by knotting its ends over my shoulder. Then I did the same for Sitara's urn and *A History of Jalapashu* and handed them to Leena.

We waited–three sisters and a hare–for the guards to stop their tall tales about the state of the king, the men and women of the court to peel off their finery, and the faint sounds of a sitar to quiet. Then, with careful footsteps, Leena and I followed the shimmering mist of our ghost sister down the winding turret stairs and along endless runs of palace corridors. By the time she stopped at a grand tapestry of a Bengal tiger, I'd lost my bearings.

"In here." Sitara drifted clean through the wall.

Heart in my mouth, I slid the tapestry aside and inched my hands across the wall to find an opening. Nothing. Nothing but smooth wall and the faint scent of incense that the tapestry had absorbed.

Sitara's head popped out of the wall again, her eyebrows raised with impatience.

Leena jumped three feet high. "What the–? Is it part of your plan to scare us to death?"

"This is like that time when you two didn't want to step around the corner at the House of Terror at the funfair," said Sitara.

"Well, if you're poltergeist skills were up to crack, we would be tucked up nicely in bed while you retrieved these yourself," said Leena.

"Stop it. That's not helping," I said. "If we're going to pull this off, we have to be on the same page."

Sitara harrumphed. "There's a groove in the wall parallel to the tip of the tiger's tail."

I found the groove and pressed a button hidden within it. A thin door eased open with the slightest hum. Merlin went first, scouting ahead to check the coast was clear. His colouring camouflaged him in the shadows. Leena followed him, her face tight with nerves. I shuffled the tapestry back into place and eased the door shut, then headed after them. Inside, the passageway was cramped and claustrophobic. I crept forward, one hand on my improvised bag to prevent the pots from clattering or breaking. Flickering torches cast eerie shadows on the walls that made my heart clatter in my chest. The air was thick with the scent of damp and the weight of secrets. The kind of secrets that could topple empires and change the course of history. It was easy to imagine mistresses and murderers stalking these inner walls like rats. I jumped at a scuttling in the walls.

Sitara's wispy form was barely visible in the dim light. Her whisper echoed. "Just a little further," she said before resuming her count of the oil lamps.

The muffled thud of Merlin's leaps returned. His words brimmed with bravado, but I could tell by the quiver in his voice that he, too, was anxious. "All clear up ahead. Kiya and Leena, you sound like panting bulldogs on a summer's day.

Thankfully, heavy breathing is no longer a problem Sitara suffers from."

At the fourteenth pair of oil lamps, our ghost sister crouched down low. "See that faint line? That's our way in. It's not been used in an age, but it should do the trick. Merlin, you're up. Stand back, everyone."

Merlin gave a great, heaving sigh and positioned himself with his back to the jammed opening. His liquid-gold eyes swept over all three of us. Then, with a slight twitch of his nose, he kicked out his muscly hind legs with force and speed. Once, twice, and then with fierce concentration and a thrust of momentum, a third time. A half-sized door flew open.

A door that led directly to the raja's bathroom.

I scooped him up into my arms. "You did it."

He grunted. "Let's hope he's out cold after all that partying. If he comes to and the old stories are true, there is little a hare can do against a bear, a wolverine or a mountain cat. I'd be like a snack to him. A cocktail sausage."

I set him down, anxiety spiking as Sitara floated ahead. Leena and I manoeuvred through the half-sized door on hands and knees. There, just as Sitara had described, we found a small room with limited headspace and scarcely room to swing a cat. On one wall, an ivory panel of wood stood out: the back of a linen closet. Together–barely speaking for fear of being found out–Leena and I jiggled the back off the closet and laid it to one side. With ashen faces and trembling hands, we pushed aside piles of plush towels and crawled through the shelving into the raja's bathroom.

I set down my makeshift bag alongside Leena's. "Keep watch at the passageway," I said to Merlin.

It was hard to imagine living in such opulence. In the moonlight, I discerned a bronze bathtub on marble floors, a his-and-hers sink, and a chandelier fit for a ballroom. A large window framed with clusters of honeysuckle looked out across the kingdom. I caught their cloying scent as Leena, and I tiptoed towards the raja's sleeping quarters behind the mist of our sister.

Already we could hear his snoring, like a monster in his cave.

The soft glow of oil lamps illuminated his thickly carpeted room. I frowned at deep gouges in the carpet and claw marks on the drapes in the otherwise luxurious room. Tapestries of jungle and forest settings lined the walls. The ceiling was high, decorated with frescoes of a stormy sky, its clouds flickering in the light of the lamps. At the centre of the room was a colossal bed draped in sumptuous silks. The raja slept naked at the top corner of the bed, his bare bottom giving us a rude welcome.

Two bedside tables, carved from the finest teak wood, bookended the raja's bed. It was the right one we needed. But Prem's arm lay strewn across it next to a jug of water, his elbow dipped right by the handle.

Sitara gave him a death stare. "Just perfect. You'll have to be careful. Top drawer. Avoid the box of sex toys. I almost seared my eyeballs seeing those."

I could feel the magnetic pull of the jewel fragments as if they knew they had been coded to us. They belonged to us, not the raja. Only, to get to them, we'd need to lift his arm or roll him over. I didn't fancy our chances, but if anyone could do it, it was Leena. I waggled my brows at her.

Her brown eyes flashed with terror in the flickering shadows. "What? Me?"

"Yes," I whispered as another snore rocked the royal chamber. "You do all that manoeuvring of patients at the hospital. Go on. He's out cold."

Leena inhaled deeply, blew out her breath and rubbed her palms together. Taking care not to loom over the raja, she nudged his arm away from the bedside table. We froze as the raja's drunken snoring changed its pattern, and he grumbled, on the verge of waking up. Time stopped. My brain whizzed through a dozen outcomes of being caught at his bedside until Leena opened her palm and spilt a clutch of lavender petals on his bed. The raja breathed in their scent, and the rumbling pattern of his drunken slumber resumed again.

Relief washed over me, but his arm had moved only by a whisker.

We still couldn't access the drawer.

"I thought I was going to wet myself," said Leena. "What now?"

Honey-hued eyes glimmered in the shadows as they came closer. The solution came to me before Merlin released the tiny cup I had fired in the kiln from his jaw. "Your spells, Kiya. Trust yourself."

Nidrāṃ dhāvatu. The spell drifted back into my mind as I picked up the cup. When my eyes met the hare's, I understood it was a sleep spell. I padded back across the carpet, set the cup carefully on the bedside table next to the raja's jug of water and said the spell out loud. A muted glow transferred itself from the cup and travelled across the raja's brown skin. His grunting snores ebbed away, and his breathing grew gentle. The slight frown on his face disappeared as if he'd suddenly fallen into a restorative sleep.

With a sudden burst of courage, I picked up his arm and moved it, none too gently.

The raja stayed sleeping.

So much for the bear, wolverine or mountain lion. He was as harmless as a toothless hamster. A wave of euphoria crashed through me, together with a need for payback. The power had clearly gone to my head. With a grin at Leena, I shifted his body. We moved him like a life-size ragdoll, positioning his arms and legs in absurd angles until we settled on a pose that had us doubled over in silent laughter. The raja's body was now contorted into a sleeping baby pose, with his knees tucked in and his bare bum high in the air. I put one thumb in his mouth. Leena put his other thumb in his bottom.

Sitara paced around. "For heaven's sake, you two. Get the job done."

The hare leapt onto the bed to have a look. "You've forgotten how to play, Sitara."

"Damn, I wish we had a camera," said Leena.

There was no more need for careful movements. I stifled a laugh and opened the drawer. It was deep and lined with velvet. To one side was a black satin pouch tied with a yellow ribbon. I picked it up, my heart beating impossibly fast, blood rushing to my head. The weight of the pouch surprised me.

"And?" said Sitara.

Leena inched closer. "Do you have them?"

I untied the ribbon and let the jewels fall into my hand. My mind flashed back to Sitara holding a palm-sized bronze-hued stone in our kitchen the day she died. Now, one smooth oval topaz stone had become three perfect jagged fragments. They were evenly sized as if they had been made for us: for three magical sisters. One in particular called to me. At its touch, a jolt of electricity coursed through my body and radiated outwards. I rocked with sudden vertigo as if standing on the edge of a cliff, falling, falling ever deeper. With the next breath, the dizziness abated, leaving only a sense of exhilaration. I looked at my sisters. Could it be that despite the breakage, they still worked?

I forced myself to focus. "I have them." I slipped the jewels back into their pouch.

Sitara nodded, her face determined. "Then it's time to leave this hellhole."

With one last look at the raja's comically contorted form, we turned back towards the passageway. But Merlin stopped, ears twitching at the sound of a click behind us.

I swung around, thinking my sleeping spell had been

broken. I knew so little about my magic. About how long spells lasted and how to maintain them. Whether they were dependent more on my ingredients–clay to water proportions and the precise temperature of the kiln–or whether they were dependent on my nearness to Merlin or my own concentration. We shouldn't have stopped for the antics with the sleeping raja. We should have just made haste.

But the raja was still in his sleeping baby pose with his thumbs in his orifices.

However, there was someone else in the royal chamber with us. A figure stood inside the main door to the raja's suite. A figure who, by his stealth and stature, was a soldier. He stepped towards us with purpose, and by the light of the oil lamps, I recognised Deven.

His hand rested on his belt of daggers, and his voice promised trouble. "What the hell are you doing in here?"

We froze. A confrontation was in nobody's interest. Not in Deven's interest if Sitara went all poltergeist, not in our interest if more guards came to the raja's aid, and not in the macho raja's interest given he'd been subdued in his chambers by three women and a hare.

He'd taken off his dress coat and wore a translucent shirt over trousers, but by his furious expression, he was committed to his duties. "How? How did you get in here?"

My mind whirred. Neither of us could back down. There was only one way this could end.

He observed how Leena inched backwards towards the bathroom and the towels spilling across the floor, and realisation dawned. "I *told* him we should have that concreted up. He thought having free rein for his mistresses to come was more important."

I clenched my fists tightly around the pouch as my magic coursed through my veins. My heart thrummed like a hummingbird's wings. "Turn back the way you came. Pretend you didn't see us."

Deven darted a glance at the raja. "Why is he sleeping like that?" His jawline hardened at the faint glow of my magic on Prem's body. "Are you here to kill him? There are other witches in Jalapashu. You do this, and the consequences will get out of hand."

"We're not here to kill him." I opened my palm to show him the pouch, then tossed it towards Leena, hoping her catching skills had improved since school. But it turned out that my ball throwing skills–unlike my pottery throwing–hadn't improved either. "Run, Leena!"

My stomach plummeted as the pouch flew off kilter.

Deven caught it easily before circling my wrist and spinning me against him. "You'll be the death of us."

At our feet, the hare squared up to him. "Let go of her, or your ankles will feel the full force of my gnashers."

My eyes locked onto Deven's. "Let me go."

His grip tightened. "I went to your room. I found it empty. Then I found the casserole dish with the magic. You're playing a dangerous game. Why do you make me forget my fear?"

My breath quickened. My spell drifted up through the layers of my consciousness. *Abhayam.* Be without fear. Was my magic why he was speaking so plainly? I countered his question. "Why do you protect the raja? He doesn't deserve your loyalty."

His nails bit into the soft skin of my wrist. He lowered his voice until it was a murmur only I could hear. "He is family as well as my king. My cousin on my father's side."

To our left, the raja's snores reached a new crescendo.

Warmth flooded through my body at his touch. "Families don't get a free pass to be jerks." I wrenched my wrist away, but he held fast as a cold breeze circled around us. *Sitara.* I willed her not to show herself. I willed her not to hurt him. Yet. "Let my sister and the hare go."

His brows pulled in. He darted a glance at his sleeping cousin. "Fine."

My eyes didn't leave his face. "I'll be right behind you, Leena. Go."

She left, followed by the hare and the cold wind of our ghost sister, who knew better than to reveal herself to the enemy.

I knew by the tingle of my nerve endings and the confusion clouding Deven's face that a strange connection had formed between us. He released my wrist and trailed his thumb across my cheek. The chiselled lines of his face softened when I tilted my head slightly to enjoy his touch, there, in the most dangerous place in Jalapashu.

Then he cupped my hand, placed the pouch of jewel fragments in my palm, and closed my fingers over it. His voice was harsh. "You've been one step ahead of me this whole time, haven't you?" A pause. "The least competent watchman is posted at the east palace gates. I'll clear away all signs of your caper before he wakes. Go, Kiya." He said my name like a prayer.

My knees loosened, and a clumsiness came over me as I turned away from him, but I didn't need to be told twice. My family waited. I escaped after them into the twisting passageway, coal-black eyes at my back, leaving the drunken raja in a state of blissful unconsciousness on his bed.

My hand tightened around the jewel pouch, but my mind was elsewhere. A wayward curl, heat on my wrist, a stern man softening for me. Deven had risked his reputation for me tonight, but it wasn't enough to earn my forgiveness. Soon Jalapashu would be mere dust in our rearview mirror. It's what we had been working towards.

Why, then, did it feel so wrong?

CHAPTER 19

We didn't bother to close the passageway behind us. Time was of the essence. All that mattered was reaching Boundless Bay. Our footsteps echoed down the cramped passageways.

Leena whispered over her shoulder. "Thank God you managed to get away."

My bag clattered as I caught up. "He let me go."

"I smell a booby trap," said Merlin.

Sitara nodded. "We'll have to be quick before he raises the alarm."

Despite the late hour, the guards still patrolled the grounds, and so we pushed forward on quick and light feet. Weaving through the dank tunnels disoriented me. The oil lamps cast long shadows, and the walls blended together. Every change of direction led to another corridor, twisting and turning without end. Some passages were so narrow that we had to squeeze through sideways, our shoulders scraping against rough walls. Other passages opened into vast caverns filled with dusty paintings and forgotten rails of clothing.

How many mortal bodies had rotted to skeletons and dust down here, unfound? But Sitara's divination magic kept us moving in the right direction. She had planned for every eventuality. She knew the guards' routines, and with Deven's advice about the incompetent watch at the east palace gates, our escape was almost certain. In spite of the musty odour, dead ends and locked doors, a new vibrancy filled our every cell. Butterflies fluttered in my belly at the thought of the bay and our home. I sensed the same glee in my companions, too, in the spontaneous laughter that bubbled through Leena and in the hare's eager bounds.

We were running towards danger, but soon we would be safe.

Still, our adventure had turned up the volume of the familiar chant in my mind—m*agic, magic, magic.*

A thought had sprouted in me the moment I held the jewel fragments in my palm in the royal chamber. With every step, the thought took root, growing stronger. At the final tunnel, I stopped short. The black pouch weighed heavy with promise and longing in my hand. "We need these jewel fragments. We need to embrace their power to get out of here."

"Now we're talking," came Merlin's sage voice from the shadows. "Those gemstones are coded to you, and this isn't a walk in the park. Of course, you use them. I'm for any measure that keeps me from a butcher's block."

Sitara's orange and magnolia perfume reached my nose before she did. "One last hoorah then."

Leena's eyes shone with excitement. "I'm in."

I tipped the topaz onto my hand, swallowing my possessive instinct when she hovered over the jewel I considered mine. When she chose another, the tightness in my chest eased. Leena's eyes widened with heightened awareness. She stared at the tips of her fingers and flexed her hands, and her gaze moved upwards to her arms as if her magic had been jump-started.

Dense shadows moved around Sitara's shift dress. Her face was solemn. "Feels good, doesn't it?"

"What about yours?" I asked.

She gave a wry smile. "Place it in my urn. It has to be worn close to your body. In this kingdom, the topaz is worn as jewellery, but it will work as well to stash yours in your bra. It doesn't matter whether you choose your larger or smaller boob. And yes, we all have them. Be careful of those jagged edges."

Merlin waited impatiently, his nose twitching, yearning to leave the confines of the stuffy passageway.

I reached under my embroidered top and did as I was told. Once suspended above my heart space, the topaz was cool against my skin. An esoteric jolt raced through me as if a switch had been flipped inside me, making my magic more potent and bringing clarity and focus. It was both exhilarating and terrifying.

Leena slipped her own gemstone into her bra, then extracted the urn from her bag and carefully laid the last jewel amongst our sister's ashes. Almost immediately, Sitara's ghostly sea-foam eyes glimmered a deeper shade as she reestablished her connection to its magical properties.

"Come on," she said, driving forward in a surge of mists.

We hurried after her through the final stretch of the passageway. The musty scent gradually faded away, replaced by a faint scent of fresh air. The cramped tunnels widened, and the rough, uneven walls gave way to smooth ones. Shining marble floors replaced the dull concrete ones, changing the sound of our footsteps. We paused in front of a small wooden door, hearts ricocheting, and then Sitara floated through it. With the hare agitating at my feet, I steeled myself and opened the door onto a narrow alleyway within the palace compound. Merlin bounded away lightning quick, his ears alert for any signs of danger, without even a word of polite explanation. Not that I blamed him. I set down my bag, knowing I needed a moment, too. The cool air was welcome on my skin. I rested, filling my lungs with great gulps of clean air, before taking stock. Tall brick walls rose on either side of us, lined with fearsome gargoyles. Up above, the summer night shone with a thousand stars. At the end of the alleyway, I glimpsed a babbling fountain and the thorny pink roses tipped with white that reminded me of our mother.

I liked to think that somewhere, somehow, she willed her girls to succeed.

Now all we had to do was to skirt around the compound towards the east palace gates, avoiding the detection of guards and strange beasts in the grounds, find the magical channel to slip through the foliage back to Boundless Bay, make it on foot to replace the gemstones in the Crypts, and survive the night until the train station opened to get us the heck away from Jalapashu—all with a hare in tow and looking like we were extras from a Bollywood movie.

I told myself it was a piece of cake, but my gut still churned.

"I don't know about you, but I'm knackered." Somewhere along the route, Leena's hairband had snapped. Her golden hair was less a blunt-edged asymmetric fashion statement and more a scarecrow taking a walk on the wild side. "More knackered than after a week of night shifts at the hospital."

I nodded. It was enough to make a woman want to lie down and take a nap. Or at least a tea break, complete with an entire packet of shortbread. But that wasn't constructive. Sitara might have returned, but she wasn't on the earthly plane. Not really. It was still up to me to step up for Leena. "We push on like Sitara says. Otherwise, it'll all have been for nothing."

"I keep thinking about Aanya. I like her. She's gentle and quiet and so bloody cool. With hidden depths, you know? I wanted to get underneath her layers."

I pushed down the thoughts of Deven that surfaced in my mind–how he had spun me against him, trailed a finger down my cheek and let me leave–and cocked an eyebrow. "I bet you did."

"Not that it could have worked. Another relationship doomed to failure."

"For what it's worth, I was a cow in Lokesh Saheb's atelier. I've always admired you for giving your heart away so readily."

Leena grinned. "Whoever wins yours will have to work damn hard for it. But maybe you can meet them halfway. Not every man loves as purely as Dad. But some do."

"You two are having a girl chat without me?" said Sitara. "Grab your stuff. It's three in the morning already. We only have a few hours of darkness left before this escape gets a whole lot harder."

I double-wrapped the plate I had made, determined to have one memento of my stay and combined the contents of the two bags into one. As I stood upright, a low rumbling filled the air. The sort of rumbling that didn't belong in a quiet alleyway in the dead of night or a palace garden. We would have been unmoved by a chorus of crickets, the hooting of an owl or leaves blown by a summer breeze. But the deep grinding noise, like boulders dragged over rough ground, made my blood curdle.

Leena jerked with terror. "Oh, shit."

I looked up. Six gargoyles standing sentinel on the tall brick walls shifted in the moonlight. As they tore their clawed feet, talons and coiled serpentine tails from their perch, the brickwork around them cracked, dusting the ground with mortar and stone. Their once-still eyes glimmered with a sinister light, and their stone mouths twisted into menacing grins.

They lunged forward en masse, their razor-sharp talons at the ready, leathery wings beating with thunderous force. I winced as they hit the ground with a thud. Leena's eyes darted frantically around the darkened alleyway. But Sitara didn't hesitate. She sprang into action but hadn't figured out how to land punches as a ghost, and the emotions she channelled into her swinging movements didn't pay off. They were mere flicks on tough gargoyle skin.

Sitara straightened her spine. "I know my lore, arseholes. You hate water, and I'm a blue witch."

We would have been helpless mere moments before, but we stood a chance with the jewels amplifying our magical talents. Sitara raised her hands, called forth a torrent of water from the nearby fountain and became the goddess we had witnessed in our kitchen. Her ebony hair whipped in the wind as she beckoned the water to her and directed the water at the six gargoyles with a soldier's precision. They stumbled with the first attack, shrinking back and snarling. Sitara didn't waste a drop. With cupped hands, she called every droplet back to her and struck the gargoyles with icy arrows that tore chips of stony flesh from their bodies. We remained entirely dry.

They came towards us, undeterred, shaking water off their wings. My heart pounded as Merlin returned and bounded through their legs, panic evident in his lurching movements but determined to do his part and topple some. My heart hammered in my chest as he rammed one and was almost crushed under the weight of another. I reached for my magic, feeling the thrum of power coursing through my veins. Almost by instinct, I tore bricks from the wall and sent them arcing through the air with a sweep of my arm.

Relief flooded me when Merlin made it to my side.

"Bollocks to this." Leena flung out her palms, and looping vines emerged, targeting the two closest gargoyles. The vines wove around their limbs, but they broke free easily, their stony hides unyielding to her plant magic. So she raised a dense thicket of brambles between us, with utter effortlessness, when a few hours previously, palm flowers had been the pinnacle of her magic.

Now both the thicket and the gargoyles blocked our route out of the alley. It would be folly to go back into the passageway.

I frowned. The gargoyles could have flown over the top of the thicket, but they chose not to. Instead, they shuddered to a halt. Although they looked fearsome with their teeth and claws and grotesque expressions, they seemed forlorn.

"Stop!" My cry echoed off the brick walls. The gargoyles outnumbered us, but there was hesitation in their movements. "They're not serving the raja."

Sitara's form was less light than shadows again as if her efforts had taken their toll. "Of course they are."

My mind reeled as I stepped over the thicket. "They're defending themselves. Not attacking us."

"Stop," Leena called out. "We'll find another way."

It didn't make sense to them, but I felt the truth of it in my bones and in the warm pulse of the gemstone on my skin. I approached the gargoyles cautiously, stopping next to one with a lion's head and mane. It was half my height, with a muscly humanoid bottom body and a ridged tail with a pointed arrow tip. Pulse racing, I placed my hand on its cold, battle-hardened skin.

The gargoyle bowed, deep and low, and the other gargoyles followed suit. His voice was low and guttural like gravel being ground together. I could have easily mistaken it for creaking branches or the call of the wind. "We wake for you, mistress."

His declaration sent shivers down my spine.

The hare leapt over the thicket to sit by my side. "They're loyal to you."

"Yes. I think they are." Adrenalin tingled through my body, dulled by a pang of pity. We journeyed towards the end of our magical destiny, but I had barely begun to fathom what might be possible.

"Not going to lie. This is awesome," sang Leena.

Sitara and I exchanged sombre glances, and I understood at last why she had hidden our magic from us.

How harsh to revel in a new gift, only to have it stolen from you or for it to bring pain.

The gargoyles fell into step behind us, forming a protective shield. As we left the alley, their wings rustled in the night breeze. The air was thick with the smell of damp stone, mother's thorny roses, and the sound of our ragged breaths.

CHAPTER 20

We made our way through the palace gardens, praying that our skirmish in the alley hadn't been heard and nobody cared enough about that abandoned corner of the grounds to notice the damage we had left behind until we were gone. Our group of ten moved in careful choreography, the gargoyles acting as silent protectors, their stony skin a stark contrast to my warm flesh. The scent of blooming flowers filled the air, their sweet fragrance mingling with the crisp aroma of freshly trimmed hedges. Beneath our feet, the ground was soft and yielding. The grass cushioned our steps as we made our way across the grounds towards the east palace gates, as Deven had advised.

Together, we navigated the garden maze, our senses heightened. The rattling breathing of the gargoyles, the anxious whoosh of our ghost sister, the shadows cast by trees, the song of a nightingale, the gleam of the moon: every sight, sound, and smell was more vivid than ever before. The maze shifted and changed before our very eyes, but Sitara had determined this was the safest way to our destination. Who would willingly venture into a maze at night? The hedges towered above us as though we were locked in a fortress, and even the gargoyles grew agitated. They muttered between themselves, like the grunting of wild animals or the rumble of a distant thunderstorm, but I couldn't decipher their language. It wasn't meant for my ears. But despite the complexities of the maze, we had Sitara and Merlin. When we took the wrong turn, they scouted ahead so we could retrace our steps.

When we were almost at the exit, Sitara pointed. Her whisper was the static of a car radio. "The gates are a hundred yards over there."

My gut wrenched. The closer we got to our goal, the closer we were to losing her all over again.

I wasn't ready to say another goodbye. I wasn't ready to scatter her ashes.

"Then it's twenty minutes on foot to reach the access point to Boundless Bay." Sitara gave the gargoyles a suspicious look. "They're not coming with us, though."

The gargoyles–either scrupulously polite or a little deaf– didn't react. When Leena winked at one, it spread its lips into a gruesome toothy response, then covered its face like it was shy.

The hare rose between us on his hind legs. "I'll scout ahead as lookout."

Sitara shook her head. "No need. We know there will be one guard positioned there. We can't let him raise the alarm. No one can know we are gone until the kingdom wakes. Either we tie him up or ask the gargoyles to hold him in situ, preferably with his mouth clamped shut."

Leena smiled with false bravado. "This is it then. One last rush of magic."

"Tomorrow, I will be a simple hare again," said Merlin. "And you will be back to normality with a lump."

"Back to normality with a bump, you mean," said Sitara.

As my sisters teased Merlin, it seemed to me I could

already hear the seagulls of Boundless Bay and the crash of the ocean against the shore. Part of me yearned for the familiarity of our family home, the rugged terrain of coastal walks and the gentle peace of Soul Pottery. Even though staying would be impossible.

Even though in midlife, we had to start our lives all over again somewhere new.

I surfaced from my thoughts and inhaled deeply. Then I turned to my sisters, our gargoyle protectors and the black and tan hare. "Ready?" The faint rustling of leaves and the occasional chirp of a cricket met my ears, but other than that, the gardens were still and silent.

On the count of three, we edged around the exit to the maze, peering cautiously into the darkness ahead. Merlin tore across the grass, and the rest of us followed. The gargoyles moved with surprising grace for their size, their massive wings slicing through the air as they followed us, their heavy footfalls absorbed by the lawn. Between us and the gates was a vast expanse of open land, with no statues or high hedging or pavilions to hide behind. We held our nerve and pressed on to the last turn.

When Merlin screeched in alarm, we should have turned back, but I couldn't do that to him. I couldn't leave him alone and in trouble.

We froze. Then I raced ahead, and my gargoyles surged with me, despite the cursing of my sisters and Leena's frenzied yell about the blasted urn, the damn plate and our fragile bodies and what the blooming hell we had gotten ourselves into. I ran towards Merlin, tired and bruised but determined for us all to be safe, including the hare I now loved. The hare who had comforted me and made me laugh and told me the stories of my past. The hare who had stolen for us and faced up to friendly gargoyles. The hare who had been there for my mother and who desperately didn't want to end up as hare stew.

My stomach grew leaden when I turned the corner and caught sight of him. Merlin squirmed as a sniggering guard held him by his long ears. The guard was accompanied by fourteen–perhaps sixteen–others, though it was before dawn, and he should have been alone. Unlike the ivory dress coats of Deven's elite troop, these men wore uniforms of dark blue and gold, with tall turbans adorned with peacock feathers. Their armour was made of polished metal and leather. In the light of the moon, I saw no topaz jewels, though I scanned their hands and wrists and the spaces between their armour. Some carried gleaming swords, others long spears and a few wielded heavy iron maces. Though the smiles slipped from their faces at the sight of the gargoyles, they stood in formation to face us.

For a group of women who had never even been in a catfight, this promised to be a tall order.

But we had gargoyles and our magic.

They had my hare, and my mama instincts were in overdrive.

I glanced at my sisters, and we proceeded in silent agreement, each of us calling upon our respective powers while the gargoyles moved two apiece to back us up. It all happened so fast, as if by instinct. The guards charged at us, their weapons glinting in the dim light. We moved as one, dodging their blows and striking back with our magic. Merlin's captor hung back. Even as the remaining guards ran in our direction, I focused my efforts on the hare. I clenched my fists, tearing clumps of earth from the lawn that solidified into rock and travelled through the air, hitting the grinning, self-congratulating soldier clean in the face. He howled and released Merlin as one eye streamed with blood. Merlin tripped him up and trampled him with glee while the man writhed on the floor.

My heart soared at his escape. My fear ebbed away. I kicked off my sandals, giving in to the need to feel the soil beneath my feet, connecting to the life that teemed within it: earthworms, insects, and seeds of flowers burrowed deep with the promise of tomorrow. The magic that flowed within me was familiar. Just like clay, I could shape and manipulate the earth to my will. I could harden it like in a kiln or soften it like wet clay on a wheel. With a flick of my wrist, I could make the earth rise like a pot shaped by a skilled potter. Just like in my studio, I felt the need for playfulness, to create new shapes from the earth at my feet.

With a flick of my hands, I protected Merlin's progress across the field, shielding him with a cocoon of earth that moved as he did. I sent projectiles in the blink of an eye, with utmost precision, and looped them around, hitting the guards from unexpected angles, disorienting them. I created mounds to slow them down and walls of protection when the guards' spears flew through the air.

My mind and body worked seamlessly as if the gemstone suspended above my heart space somehow unblocked all the doubt that otherwise made me second-guess myself like silt being washed away from a riverbed. In that moment of power, anything was possible, even three women winning a battle against trained soldiers. I didn't fear making mistakes because the gargoyles proved to be powerful allies. They grunted with exertion, shielding us with their bodies, striking crushing blows with bare leathery fists or flinging the guards' weapons far away. Bat-like wings propelled them into the air, and they hauled the guards up, dropping them a few feet, their intention to wind not to kill them.

Their connection to me told them it wasn't bloodshed we wanted. It was freedom.

My sisters acted with the same joy and abandon, their magic surging and evolving with every moment. The scent of fresh foliage filled my nose as Leena worked her magic. Her vines, once small and thin, grew rapidly in size and thickness as she battled the guards. It didn't matter that they carried weapons. She didn't have to get close. Plants snaked around the guards' ankles, tightening like a vice. The guards stumbled, toppling like bowling pins, and cried out *witch, witch*. They slashed at the vines with their swords, but they couldn't break free. There was no limit to Leena's imagination. She created barriers that shot up from the ground where there had been nothing before, shielding the shy gargoyle from a brutal mace attack. The leaves of nearby trees shook as if in a storm as if she vibrated at her truest frequency, and they couldn't help but join in. All the while, her face shone with joy.

We fought on, side by side. Sitara was in her element. Her brow furrowed in concentration as she summoned a jet of water from the ground. The guards ogled, first at her shimmering ghost form, then her magical prowess, as the fountain sprayed high into the air, scattering the gargoyles. The ogling guards expected to be splashed, but my cunning sister scalded them. As they groaned and regrouped, Sitara called the water droplets back to her and thrust her hands forward, sending a barrage of icy darts shooting towards them. But she wasn't finished. Only two guards remained standing. With a dancer's grace, she turned her palms upwards, and the icy darts regrouped above the guards' heads. When she pulled her hands apart, the darts broke into a cascade of droplets that shimmered in the moonlight. She clapped her hands together, sending a shockwave through the water. It erupted into a wall of crushing force, felling the guards beneath it like rag dolls.

I had never felt stronger than at that moment, together with my sisters.

It was a perfect symphony, a deep connection to my own purpose, to other witches and the world, as if we hummed in harmony with the natural world and our souls. The air was charged and tingling, but a peace pervaded my very bones. My breathing was calm, my expression serene. At that moment, I was both uplifted and supported by our fledgling coven.

Coven. The very word sent a frisson of excitement up my spine.

The guards tired long before us. The few that stood up were quickly felled again, their weapons scattered across the field. Though we were outnumbered, we were not outmatched. The sour scent of sweat and fear emanated from the guards as we bound them.

"The raja won't let this stand," said the sniggering fool who had hurt Merlin. But there was no oomph behind his words, only humiliation and awe at the sight of gargoyles that had not woken in decades and witches far more powerful than he had expected.

"Collect their weapons," I said to the gargoyles. "And make sure every last one is tied up, or wrap them in your arms to subdue them. Thank you," I added as an afterthought.

Sitara's mossy eyes were alight with triumph. "I think gargoyles respond more to strength than softness."

"Really?" asked Leena, gesturing towards the shy one with the fishtail that still made eyes at her.

My chest tightened. "Do you think anyone heard the sounds of battle?" I couldn't think of anything worse than round two. The magical surge had drained us all, and I shivered now the battle was over despite the warm summer night.

Leena shook her head. "They would have been here by now. This is the furthest gate from the palace."

Sitara frowned. "But why were so many more guards here than we expected?"

"I don't know." Merlin nuzzled my legs. "I thought I was barbecue meat right there."

I bent down to caress him and tried not to wince at the tear on his ear. "Not on my watch. You're family. And I'm pretty sure most of the inhabitants here are vegetarian anyway if that helps you sleep more soundly." Stroking him brought us both ease.

He gave a sweet sigh of anticipation. "I always sleep soundly in grasses by the ocean."

With a great sense of relief, we turned our attention to the imposing iron gates just beyond our huddled prisoners. My heartbeat quickened at the intricate tiger designs on the gates, lit by flickering torches attached to the soaring palace walls. The gates were locked, but it was nothing we couldn't manage with our combined strength or perhaps with the intervention of a muscular gargoyle. All our patient scheming, all our risks and bravery had brought us this far. Our exertions were nearly over.

I tensed at a familiar squawk.

"Dirty hare. Ugly gargoyles." Babbu, the parrot, swooped down from a tree on luminous green wings and landed on the top of the gate. He gave me a beady-eyed stare. "She said you would come."

The hare sprang up. "Let me have him. You and me, parrot. You and me in the ring. Here and now. If I win, the witches go free. If you win, the witches go free."

Babbu's cackling squalls filled the air. "Let me have him. Dirty hare."

"No need for that," said Mahi as she and Aanya emerged outside the palace walls, their faces obscured by the iron bars. She inserted a sturdy bronze key into the gates, entered and locked the gates firmly behind them. Then she reached under her T-shirt of Boy George in his Karma Chameleon era and tucked the key into her bra. "Handy places for odd bits and bobs, aren't they?"

"No," said Sitara. "It can't be. We can't have failed."

"Not quite failed, dear." Shadows flickered across Mahi's face. "Foiled, maybe. But you were still fairly successful. It's nice to see you somewhat returned to your former glory. A horrible business, what happened to you."

"I knew it." A quiet confidence brimmed in Aanya. "I knew the ghost sister had returned."

My stomach plummeted. Next to me, Leena shuddered. We had been so close to pulling the wool over their eyes and winning back our freedom. We could only hope that our punishment would not be too severe.

A chorus of calls erupted from the bound men. "Seer! Seer!"

Mahi ignored them. "Let me tell you how impressive that feat was. Jalapashu hasn't seen a battle like that in close to a century. A blue witch, green witch and black witch working as one. Let me tell you, Kiya, your hair danced like a nest of snakes as you worked. It's been decades since the gargoyles woke. They are loyal to you. I hoped that particular piece of the puzzle might fall in place."

Her crowing made the air leave my lungs. How long had she been there? What did she want with us? Merlin, too, couldn't contain his agitation. I caught him as he growled and bounced, his forelegs circling like a 1920s boxer in prefight theatrics, bobbing his head back and forth in an exaggerated fashion.

"Seer!" said a guard soaked to the skin by Sitara's magic. "Free us from these dangerous women."

Babbu flew down to perch on her shoulder, head cocked as he glared at us.

"Oh, do be quiet." Mahi's face soured. "Don't you know I am a dangerous woman, too?"

CHAPTER 21

By now, the darkest hour of the night had passed. Faint glimmers of starlight were visible in rich hues of the purple-black sky. With each passing minute, the colours softened into an ethereal blue.

The bound guards wriggled on the ground, their eyes skittish. The gargoyles gave them the odd boot to subdue them. One grabbed the vines in its sharp talons, pulling them taut.

Mahi scraped her hand over her lined face and pursed her lips. "What does an old woman have to do to make young people see sense? We tried everything to nudge you in the right direction. Aanya and I brought you solace when you first arrived. I arranged for you to experience the wonders of your magic. Aanya's potion helped the hare get his voice back. I kept stumm when he stole *The History of Jalapashu* from the palace library even though I suffered three days of visions about it. Then, when you revealed your magic in the gladiator ring, I risked the raja's anger. I even persuaded him to place your maternal grandparents on the invitation list at Biryani Junction. None of it was enough to make you want to stay." She surveyed the destroyed lawn and the struggling guards and lingered a long moment on the gargoyles. "Look at what you can do. Would you really give all of this up?"

The gargoyles grew so still, I feared they had solidified there and then on the roughened green.

My throat clawed, painfully tight. The coolness of the gemstone radiated through my chest. The flow of magic through my body was intoxicating. My hands were my tools, and the earth was my canvas. With every breath, I felt the hum of the world around me, the vibration of the soil, the stillness of the rock, the waking of the gargoyles and cycles of renewal. It was a symphony only I could hear, a dance only I could revel in. Stripping away this connection would be like a sailor without a compass. The thought of losing my connection to something so elemental was unbearable. I knew in my bones that Leena felt the same. But our pattern was set: big sisters knew best. It wasn't too late to see Sitara's plan through if we could persuade Mahi to let us go.

"Yes, we would give all of this up," I said. "Step aside, Mahi. Please."

The seer took off a shoe and slapped it against her palm as if she weighed up whether to take it to our behinds. "I warned you not to let the dead drive mortal decisions. You have no respect for your elders. How can I explain to you all that I have seen? Vision upon vision about the rot in this kingdom. Jalapashu is lost without your help." She flew at us in a fit of frustration, threatening to whack us with her sturdy trainer.

Above us, Babbu the parrot chattered with excitement and tormented the hare with bursts of flight and sharp turns wherever he ventured. Just when I thought we'd have to dodge and weave to avoid Mahi's ire, Aayna broke into a song so sweet that the seer stopped in her tracks and the guards, too, ceased to struggle. Even the gargoyles seemed to soften with the swell of her voice.

Despite her anger and eccentricity, Mahi had endeared herself to us. This precise moment wasn't a threat. We had faced far worse. It was what came next that worried me.

The seer sighed as if her puff of indignation had simply evaporated.

Sitara folded her arms across her chest. "Give us the gate key, Mahi. Don't make us rummage in there."

Mahi's face turned red. "Rummage away. My lady parts need a little love."

My mind whirred through the options. We could overpower her and Aanya with ease. We could leave them tied up. We could still make it back to the Crypts, return the gemstones and disappear into new lives.

Sitara's spectral hands clenched into fists, and her normally serene features twisted into a scowl. "Just command the gargoyles to tear them limb from limb."

Leena didn't take her eyes off Aanya. "No, they were kind to us."

A grinding of stone filled the air as the gargoyles turned in my direction, expectant.

I gave a slight shake of my head, staying them. Was this always who Sitara had been? Just as Leena's nursing profession made her want to heal, did Sitara's archaeology background, with its focus on lost civilisations, make her more ruthless? Or was her maternal need to protect us the driver of her violent instinct? Worse still, had death extinguished her humanity?

The seer put on her shoe, straightened with difficulty and cracked her spine with a moan. "There was a time when I made moaning noises during hanky panky. Now I make them during strenuous activity like standing up straight."

"What do you want from us?" I asked.

Mahi's shoulders slumped. "Your gargoyles can rip me limb from limb. I have lived a good life. It would be a sad end, but most people would say I've had my fair share of years and a considerable share of power. But what I want… that's another thing entirely." She clasped her hands at her belly. "I want what most old people want. I want to see a changed world."

Babbu zigzagged through the air, his ruddy beak squawking. "Change is coming."

Mahi's eyes shone in the moonlight. Her words dovetailed into Babbu's squalls. "I want to live out my days, not jaundiced by all the wrongdoing around me. I was so proud of Jalapashu once. I remember wisps of our time of plenty when magic was shared, and families didn't have to choose between medicine and meals. When previous rajas wouldn't lash an animal, let alone a person. Under Prem Kumar, every day brings a new tragedy, a new injustice."

I bit my lip. "You have been at his side all these years, Mahi. You could have done something."

The seer gave a sad smile. "Not without you. My visions told me as much… But seeing you work together tonight… It's what I hoped would come to fruition and more."

Aanya's humming petered out. "It's not often Mahi speaks so frankly. This is your destiny, Marlowe sisters. We are allies. Stay and fight with us. Others will join us, too."

My scalp prickled at the sudden realisation that Leena's and Aanya's hands were entwined and that by the set of Leena's mouth, she had reached the limits of meekly going along with the plan. The shy fishtail gargoyle edged in their direction, seemingly as uneasy as I was about their nearness.

Sitara crackled with anger that radiated outwards in waves of energy. The air around her buzzed with static. "Oh, yes. We have allies. Allies who have been puppet masters rather than truthful. Allies who did nothing as I was killed and my sisters imprisoned."

"I see we've got a real boss lady in our midst." A wave of sadness came over Mahi. "You remind me of my older brother, always telling me what to do and how to do it. But

Sitara, as much as your sisters love you, your time is already up. But there are people here that can help your sisters."

Sitara pursed her lips. "Like the general? The man who allowed us a whiff of freedom then trapped us like dogs in cahoots with you."

Mahi smiled. "Deven? The man who gave you the turquoise chamber with its ocean feel because he knew you'd miss the bay? He's incapable of betrayal unless pushed to his limits."

The midnight mass of our ghost sister's hair electrified around her face. "Why you–"

Leena was now sandwiched between Aanya and the shy gargoyle. "Sitara's right. It was the general. He must have given us up."

Icy coldness hit me at my core as I replayed the events in the royal chambers in my mind.

Merlin bounded to my side, gilded eyes glimmering like tiny suns. "Trust your instincts."

None of this felt right. Our disharmony, our bickering, our unease with our decisions. We were sisters, bound by blood and magic. For one moment, when we had battled the guards, we had worked together seamlessly, our magic flowing in perfect unison. But in reality, our once-tight bond was frayed. We'd been lying to ourselves and each other, and it was time for that to stop.

My voice cut through their griping like a siren in the night, causing the gargoyles to stand at attention like my own private army. "That's enough." My heart raced as I recalled Deven's touch and the words that had ignited a fire in my belly even as I ran from him. *You'll be the death of us.* He had said my name like a prayer. "It wasn't the general. Deven didn't give us up."

Mahi's papery lips curved into a smile. "Maybe you're learning to follow your heart, after all. Deven didn't give you up." Her forehead rippled, and her violet eye came into being once more. "I have known this particular scenario was a possibility from the moment we met. In some versions, the raja woke and tried to seduce you. In others, you refused to lock onto the gemstone, and your truest potential went untapped. In most, the gargoyles stayed sleeping. In all but one, you walked away from Jalapashu, never to return." She looked at Aanya. "But we had to try."

Aanya dipped her head and toyed with the tiny row of hoop earrings on her cartilage. Her singsong voice filled the still predawn air, and it seemed that even the bound guards held their breath. "If you want to leave, we won't stop you."

Sitara lifted her chin. "Let's go."

Leena inhaled deeply through the nose and then exhaled through the mouth. "No."

"Yikes. That's one all." The hare's whiskers twitched. "Kiya, you have the deciding vote. I may be an Einstein amongst hares, but I get decision anxiety. However, once we have resolved this stressful day, I will happily perform a dance to celebrate and give it my best Fred Astaire. Smooth, effortless, graceful. Or perhaps you're after a more energetic, acrobatic style à la Gene Kelly. I can do that, too. Or even a playful Bojangles stair dance."

I grimaced. "Later, Merlin. I have to think."

He sniffed. "Party blooper."

"A parrot never makes such linguistic errors," said Mahi.

"Maybe not." The hare turned his back on her. "But you can't cuddle up to a parrot in bed, can you?"

My thoughts bubbled like a boiling cauldron. I'd allowed myself to be swept along by Sitara's thinking. She feared the price of magic, and that fear had propelled our decisions. She wanted to wrap us in cotton wool to tend to our wounds and make us safe, just as she always had. But my magic didn't make me scared; it made me soar.

Mahi unconsciously felt for the topaz medallion beneath her Boy George T-shirt. "Please Kiya and Leena. I can see it in your eyes that this isn't as clear-cut a decision for you as Sitara makes out. Is this what freedom means to you? Allowing the voice of other people to be louder than your own? Silencing your intuition?"

I *had* been silencing my own voice. What is more, I'd been chasing impossible goals.

I'd sworn to protect my sisters, but one sister was already dead, and the other didn't want saving.

We weren't children anymore. We weren't the scared young women who lost their parents. We were grown women. Adults understood that there were no guarantees in life, not for happiness or health or even love. Whether we stayed in Jalapashu or took a train to the other side of the continent, life would be a melting pot of tragedy and joy. I would find moments of peace and triumph amidst the quiet turn of an ordinary life, but no one was immune to heartbreak or pain.

That's what made life such a terrifying, exhilarating ride.

I met the seer's eyes and tried to ignore her rippling forehead. "You said you wanted a changed world. What change do you wish to see, Mahi?"

She fixed me with her shrewd gaze. "Isn't it obvious? I want the three of you, together with me, Aanya and Deven, and our various furry and nonfurry creatures–I'm not talking about my vagina, mind–to take down the raja. Because Prem Kumar is no longer who the people need. He never was."

"Not sure the guards should hear you saying that," blurted Leena.

Mahi grinned. "Oh, don't worry about them, dear. They won't be a problem much longer."

My senses were in overdrive. All the competing agendas made it hard to think.

I crouched down to the hare and buried my nose in its musty fur. The raja was a rotten king, of that there was no doubt. I wanted to stay in this magical land for us. I wanted to uncover more of our history and explore my dormant potential. Giving up magic would be giving up a part of myself. That wasn't a sacrifice I was willing to make. Not when, even now, my heartbeat drummed to the rhythm of the familiar chant. *Magic, magic, magic.* But it was more than that. What if I had been given this gift for a reason greater than myself? What if the universe intended us to help the people of Jalapashu? No, that was stupid. I was getting too big for my boots, thinking we could bring about change in a place we barely understood.

I leaned into the meditative hold of the chant on me, trying to unpick my intuition, allowing calm to wash over me like the evening tide. When I opened my eyes, my words spooled out, an instinctive reflex. "We're staying."

"Staying and playing. Praying and betraying. Swaying and slaying," squawked Babbu.

The guards let out a collective groan.

I shot them a dark look, leaning into witchy vibes, and damn, it felt good. "Just say if you prefer a quick demise. Happy to oblige."

The gargoyles grinned their gruesome toothy smiles.

"We're staying for us," I said, not wanting to give Mahi false hope. "But we won't be part of your rebellion. That's not our fight."

Sitara pressed her lips together. "I'm *not* happy about being railroaded into staying."

"Thanks for being gracious about it." I teased her with a fervent wish that we weren't making a terrible mistake. Could following your intuition ever be the wrong move?

"Democracy's a bitch," said Leena, but there was a new ease in her body language.

Mahi's sour face softened with relief, and suddenly, the distance between us closed as if there had never been a divide between us. She hooked her arm through mine. "That's settled then. Small steps. We'll pretend like this never happened." She waggled her eyebrows. "Tell me, in the royal chamber, did you draw a clown face on the raja and pose him with a feather boa?"

I frowned. "No."

"Did you make towel animals and force him to ride a buckaroo?"

"Err, no."

"What about putting his finger in cold water and making him go pee-pee? Or a monobrow?"

"No. What is this? Kindergarten?"

"What a shame. In an alternate vision, you did." Her lips puckered. "Never lose your sense of fun. That's the best anti-ageing advice I have. Anyway, you have the jewels. That's something, at least. More than something, actually. That's everything. We'll find a way to hide them on you, shall we? Oh, and Kiya dear, use that last spell in the bag Leena is carrying, will you? Otherwise, we'll have to kill the guards, and I'm far too tired for that malarkey. A face like mine needs eight hours of beauty sleep without fail, and at this rate, I'm not even going to get half of that."

The spell floated into my head. *Tvamapaśya.* I retrieved the small plate created from dark rich clay I'd made in the turquoise chamber. Though its glimmer had all but faded, I tipped it over the heads of the guards. The spell swirled in my head, the vowels stretching and contracting like elastic bands. *Tvamapaśya.* With each repetition, the incantation grew stronger, and magic coalesced around me. *Tvamapaśya.* The consonants snapped like twigs, punctuating the rhythm of my chant. When I released the spell, the world around me seemed to shimmer, and the guards scratched their heads. They looked at us blankly, even as the gargoyles broke their vines and handed them their weapons, even as they abandoned their post and began the long walk towards the palace and their beds.

As the first dawn rays broke through the sky, Leena and

Aanya stole a chaste kiss. Merlin and Babbu settled into a prickly companionship, though the hare snoozed with one eye open. I thanked the gargoyles for their service and persuaded them to return to their places of rest, even though their stony faces flattened with disappointment. Sitara floated alongside their clumping gait back to the alleyway. I watched them go, worried that I didn't know how to activate them again or how I had done it in the first place.

The early morning skies put the damage to the palace gardens into sharp focus.

"What about the lawn?" I asked.

Mahi shrugged. "Use your earth magic to heal and restore it."

My eyelids had never felt so heavy. "How do I do that?"

"Never mind, dear," said Mahi. "We'll blame it on the elephants."

CHAPTER 22

Back in our unguarded chamber, we tended to Merlin's torn ear. Falling into bed, we snatched pockets of sleep woven with wild dreams of stone monsters and luminous birds. Once the sounds of palace life grew impossible to ignore, we untangled ourselves from the bedsheets and washed the caked dirt and sweat from our bodies. Our choice resonated deep within me, shaking me to the core.

It was easier to run than to stay.

Merlin devoured what food remained in his bowl while Sitara waited impatiently for us to dress. She didn't have to worry about unclean hair, oral hygiene or changing her clothes. She just existed, forever frozen in the state she had died in. "Hurry, will you? We don't know if the general managed to clear away signs of our presence from the royal chamber. We don't know how the raja will react when he realises the jewel fragments are gone or who he will blame."

Leena sighed. "Based on his small dick energy, it won't be pretty."

With a nurse's strong gut for unpleasantness, she retrieved the gemstone from Sitara's urn. Once I'd hidden the urn in the dresser, Sitara faded from sight, and we made our way across the kingdom to Mahi's tall house as agreed. Anxiety bubbled in the pit of my stomach, but we needn't have worried. Maids bobbed their heads as we passed them in the palace corridors. Guards smiled in greeting when they opened the gates, as if the previous night's battle was the wisp of a dream, and talked of how the elephants had been on a rampage through the gardens under the light of the new moon.

Jalapashu was peaceful in the midmorning wash of light. A few people scurried about their business and stopped to stare. The scent of fresh *chapatis* and chutneys filled my senses. But it was the rooftop gargoyles that caught my attention; their stone faces looking down at us with an air of solemnity. I smiled at them, grimaced, and puffed out my cheeks, but they remained motionless.

Leena hissed. "Pack it in, or they'll lock us up again."

Mahi and Babbu waited for us on the threshold of her three-storey house. The withering plants on its balconies now bloomed as if they had been replenished by attentive care or clever magic. Only when the weathered door had closed behind us did the parrot squawk a hello.

He flapped in the air before our noses. "Welcome witches and dirty hare."

Sitara materialised, shimmering against the deep burgundy of the hallway. When Mahi raised her fingers to her lips and pointed to the chapel-like windows, we retreated to a dim inner room with stale air and brimming with mystical objects.

"That's better," said Mahi. "I find staying away from windows a good precaution against prying eyes. Magic seeps out, but sometimes it finds its way in." Mahi swept her arm across a table full of tarot decks and jars of tea leaves. "Now come and sit down, all of you and pop your gemstones on the table."

We did as we were told as the hare bounded about investigating every nook and cranny of her house, pursued by the cackling parrot calling him all manner of names under the sun.

Mahi held the gemstones under a magnifying glass and squinted at them. "Exquisite. You see here? They are already adapting to your particular bodies, changing at a molecular level. Sitara's is the most advanced, with this thread of blue. Yours, Leena, has a tinge of green. And Kiya, see this corner? Just a touch of a black shadow mixed with that glorious amber."

I leaned forward to get a closer look. "What about yours?"

She pulled it from beneath her T-shirt: a flat yellow medallion, as I had thought, but its edge was a thin violet line, making it look like an eye.

I suppressed a shudder. We waited in agitated silence as Mahi hurried about the room, collecting ingredients and checking scrolls. The hare bounded across floorboards under the parrot's sharp eye as Mahi worked.

The seer crushed various herbs and powders in a mortar and pestle: belladonna, a pinch of hemlock, slithers of moonstone, black salt and a gloop of wax. Next, Mahi ground the ingredients, releasing a pungent scent that made us wrinkle our noses. Chanting under her breath, she mixed the ingredients and, after a moment of hesitation, spat into the bowl before stirring again. Then she collected two tiny teaspoons from a drawer, scooped up some mixture, and turned the weight of her gaze on Leena and me. "Open wide."

"Not on your nelly." Leena covered her mouth. "I would have considered it until that ball of spit."

"Uh-uh. Not for me, either," I said. "That is not going to agree with my digestive system."

Sitara laughed hysterically. "The joke's on you. Another advantage to being dead."

Mahi's kohl eyebrows shot up. "I'm afraid no isn't an option. It's the custom for magicals in this kingdom to wear their gemstones proudly. They are a sign of belonging to the highest class of citizens, a sign of power and magic. The jewellery fashioned from these pieces is the talk of the kingdom: medallions like mine, manly rings or dainty ones, earring cuffs or solid watches, necklaces that glitter like chandeliers or bracelets with a gem suspended within intricate lacework, like your mother's. Even nose rings, although personally, I think that's a little unhygienic." Her shoulders drooped. "But if you wear yours like that, the raja is going to set his entire guard on you, and there'll be nothing you can do apart from having the end of days showdown or submitting to his often quite violent will. So it's up to you, witches. Are you going to ingest this bad boy? Or are you going to let minor discomfort get in the way of surviving this day? I'll wait for you to make up your mind." She tapped her foot, a sly smile on her wrinkled face.

"I hate it when someone calls my bluff," said Leena.

I peered at the spoon Mahi waved in front of my face and dry heaved. The mixture was a deep red, almost like blood. With a sigh of resignation, I closed my eyes and opened my mouth. When nothing happened, I prised open an eye.

Mahi chuckled. "The gemstone isn't just going to float its way over to you. Hold it above the space where you want it hidden."

With a huff, I picked up the gem and ran a finger over its jagged edges. Then, feeling a fool, I rolled down my leggings and held the jewel on the upper thigh of my left leg, an inch below the pelvic bone.

Merlin hopped to my side, a little anxious. "Don't worry, I'm here, Kiya."

I shut my eyes and opened my mouth. She pushed the spoon in with the finesse of a bear learning how to use cutlery. I hesitated for a moment but then swallowed in one gulp, still holding the jewel against my upper leg. The taste was bitter, with a gritty, oily texture. My eyes flashed open. I cringed away from the remnants on the spoon, my toes curling. The magic seeped into me, settling into my bones. The jewel fragment grew warm against my skin. I gasped as it sizzled and steamed and took on a life of its own, boring into my skin. At my feet, Merlin turned in frantic circles, and somewhere my sisters called to me. My vision swam as the pain peaked, and I bit down on my lip to stay quiet. But as soon as it peaked, the pain subsided, like riding a wave. When I looked down at my leg, the jewel was gone, and there was no mark. My thigh was smooth to the touch, and only my heightened pulse remained as proof of what had just occurred. I pulled up my leggings, winded.

Mahi touched my cheek. "Well done."

Then it was Leena's turn. She retched at the taste of the potion and stamped her feet as she swallowed it. As the magic took root, she bit her lip to contain her screams. The gemstone drove into her upper arm, where she had a scar from a childhood injection. I looked on in mute horror as veins pulsed under her skin and writhed as the jewel burrowed deeper. The pain etched on her face was almost my undoing. A long minute passed before the jewel was gone and her scar with it. She touched her arm in awe and slicked away beads of sweat that had formed on her forehead. "Holy shit."

Sitara's brow furrowed. "My jewel can stay hidden in my ashes. Not without a body. I don't even have a gag reflex anymore, let alone muscle and sinew to hide a jewel."

Mahi cocked an eyebrow. "You are a fledgling witch, young lady. *I* am an experienced one. Watch and marvel." She reached back to a dusty shelving unit filled with yellowing vials, measuring spoons, serrated knives, gleaming animal bones, clumps of charcoal, and baskets of roots and bark. With a natural flair for drama and the sense of a cook who knew the precise contents of every square centimetre of their kitchen, she picked out an old jam jar. "This should do it. A drop of silvered honey." Popping the lid off, she took a clean spoon and added a smidgen of the contents to the bowl before stirring a final time. At the precise moment it fizzed, she dipped a muslin into the potion, wrapped the cloth around the jewel and handed it to me. "Kiya, hold the final fragment in the centre of Sitara's mass."

Anxiety swirled in Sitara's mossy eyes. "Seer, if this goes wrong and I lose the connection to my sisters, I'll never–"

"Don't worry," said Mahi. "Much as sometimes I'd like to send you spiralling into the afterlife, I don't have that power. Now, please, I really do need a nap."

Babbu loomed up behind her. "A seer siesta," he squawked. "Or a beer fiesta."

Ignoring him, I faced my beloved sister and took a deep breath. "Ready?" At Sitara's nod, I plunged the wrapped jewel with its dripping goop through her heart space. I held it there as a strange vibration ran through her shimmering form. My hand stiffened like it had been submerged in an icy lake.

Sitara's face contorted in agony, then she flickered like a faulty lightbulb. Her ghostly form glowed with a pulsating energy that was palpable. The air around us crackled with electricity. Mahi's vials and jars rattled, and the parrot flapped his luminous wings and shrieked with fear. Sitara's eyes rolled back in her head. She let out a blood-curdling scream as the jewel slowly faded from sight into the cavity where her heartbeat had once drummed.

For a moment, I feared we'd made a terrible mistake, but then, just as suddenly as it had begun, the flickering stopped, and Sitara's form stabilised.

Merlin crept out from beneath a chair, his warm gold eyes wide in the dim light. "It worked."

TO SAVE A SISTER

Mahi crowed with delight. "That, my dears, was the power of magic. Now, even if he suspects you are the thieves, the raja won't be able to find them." Her violet eye deepened to the hues of a faraway galaxy. "He'll concoct some excuse to search your chamber and perhaps your bodies. But I imagine when he finds nothing, he'll bite his tongue. After all, courtly life is a game of chess. If the court finds out how he was hoodwinked by you ladies *and* that you managed to steal the jewels in such delightful fashion, he will lose face." She grinned. "And that, my fledgling witches, is very dangerous for a king. Now Babbu, be a good boy and check that we haven't attracted any unwanted attention during our exploits today."

With a flash of a scarlet beak, the parrot soared out of the dark room, leaving behind a trail of shimmering feathers and the whisper of wings.

THAT AFTERNOON, LEENA CHATTED WITH AANYA UNDER A brilliant blue sky, with cirrus clouds drifting overhead and the sound of ride-on lawnmowers in the gardens. I left their company to retrace my steps to the tiger tapestry, where I met Deven at Mahi's request.

I walked towards him, my heart hammering in my chest. I'd thought about him more than necessary since our encounter in the royal chamber—more than I'd wanted to. Under the moonlight by the east palace gates, Mahi had named him in her roll call of allies, but him being the seer's ally didn't make him mine.

He leaned against the cool palace walls, his strong arms folded, his obsidian eyes following every movement: the sway of my hips, the swish of my dark hair, the way I wrung my hands together. He wore joggers and a grey T-shirt moulded to his skin. It surprised me to see him off duty when it seemed he was always in uniform, always shielding the raja or on standby for duty, big or small. It occurred to me that he must have his own chambers in the palace, even though he had family in the kingdom: his sister and a nephew, at the very least.

He pushed himself off the wall when I reached him. His lips pressed into a white slash, and his eyes dropped to my left upper thigh. "Did it hurt?"

So the seer had told him everything. "It's fine."

Cords twanged in his neck. "You should have left this all behind."

I swallowed. "What can I say? Like a moth to a flame."

His hair was shorter than usual, and I missed the curl, even though he wasn't mine, and I'd never run my hands through his hair. My brain betrayed me by making me think these things when we weren't anything to each other. We were closer to enemies than friends.

His gaze bored into my soul. "I never thought I'd see the gargoyles wake. My father talked about them when I was a boy. He never forgot the sight of them." He lifted a wry eyebrow, and his silver scar glistened against his skin. "I worked it out. Why they answer to you. The seer tricked me into bringing you Vikram Reddy's old kiln. He was the last one they called master. Your magic must rival his."

"My magic is my own."

"You and your coven made quite the mess."

I lifted my chin. "We cleaned up as best we could."

He bent to murmur in my ear, and a shiver ran up my spine. "By the looks of it, you're born to destroy." He pulled back. "Come on. We'd better get it over with." He checked we were still alone, lifted the tapestry, found the groove in the wall, and waited for me to slip into the passageway before following.

My chest tightened at the sound of Deven's footsteps behind me. Torches lit our way along the damp passage, casting strange shapes. Even though I knew my way, I flinched from shadows crawling up the wall, and the damp settled into my bones. Nothing good could happen in a place like this. When I stumbled over a loose stone and almost fell, Deven caught me by the arm.

I flushed at his touch. "Did Mahi tell you why this was so important?"

"Just that we had to be there at this precise hour." He urged me onwards, and when we got to the half-sized door, he dropped to his knees and shoved it open, waiting for me in the inner space. As soon as we removed the back of the linen closet, two muffled male voices reached us.

My breath quickened. "This is ridiculous. Let's go back," I whispered.

Deven held his finger to his lips, brow furrowed. He shifted a pile of towels aside and eased the outer closet door open as if a careless maid had left it that way. The voices grew clearer and more easily discernible. If we manoeuvred our bodies into a certain angle and tilted our heads to a position of discomfort, it was possible to glimpse a slither of the raja's bedroom. Deven peeked through first.

Then it was my turn. I stood on a brick and pressed close to our viewing crack, the scent of fresh linen in my nostrils. When I realised who was with the raja, fear snaked up my spine.

"You promised I could take his position if I did as you asked," said Mustachio.

"It's just a matter of time," came the raja's voice. "These things are sensitive. The court expects certain norms, and he is respected. Acting impulsively will raise too many questions."

Deven went rigid at my side. His fingers clutched the edges of the closet, knuckles white.

"If you want me to keep my mouth shut, it'll take more than a handful of gold coins," said Mustachio.

"Calm down. We'll have to nudge him into showing a failing," said the raja. "It won't be easy. He rarely puts a foot wrong. Our plan for the Summer Soiree should force his hand. It's the perfect stage for tragedy. Still, I'm fond enough of him not to wish him a violent death. This will merely be a reshuffle. After all, power ebbs and flows."

"Are you so keen to knife your cousin in the back? I almost pity him."

"He might be my cousin, but I need someone with a stronger stomach."

I jerked a look at Deven. His face was twisted in anger, and his eyes were cold.

Mustachio laughed. "He wouldn't have obeyed your orders to kill the oldest Marlowe sister."

"Lucky I had an inside man."

The ground rocked beneath my feet. Deven's hand pressed against the small of my back, steadying me. My thoughts whirled. Despite everything, despite the raja's callous behaviour, I'd still given him the benefit of the doubt. I'd convinced myself that maybe Sitara's death had been unplanned. It had been a horrific act of violence, two cultures clashing, not understanding each other. I'd believed him when he said he'd longed for our return and even a little flattered when he'd shown interest in me. I'd resisted taking part in an active rebellion. But the bastard had intended to kill Sitara all along.

He'd wanted her dead before the troop of soldiers had even stepped into our house.

Deven hadn't known about it. He was as much a pawn in this game as I was.

A moment of lost focus, and my foot slipped from the brick. We froze, holding our breath, waiting to see if we had been discovered. There was a sudden shift in the air, a rustling of fur and deep growls that made my pulse leap to the beat of a thousand drums. Deven's hand clamped over my mouth as we both peered through the crack, his breath mingling with mine.

Two jungle cats prowled into the bathroom. Mustachio had shifted into the strong, sleek panther with bright yellow eyes I had first seen in the south courtyard. But it was the raja who made me heave with anxiety. He wasn't a bear or a wolverine or a mountain lion. He was a Bengal tiger, twice as big as the panther. The bathroom seemed to shrink in size as he moved. His coat was a symphony of colours, a fiery orange that glimmered in the sunrays filtering through the window, with thick black stripes that accentuated his powerful form. Muscles rippled beneath his taut skin, and his teeth were like jagged tombstones. I realised the palace guard were just window dressing. Prem Kumar was a killing machine. One swipe of his paws could do untold damage.

His icy blue eyes scanned the room for a sign of danger.

In the linen closet, we didn't dare move a muscle.

But by shifting out of their human forms, they had upgraded their sense of smell.

They sniffed the air, catching the scent of our fear and sweat, and charged towards the linen closet. The tiger growled low in his throat, warning us not to make a move. As they scratched and snarled at the door, sheer panic floored me, but Deven already had his hand around my wrist and was already dragging me backwards through the half-sized door as the tiger let out a deafening roar.

His fingers dug into my skin in the main passageway, and the torchlight spun shadows across his face. "Block it," he said harshly, trying to stun me into action as the beasts broke through the closet. "Block it off with your earth magic, or we die right here."

I nodded wordlessly and raised my hands. Magic swirled within me, pulsing through my veins and radiating to my fingertips. The ground shook as my magic collided with solid stone, sending cracks spiderwebbing outwards. I gritted my teeth and turned it inwards again, beads of sweat pooling on my forehead. Finally, with a burst of power that exhausted me, the stone crumbled to pieces, blocking the tiger and panther.

We ran. We ran hand in hand through the dank passage and crawling shadows. Him dragging me. Me stumbling, half-blinded by terror. The tiger's roars thundered after us, a deep bone-rattling sound that sent rats scurrying along the tunnel and would send birds flying from the trees.

When we finally reached the tiger tapestry and ducked into the cool air of the palace corridors, we patted down our clothes and prayed nobody noticed our ragged breathing and darting eyes.

Waves of terror rolled through me still. I looked at Deven's topaz ring, the sound of my heartbeat thrashing in my ears. I didn't dare ask what layers of himself he hid from me when all around there were monsters. I chose another question instead, one that was simpler than secrets between strangers. "Do you think he knows it was us?"

He gave a wry smile. "If we survive the next hour, we'll know we've been lucky."

"That must have been hard to hear. He is your family. You were loyal to him."

His jaw clenched. "Your sister never stood a chance."

A wail formed in my throat. "Mahi knew we'd overhear. That's why she wanted us there."

"The seer is always pulling strings. It is the worst and best thing about her." A wild storm raged in his black eyes. "I can tell you one thing. I'm not loyal to him now."

The general wasn't my enemy anymore. Along the way, we had become something more.

CHAPTER 23

The Maharaja's Summer Soiree marked the height of the summer in Jalapashu. In the tradition of previous rajas and ranis, Prem Kumar threw open the doors of the palace for four hours of revelry until the clock struck midnight.

For the kingdom's subjects, the soiree was the highlight of the year, the only occasion on which courtiers entertained them with grand displays of magic. Not that Merlin was interested. The rituals of humans couldn't compete with the call of fresh grasses now that we weren't confined to our chamber. Sitara had warned me it was too dangerous to come, but I felt the opposite was true: if I stayed away, the raja would grow suspicious. Besides, he couldn't act out against me in front of a whole ballroom of people. He liked to be seen as a generous king, not a fearsome one. So, for the second time, I disagreed with my eldest sister and this time, we came to a compromise that she would shimmer in dark corners to preserve the secret of her return in case we needed her.

My breath caught in my throat as I entered the ballroom with Leena and Aanya, all three of us clad in Lokesh Saheb's creations. The Summer Soiree was in full swing. The light of crystal chandeliers reflected off glistening marble floors. Colourful lanterns and garlands of flowers hung from the ceiling. The aroma of exotic spices mingled with the heady scent of jasmine in the air. My heavy skirts swished as we made our way through the ballroom, accompanied by a buzz of whispers and the giggle of children. Nonmagicals mingled with courtiers in perfect harmony. Women wore flowing silk *saris* in a rainbow of colours. Men wore gleaming turbans with intricately embroidered *sherwanis*. I noticed Jilu and Radha, the chefs from Biryani Junction, enjoying themselves rather than working for once, and courtiers I had broken bread with there. A beautiful woman with a striking resemblance to Deven held little Ishaan's hand. The royal tailor stalked the room with his feathered walking stick, dapper in his white *kurta* and black *churidar*, his chest puffed with pride as he surveyed his creations.

"You look radiant. The forest green brings out your hazel eyes. Just as I imagined," said Lokesh Saheb.

"With deep thanks to you." I hadn't wanted to have my shoulders bare or my ribs enclosed by whalebone again, but it was the only option he had offered me with pockets. I slipped my hand into the deep folds of my right pocket. The tension in my chest eased a notch when my fingers found the bulb-shaped pot I had fired in the kiln.

"Swirl for me. Let me see how the sequins come alive under the chandeliers."

My heart raced as I spotted the raja cutting diagonally across the room, making a beeline for me. "Later maybe. My sister has gone ahead without me."

He inclined his head. "Perhaps a dance later."

I rushed away, Lokesh Saheb's voice at my back, and lost myself in the crowds. Like the guests, I found myself mesmerised by the magic on display. A juggler performed with balls that glowed like stars in the night sky. Conjurers wove intricate illusions: gold coins disappeared and reappeared in impossible places; cards changed suit and rank with a flick of the wrist; Babbu the parrot became a red and green disco ball and returned a moment later, his feathers in disarray. On a far-flung stage away from the alcohol, a group of fire-eaters breathed flames with reckless abandon. A performance by classical dancers blurred the lines of reality, multiplying and morphing, creating the impression that there were dozens of dancers on the floor at once, their *ghungroos* jingling with the rhythmic footwork. Then there was Mahi, slumped at a table reading fortunes with eerie accuracy, surrounded by a crowd of nosy onlookers.

By then, I'd lost track of Leena, and when I found her, she leaned on a circular podium where Aanya stood, enchanting the revellers and Leena most of all with a voice like velvet, her songs a journey of healing and comfort. But when I stopped, curious glances lingered on me, and Aanya and Leena only had eyes for each other. I left them to it, searching for Deven, hoping he had decided to attend, though I hadn't dared to inquire in advance for fear of outing us as allies.

I made my way through throngs of people devouring tiny *samosas*, succulent pastries, rich *biryanis*, pungent curries, *poppadoms* and naan breads as if they had never seen food before. Along the edge of one wall, the drinks table filled with tall glasses of *lassi*, *chaas*, mango juice, lemonade and champagne flutes decorated with sugared raspberries. Glass in hand, the court poet Nitin regaled a large group with his newest work. It was more than a poem. More than words. When the small square stone on his simple necklace shone, I knew it to be magic. Nearby musicians wove the sitar and *tabla* drums into a hypnotic tapestry, and my head spun as though their melodies stretched and twisted the very fabric of reality.

My head whirled with the expansion of my horizons. I

was ready for quiet, to strip off my clothes and rest alongside Merlin, when I came face to face with my grandparents.

My grandmother's henna-coloured hair was plaited down one shoulder, and her simple *sari* hung off her bird-like bones. She offered me her hand. "Kiya. I was hoping I would see you again."

I gulped and took her hand. It was cool to the touch. What do you say to grandparents you have never met? Who never tried to meet you? "Why did you wait so long?" I didn't mean the weeks since we had arrived in Jalapashu. I meant the forty-five years before.

Her eyes filled with tears. "Life is complicated. I am sorry for the loss of your mother and Sitara."

My grandfather's swarthy skin grew ruddy. "Come, Kavita. We mustn't talk to her."

My grandmother twisted her neck to see me as he ushered her away. Her necklace glittered like a thousand suns. "If not now, when?"

I stood, rooted to the spot, as the crowd swallowed them. When a hand yanked my elbow, I swung around. Only then did I realise my mistake in standing so close to the edge of the crowd. Mustachio grinned down at me like a predator with a bird in his grip. I masked my fear as he hauled me to a quiet spot, past laughing guests and the clinking of glasses. In all the extravagance and my manoeuvres to avoid the raja, he'd slipped my mind. I didn't dare make a scene. Not with so many people around.

"It was you in the secret passageway. Your scent is distinctive." He leered at me. "Unforgettable."

He'd killed my sister. I wanted him dead. I bit my lip, tasting iron. "What do you want?"

"He suspects, you know. The raja suspects you took the pouch of jewels." Mustachio gave a bark of laughter. His foul breath was hot against my cheek. "You being trouble makes him want you all the more. You're a riddle to him. A toy for a bored, rich git. He has some sort of delusion that he'll bed a Marlowe woman when his own father didn't manage it. But he'll tire of you. When he does, I'll take great pleasure in doing to you what I did to your sister."

My heart hammered in my chest. I tried to escape his grasp, but he held fast. "You aren't fit to breathe the same air as her." A cold breeze made me shiver, and I knew my ghost sister was nearby.

Deven stepped between us. "Get your fucking hands off her."

A thrill ran up my spine, tinged with relief. Deven didn't spare me a look, but by the frisson of energy in the air between us, I knew we were equally aware of each other.

Mustachio dropped me like a hot potato.

I backed away, adrenaline rushing through my body.

The men jostled for position. Neither wore a uniform, but both wore weapons under their embroidered fitted Indian suits. Their muscles bulged and strained as they pushed each other, grappling for the upper hand. They drowned everything out: the music, chattering, the thundering footsteps as revellers joined in *dandiya raas*, a traditional dance with sticks. They were rigid, their control close to the breaking point, eyes were locked in a silent struggle. Their movements were contained, almost imperceptible. Ruining the raja's Soiree wouldn't have been a good look.

Deven had the edge in height over the shorter man, but their strength was equally matched. "I trusted you, brother."

Mustachio spat. "We're not brothers. All that bullshit you spout. We worked together, that's all. It's every man for himself in this kingdom." His brown eyes turned yellow, and his bones cracked.

"Deven!" I flexed my hands, but my earth magic was too crude to use in the middle of the palace.

"Wait for me where the stone sleeps, Kiya." Deven kept his focus solely on his adversary. He pushed his forearm up against Mustachio's neck. "Don't be stupid. You can't shift here. Think of the people."

Mustachio's neck bulged as he strained against Deven's hold, his breath coming in quick, shallow gasps. "You would say that. You don't stand a chance against me after what he did to you. After what he turned you into."

Deven's voice was dangerously soft, anger radiated from his eyes. "Do you want to bet on that?"

Their impasse broke. The two men exchanged quick blows. I gasped as razor-sharp claws protruded from Mustachio's fists, and he took a swing. Deven's eyes narrowed as he evaded them. Why did he keep his own magic hidden? He fenced Mustachio against the wall with his body and aimed a series of punches, trying to wound, not kill. But Mustachio didn't hold back. His claws hurtled towards Deven's shoulder, and when Deven ducked, they caught his side instead.

I couldn't let him get hurt.

I delved into my pocket for the pot. The spell had been Sitara's idea. When walking into unknown danger, what better way to be prepared than with a spell of *boe kāṭe*, she had asked? *Boe kāṭe*. It meant reap what you sow. A boomerang spell because just as my intentions were good, there were those who sought to harm us. They deserved to have their intentions mirrored back to them. The incantation took hold in my mind, steady at first but rising in volume and intensity as I threw the pot's energy over the fighting men and traced out the shape of the spell in my thoughts. *Boe kāṭe*. As my spell took hold, it rippled outwards, and the air crackled with power.

Mustachio's claws turned on himself. Confusion swam across his face as he shredded through his own clothing and gouged his own chest. A choked gasp escaped his lips. He looked down at his chest in a mixture of horror and disbelief at his claws buried deep in his body. Blood and gore and muscle and sinew. Then he convulsed with pain and slid to the ground.

Deven, breathing heavily, cast me a look of surprise. "You did that?"

I nodded. "I had no choice." Another me in an ordinary world would have frozen with horror, but Mustachio had chosen his fate. Mustachio drew his last breath, and Sitara breezed around us. I didn't feel sorrow for him, only relief that he couldn't harm my loved ones again.

Deven dropped to his knees as the party music reached a crescendo behind us, and feet whirled and leapt during the *dandiya raas*. His breathing was erratic as he removed Mustachio's claws from his own chest. Then he pulled a pair of knives from his pocket and drove them into the wounds.

Bile rose in my throat. "What did you do that for?"

"Prem can't know what happened here. We need a story. Fast." He looked at me as a shadow fell over us.

My grandmother stood there, soft but proud, in her ivory *sari*. "I came to find you, Kiya." She blanched at the sight of the dead man, panic sweeping across her face as she took in the bloom of blood across his *sherwani*.

I held my hands. "I can explain."

"You don't have to. That man was a monster. I know what he did to your sister." Without missing a beat, she ripped off her glittering necklace and pressed it into my hand. Her bird-like bones pressed my fingers together. Her brow furrowed as she looked at Deven and me. "Tell the Prem-ji that the soldier tried to steal from me. Tell him the general had to intervene, and the soldier wouldn't listen. It won't be a hard story to sell. That man would have sold his soul to the devil. A little thievery was entirely within his repertoire."

I bit my lip. "I don't know how to thank you."

"My darling," said my grandmother. "I will do anything to make up for my failings."

I looked into her anxious eyes and hoped it was true. My heart raced as I turned to Deven. "He'll use this to discredit you."

Deven raked a hand through his errant curls. "I have done enough for Jalapashu to weather the storm."

In the unspoken words that hung between us before we went our separate ways, I realised he was doing this for me.

CHAPTER 24

I pushed through the crowds, relieved to see the sunshine yellow of Leena's *lehenga*, the soft blues of Aanya's *sari* and the glittering black of Mahi's *Punjabi suit*. Already, palace guards were closing off exits.

"There you are," said Leena before continuing her conversation. "What I'm worried about is how we'll get the you-know-what out of us when the time comes. From a medical perspective, it doesn't seem very sensible to have foreign objects in our bodies. It could cause all sorts of complications."

Her voice rolled over me in waves. I opened my mouth to tell them what had happened, my mind in turmoil, but I couldn't find the words. I stood there numb, thinking about how many dead bodies Leena must have seen at the hospital, how brave she was for processing hard days and just carrying on.

The clunk of the doors made me jump.

With the exits blocked, fleeing wasn't an option. Would our grandmother's story protect us?

Mahi's forehead rippled, but she was too deep in the flow of conversation to pause. "It's not a tampon, dear. Or a Gstring that has pinged upwards and is slowly separating one lower cheek from the other. Besides, even if my witchcraft fails, which is unheard of, the uterus is like a tracking device. Think about it. Men spend half an hour looking for a wallet in their back pocket. But women know where the roasting tin is from three Christmases ago. They know where to find the remote that Granddad hid when he wanted to watch a whole day of snooker and didn't want to share the television. They don't even need to use their eyes. They have a sixth sense when their toddler turns the door handle in the dead of night. And they scoop up other lost things in their communities that don't even belong to them and reunite them with their owners. Gloves. Yapping dogs. Wayward children." Mahi stared pointedly at Leena's bare shoulder, where the jewel fragment had burrowed deep. She dropped her voice. "So don't you worry. I can handle a trio of you-know-whats. And if I want to share the glory, I'm pretty sure Sitara's divination magic can find them, too."

Leena brightened. "It would be good to include Sitara. I think she's feeling a little out of sorts. Not just the whole existential crisis thing. It's not being in control. She really struggles with that. Just this morning, she crashed another plant pot. Poltergeists. You can't live with them, and you can't live—."

I couldn't get enough air. My head reeled.

There was no blood on my hands, but my hands weren't clean.

"Hush, Leena," said Aanya. "Can't you see? Something's wrong."

Leena's expression clouded with worry as she turned towards me. "Kiya?"

Sitara had told us. Sitara had warned us that Jalapashu was dark. But witches were dark too. And if they had been wronged, they could tear the darkness from themselves and cast it back at the world.

I swallowed hard. We had so much magic between us—so much promise. We had Sitara lurking in the shadows. We had the gargoyles. "If all hell breaks loose, we fight. Do you hear me?"

"You're scaring me," said Leena. "Tell us what happened."

I gripped her hand. "Mustachio's dead."

Leena's eyes widened, and Mahi's expression soured. Babbu flew squawking to her shoulder as the wild music stuttered. The revellers stopped in their tracks, and the crowd parted at Prem Kumar's feet, rolling backwards as though the sparks of his anger could burn us all.

I looked at the raja properly for the first time that night. He wore an embroidered *achkan*–a long jacket with a Mandarin collar in royal blue adorned with gold threadwork on top of a matching *dhoti* and bejewelled *jutti* shoes. A turban covered his long hair, the single feather of a peacock tucked into the folds. There, before us all, Deven whispered in his ear about Mustachio's death. My chest was weighted as I followed their facial expressions: the raja's tight-lipped smile and jolt of surprise, the tilt of his head as he listened, his frown of dismay, Deven's careful expression and his controlled breathing.

The tightness in Deven's body indicated repercussions for us all.

Prem Kumar raised his arms to address us. "Tonight, we danced, ate and marvelled at great feats of magic. But I fear our revelry has come to an end, though the clock has not yet struck midnight." His mouth was pinched, and waves of contempt rolled off him despite his physical beauty.

A ripple of sighs and whispers spread through his subjects.

"I have just learned that my favourite soldier has been killed. A hero who won your adulation during the recent slaying of a traitor."

Muffled gasps reverberated across the room. As realisation dawned that the exits were blocked, panic bubbled beneath the appearance of civility.

Cold blue eyes scanned the crowd. "I request the counsel of Kavita Malini."

My grandmother's court shoes clicked across the marble floor, her face pale, her eyes defiant. She left my grandfather trembling in her wake.

The raja spoke with the controlled fury of a brewing thunderstorm. "My general says you were the victim of thievery. Be careful before you answer. I have not forgotten the history of your family."

My grandmother's voice shook. "It is true that the dead man stole my diamonds from my neck, Prem-ji. When the general intervened, they fought. The dead man struck first with his claws, and the general killed him in self-defence."

The lies that covered up my involvement tripped from her tongue. I prayed I was the only one who sensed the falseness of her rhythm. I prayed she wouldn't be collateral damage in this kingdom that buzzed with brutal secrets. I prayed I'd get to spend time with her and find out who she was inside.

The raja flicked a glance to Deven, who stood tall despite the blood that oozed from his side. "I see. Well, this is all very inconvenient. Tell me, Kavita. Why do you think a man with such excellent prospects might have made such a choice?"

Her gaunt neck tightened like a guitar string as she swallowed. "Even your highest officials are struggling to put food on the table these days."

The raja wound his topaz ring around his finger, and I saw the flash of a tiger in his icy eyes. I wondered if he'd be capable of shifting here and tearing it all down because his little power games had played out in an unexpected way. But the raja was a patient man. Like all kings, he was a man of ample time and means. A man who could play chess over days and weeks. A man who enjoyed the secrets and shadows of kingdoms and courts. A man who revelled in small deaths and big ones as long as he was safe. He hadn't cared for Mustachio. He only cared for himself.

"He was always a greedy bugger, Kavita. With huge appetites for both coin and female flesh. Where are my footmen?" The raja pointed towards the dark corner where the dead body lay with casual disregard as if Mustachio were a cigarette end or discarded wrapper. "Clean that up, will you?"

My grandmother slumped with relief and fell into the arms of my distressed grandfather. Meanwhile, footmen dragged away Mustachio's body, watched by the still crowds. Only moments ago, they had danced.

The musicians picked up their instruments with a twang, anticipating to play once more.

When the raja's lips stretched into a cold smile and settled on me, I understood he had other plans.

The raja's voice boomed across the room. "It is from a sense of deep generosity that I throw open the doors of the palace to entertain you. But thanks to Kavita, it has dawned on me that some of my guests have been taking advantage of me. I have reason to believe that there are thieves among us. That is not something I can tolerate. Join me, courtiers. Stand by my side."

The deep unease amongst the revellers surged to breaking point. In the south courtyard, when the leopard had been slain, these very crowds had basked in their power. Now, they sensed the tide had turned, and even the smallest indiscretion could rock the raja's fragile temperament. As the courtiers cut through the room to the stand at the raja's side, families edged towards the blocked doors and begged the guards to let them leave. There were Jilu and Radha and the parents of a little girl who had imitated my dust-throwing. But the guards stood firm; better to be the hand that held the axe than to incur the raja's wrath themselves.

"Once your mother made a different choice. You have to choose a side," said Mahi to me. Then she wove her way through the crowds with the parrot muttering unwise words about mad kings, cursed kingdoms, dead princesses and stolen magic.

Leena leaned close to my ear. "We have to do something. He's itching for a fight."

"I know." A tornado of possibilities swirled in my mind. I'd used my spell to protect Deven, but there had to be something I could do.

"You're not ready to take him on openly. It would be a slaughter," whispered Aanya.

"It pains me to do this," said the raja. "All guests, including children, will submit to a magical search to ensure that no stolen goods are in your possession."

I sucked in my breath. Mahi had warned he would search us. He had found a way to do it without admitting the jewel fragments had been taken from under his nose. He'd twisted an unexpected turn of events to his advantage. The room constricted around me as Deven's shadowy eyes found mine. He gave an imperceptible shake of his head, warning me not to move.

How had I gone from hating him to depending on him for our survival?

The courtiers fanned out in a semicircle next to the raja, including my grandmother, still shaken from her encounter with him.

"Stop, Prem-ji. You must not do this." Mahi's silver pixie hair shone in the chandelier light. Her voice carried across the ballroom. "These are simple people. They live alongside magic but do not benefit from it. They shouldn't be subject to its whims."

The raja's face twisted in anger. "You, seer. You dare question me? I will not give you any more chances."

Her violet eye came to the fore. "You sow the seeds of your own destruction. What you intend here will only breed resentment and rebellion."

"Here comes trouble," squalled Babbu the parrot.

His voice was like a whip, staccato and harsh. "Quiet, seer, if you wish to remain a part of the court."

Mahi's movements jerked as she put her hand to Babbu to quiet him. She stood, expression frozen, while a trio of sorcerers stepped forward, all of whom had dined with us at Biryani Junction: the giant man with the twiddly moustache, the ageing noblewoman with oiled hair and the *jhumka* earrings and my grandfather, his face displaying religious fervour. Their sorcery was astounding to behold. This wasn't an airport frisking or a shakedown by an officer of the law. This was something else entirely. The sorcerers didn't move from their position. They chanted, and the air thickened in the room, coating first the colourful furnishings and blooms in a dense, grey fog.

Then the fog came for us all. The hair on my arms stood on end. It came in thick swirls that clogged my throat, and its heavy energy clung to everything it touched. Fear and sweat mingled with the sharp tang of magic that hung in the air like a heavy perfume. Children and adults alike cried with terror, and the crowds surged together in fright. Somewhere the parrot squalled and tumbled through the fog. I embraced Leena, wondering how it had come to this, wondering if the raja would find the jewels Mahi had gone to such lengths to hide on our bodies.

Time slowed to a crawl, and every second felt like an eternity.

As I fretted, Sitara's energy whirled around us, a reminder that we weren't alone. That despite the odds, we had allies. Despite the odds, we could succeed.

In the midst of the chaos, the solution came to me. I had walked this room. I knew the layout. The fog gave me cover. Without finding the fragments, the raja could never prove I had meddled. So, I put my trust in Mahi's cloaking spell and in myself. Focusing on the exits around the room one by one, I cleared my mind of everything else. I calmed my breath and reached deep into the earth's core with my magic. My power flowed forth with a steady hum, and the ground trembled beneath my feet. But the revellers didn't react to the vibrations, and I realised that the earth's language was for me alone, our secret.

It was a simple thing to breach the palace's defences when I put my mind to it. As if Jalapashu worked with me. As if the kingdom offered me no resistance because it wanted me to protect the people.

The locks gave a satisfying click, and the doors swung open, allowing the people of Jalapashu to pour through the exits. They stampeded past the scrambling, bellowing guard, spluttering for breath.

But Leena, Aanya and I stayed. We stayed as fresh air mixed with the fog to create tendrils of mist that twisted and curled. We stayed as almost all the revellers escaped, though Ishaan and his mother stayed as if leaving would imperil Deven. We stayed as the sorcerers halted their spell, collapsing in exhaustion in their proud places at the raja's side.

When the fog cleared, and the raja stood before me, I lifted my chin and met his gaze, uncowed.

He frowned at the doors, rage and bewilderment flitting over his face. But a raja never admits he has been outwitted, certainly not in public. He composed himself and appraised my body from head to toe. "You didn't leave."

I met his gaze. "I have nothing to fear."

He nodded, pensive. "The people like having you here. You give them hope. Hope is such a fragile thing."

My lips pressed into a thin line while a thousand thoughts buzzed in my head about how to destroy him.

He laughed, and his eyes raked over me and Leena. "I see you disapprove of my tactics... Well, it seems the Marlowe sisters are not thieves." He took my hand and pulled me away from my sister, through the revellers to stand at his side. His pressure on my hand was a promise of danger and an offer of seduction. "I looked for you this evening. I was hoping we could dance. But our fun has been ruined. You might not be a thief, but others here are. Thievery will not be tolerated in Jalapashu. We must make an example of them."

I jerked in surprise to see a young woman and a grandfather hauled before the raja, a fine black dust on their skin. With rough hands, soldiers removed napkins full of pastries from the woman's skirts and stacks of bread and fruit from the grandfather's pockets. I dreaded to think how many more subjects would have been hauled in front of him had they not escaped, their skirts and purses and pockets full of food.

My chest tightened. This was our fault. He would never have searched the people had it not been for Mustachio's death. Had it not been for the jewel fragments we had retrieved. I turned to him, ignoring the pull I felt to go to the safety of Deven's side. "Don't hurt them."

"Don't hurt them?" said the raja softly. "I take no enjoyment from this. My general will merely chastise them with a few lashes of his belt. You are soft, Kiya, from your time in England's grasp. You can't expect to have your values translated here." He grasped my chin. "I will teach you. One day you will understand. General–"

Deven stepped towards the cowering mother, grim-faced, but his hands stalled on his belt. Little Ishaan rushed to his uncle's legs to beg him to stop.

I looked up at the raja from under my lashes. "We agreed I would earn your trust by not running from Jalapashu once you removed the guard from our chamber and allowed my sister and me to roam the kingdom. Have we not earned your trust."

He gave a small smile. A tiger's smile. "Yes. You did not disappoint."

"Then, as a favour to me, show mercy tonight. Let these people go home. Let your footmen distribute the remaining food amongst the people. Show a little compassion for my sake." There was no surer way to bend the will of an egotistical man than appealing to his vanity. "In return, I will sit at your feet and learn everything you want me to learn about Jalapashu."

His cobalt eyes glinted as the rainbow lanterns spun above our heads. "Remarkable, what a man can give when a woman asks nicely." He turned to Deven. "You may let them go home. Tell your foot soldiers to distribute the remaining food. And general?"

Deven winced as he turned to face him, his hand now pressed to his sodden, bloodied side.

The raja's eyes settled on my grandfather. "Some of my courtiers have warned me not to trust the Marlowe sisters. But since Kiya has passed one test with flying colours, perhaps it is time for another. Tomorrow, general, you will accompany her to Boundless Bay to see if she will return here even after a taste of home. Of course, Leena will remain here. Think of it as insurance. I'd hate you to slip from my grasp just when we are getting to know each other."

In the darkening storm of the raja's eyes, I understood this was a test for both me and Deven.

A sense of calm filled me. The raja thought he had us trapped, but I still felt the connection to the earth. This magical place of dark enchantments and deadly secrets had allowed me to free its people. I had its trust. I knew in my gut that it would allow me and my sister to come and go as we pleased. Perhaps I would have been capable of freeing us from the turquoise chamber if I had tried.

I would venture to Boundless Bay like a tethered princess of Jalapashu.

It suited me, for now, to let the raja believe that he had won.

But my magic flowed within me, wild and untamed. I closed my eyes to the fantasy of burying him in this throne room. But just as I had my allies, the raja had his. As Prem Kumar sealed the deal with a kiss on my cheek, I vowed to do whatever it took to steal the throne from him.

CHAPTER 25

The cocoon of eucalyptus, banyan and mahogany trees grew less dense and finally disappeared altogether as Deven drove me through a shimmering curtain to Boundless Bay. Though the journey took less than fifteen minutes, the air between us was thick with anticipation and awkwardness. The only movement was the occasional darting of eyes, as if we sized each other up and neither dared to be the first to speak.

When I couldn't bear the silence anymore, I fiddled with the radio dial. R.E.M.'s 'Shiny Happy People' boomed out of the speakers. I turned the volume down with a grimace.

Deven's mouth twitched. "Not to your taste?"

"It just doesn't necessarily match my mood right now."

"What is your mood, Kiya?"

How could I explain the restless energy that refused to be still in me? Mere weeks ago, finding meditative ease as I worked the clay had been second nature to me. I had to get back to that stillness to be my best self. I had to find a way to be at one with my new identity but not lose my old sense of self. "My mood is… choppy. But time in the bay will help with that. It always does."

He'd worn jeans and a T-shirt to fit in with the locals. "Then that's what we'll do."

Merlin popped up behind us. "That suits me fine, thanks for asking. I'm not letting you out of my sight. Besides, I've longed for coastal grasses like a sailor longs for a wee."

I grinned. "You mean, like a sailor longs for the sea."

"Yes, exactly." The hare nuzzled against my shoulder. He'd been extra affectionate after what happened at the soiree.

We pulled into the gravel driveway of our ramshackle house. My breathing slowed as memories took over. How did the puzzle pieces of my life seem so long ago? A family of five had lived here, and we had been happy. Three sisters had lived here, tumbling through our lives on crisscrossing paths. We had cooked and danced and shared stories in our kitchen. A simple potter had lived here and fretted about not completing an order of teacups.

Deven waited patiently as I wrung my hands in my lap, unable to leave the car. The memories of Sitara's death and our escape were still too raw. I couldn't go in. Not yet.

One day, the house would bring me joy. It just wasn't today.

"Can we go?" I said.

"Sure." He shifted the car into gear.

We left my family house behind, and he drove us to the coast, where the rugged cliffs contrasted with gritty English sand. I opened the car door, my heart soaring, and Merlin bounded out to speed across the dunes, paying no regard to the clusters of families, hoping the grey skies would clear.

"I have a few errands to run. I'll be back within an hour," said Deven.

"Aren't you worried I'll disappear?"

"No. You've changed. You won't run."

I walked along the cliffs, trailed by Merlin, taking in the vastness of the horizon. The sound of seagulls echoed in the distance, and a light breeze rustled through my hair. When my thoughts grew calmer, I found a quiet spot on the beach and kicked off my shoes, enjoying the grains of sand between my toes. The salty air filled my lungs, and the lapping waters of Boundless Bay flooded my senses as I took out a sketch pad from my bag.

Usually, I sketched my work projects: crude charcoal drawings of lines and curves that would be the template for my latest creation. But this time was different. The waves crashed against the shore, and children squealed in the cool water as I worked. My pencil scratched the paper as I drew the outline of his tousled head of curls and his strong shoulders, paying close attention to the angles and proportions. Next, I sketched the rough shape of his features–his strong jawline, high cheekbones, slightly crooked nose and coal-black eyes, and the silvery scar across his eyebrow. Merlin frolicked in the grass banks as I lost myself in the drawing, smudging and shading with my pencil, creating depth and texture. I lingered at his eyes, capturing the intensity of his gaze, and drew the bare bones of a tattoo on his back. Frowning, I struggled to do justice to the play of light and shadow when his hair fell across his forehead.

When I finished, I slammed the sketchpad shut and stuffed it into my bag, embarrassed at how involved I'd been in the task and how Deven had occupied all my thoughts.

On a whim, though gunmetal clouds filled the sky, and the beach had cleared of people fearing a downpour, I stripped off my leggings and top and ran into the ocean over the cool sand. It didn't matter that I didn't have a swimsuit. It didn't matter that my body wasn't perfect or that my thighs jiggled. The ocean stretched out before me, blue and deep and vast. Goosebumps dotted my skin as I dove in, saltwater stinging my eyes and filling my nose as I dipped my head beneath the waves. With each stroke, I felt more alive, more connected to the world around me. I wasn't cold anymore. Blue water enveloped my body, and I was refreshed, renewed, and baptised. The sight of the Crypts, home to the gemstones and the root of our magic, didn't frighten me at all. I swam farther out as the weight of the world lifted off my shoulders.

Suddenly, strong arms gripped my waist. "What the hell are you doing?"

A jolt of electricity ran through me at the touch of his hands. "Swimming, of course." But I'd lost my rhythm, and my words came out garbled as I swallowed a mouthful of water and spluttered against him.

"Are you determined to die?" He turned me towards the shore as the heavens opened above us.

"I don't have a death wish. I was doing breaststroke." I was determined to keep my dignity even though I was in my underwear.

We swam together through the rain. I changed my stroke to front crawl to match his, intent on not being outdone. He threw me glances, ensuring I followed. I threw him glances, my eyes widening at the geometrical tattoo that covered almost the entire expanse of his back but appeared unfinished.

We reached the shallows, and I cringed at the state of me in my sopping–thankfully black–underwear.

A sneaky glance told me he hadn't fared any better. He stood in his boxers in the pouring rain, silhouetted against the grey, with a body that reflected the physicality of his job.

I looked away, and we pulled on our clothes in silence as the rain eased. Curiosity got the better of me. "What took you so long?"

He grunted. "I had to send the watchman from Jalapashu on a wild goose chase to protect your privacy, for one. A good thing, too. If he had seen you like this, you would have fuelled his fantasies for the foreseeable future."

My heart thrummed in my chest.

Already bedraggled and without towels, we sat side by side on the wet sand next to the bag in which I had hidden the drawing of him and a carrier bag from the local hardware store that must have been his.

"Why did you jump in after me? Your wound is barely healed," I said. "Leena's going to have something to say about her patching you up and you being so reckless."

He touched his fingers to his side to check the stitches. "It looked like you needed help."

"I've lived on the coast all my life. Of course, I didn't need help."

He gave me a dubious look. "Your head went under… I thought, maybe–"

I sighed. "You thought wrong. The ocean is my place of comfort."

"I did something right then. I insisted the two of you were given the turquoise chamber. It's the only palace room where the decor is inspired by the sea." He bowed his head. "I hate myself for what happened to Sitara on my watch. I had no idea that Prem had decided to have her killed."

I stared out across the ocean. "I know."

He hesitated, then reached across me for the carrier bag. "I have something for you." He lifted out the oddly shaped plate I had made at summer camp with our five entwined handprints, its broken parts fixed with super glue.

My heart skipped a beat as I turned the plate over in my hands. It was imperfect, but it still existed. At that moment, a part of me healed. "You rescued it. Thank you."

He raked a hand through his salt-spray hair. "An apology wasn't enough. I fix what I break."

My tongue tangled. "Why did you smash the vase that would have made the raja forget us?"

His voice was solemn. "Because I didn't want you to leave. For the first time in years, I think we can change things in Jalapashu. I think we can do it together. You believe it too.

Otherwise, you would have left that night at the east palace gates. You would have left and never come back."

My stomach hardened at the thought of all that lay before us. I remembered the words Mustachio threw at him. *You don't stand a chance against me after what he did to you. After what he made you into.* As the drizzle started again, I shifted position and faced him side-on. There couldn't be any secrets if we were going to do this. If he expected me to trust him, he had to trust me too.

He flinched as I peeled up his T-shirt.

"Tell me what this means," I said. "Tell me why that man said you didn't stand a chance against him."

Inky eyes met mine. "Because of the curse. Because I can no longer change into what I once was. Because Prem took that away from me when he took the throne." His voice was monotone. "This tattoo is a hidden sign of rebellion. Each year, I add a small section to it. It's a promise to myself. I pledged to free myself of the curse before my back is fully covered." He gave a wry smile. "I had almost given up hope until you–"

I knelt, reaching up to swallow his words in a kiss. We were both soaked to the bone, but the shivers running up my spine didn't come from the chill. He wrapped his arms around me and pulled me against his hard chest. I closed my eyes and let the world fade away. His lips were gentle on mine. He didn't demand. He probed like he couldn't be sure what I wanted. He tasted of saltwater and smoke, like a campfire on the beach. When we finally pulled apart, the world reformed around us: wet sand between my toes, the crashing waves against the shore, the drizzle on my skin.

The softness in his eyes made me want to go back for more.

"Well, aren't you a sight for sore eyes?" said a male voice.

My heart leapt a beat as I sprang up and threw myself into my old friend's arms. "Tommy!"

He grinned from ear to ear. He was of medium height and rugged, with neatly styled blond hair and warm cornflower blue eyes. A dusting of stubble darkened his jaw. I'd missed his easy smile.

"It looks like I interrupted something." Tommy extended his hand to Deven. "I thought I knew all Kiya's friends."

Deven stood and shook Tommy's hand. His face was a mix of wariness and discomfort. "Deven."

"Tommy and I went to school together," I said. "He runs the local chippy."

"Been abroad, have you?" said Tommy. "It was just strange you taking up and leaving without a word."

"That's my fault." Deven's voice sent shivers up my spine. "I whisked her away. In fact, she's so delicious that I may do it again."

"Oh." Tommy's face fell. He composed himself and put on a smile. "I've been keeping an eye on the house, Kiya. You know what it's like around here. You don't want squatters moving in."

It was unfair not to tell him about Sitara's death or what had really happened when we'd known him all our lives, and he was pretty much family. But telling him would raise questions I couldn't answer. Telling him would only put him in jeopardy. I kissed his cheek. "Thanks for always looking out for us."

His azure eyes flashed with confusion at my tone of goodbye. "Well, I should get going. The cod won't batter itself. Don't be a stranger, Kiya."

I watched his retreating back with an aching heart. My life in Boundless Bay hadn't seemed small at the time, but that had changed. This life felt like another me. Slowly, during my days in Jalapashu, my dreams had changed, and my wisdom had grown. How could I go back to my comfort zone?

Deven's hand moved to the nape of my neck. "Prem can't know about this."

"I know." I melted into his touch. His lips were soft and warm against mine, the taste of his kiss heady as cold droplets of rain slid down my skin. We pulled apart only at the insistent hopping of the hare at our feet.

"What did I miss? Did you just Lothario my witch?" He bared his teeth at Deven but appeared more endearing than menacing.

"Stop that, Merlin." I collected our things and scooped him up in my arms. As we headed back to the car, I covered up my shyness with a flurry of conversation. "Mahi standing up to Prem yesterday was quite something. She puts a brave face on it, but I'm sure she's out of sorts. I think I'll look in on her later."

Deven dug his keys out of his damp pocket as we made our way up the sand dunes under circling seagulls. "She'll have to be careful. Prem doesn't like it when alliances build without him. Elsewhere, families standing together might be strength, but in Jalapashu, splitting up families is the real currency. At least for this raja. The seer has survived this long and retained her seat of power because she told Prem what he wanted to hear. It'll be tricky for her now that has changed."

Twilight had fallen by the time I had bathed and reached the seer's tall narrow house. Merlin hopped ahead of me but stopped at the end of the alley. The plants on Mahi's balcony were dry and dead like they'd given up overnight.

"That's weird," I said. "Her door is open, but there's no sign of Babbu. It's not like him to shirk his guard duties."

Merlin perked up. "I wouldn't complain. Let's count our

lucky stars. Five minutes in that delinquent's company is enough to give a hare a headache."

We crossed the threshold into the burgundy cocoon of Mahi's home. The hair on my nape stood on edge. No lamps were lit, even though Mahi had poor eyesight and frequently needed magnifying glasses. Mahi invariably kept her windows locked and the curtains drawn, but a fresh current of air drifted through the house, which she would never have allowed.

The hare's ears twitched. "Something's wrong."

I held my index finger to my lips and tiptoed through the lower floors, trying not to give myself jump scares. My eyes fell across glowing bones, a rack of dried herbs whirling on the ceiling and tarot cards scattered on a table as if she had been disturbed mid-reading.

"Mahi?" I whispered. "Are you here?"

Nothing. Nothing until a steady bumping started on an upper floor.

I cursed under my breath. "Guess we'd better be brave then. It's just a witch's house. Nothing to be scared of."

The narrow staircase creaked beneath us as we climbed to the second floor. An eerie feeling settled in my stomach. I clung to the railing, grateful for the crescent moon that cast a soft glow through a chapel-like window. The hare trembled as he scampered alongside me. We followed the thudding noise to the third floor. Like the rest of the house, Mahi's bedroom was a hoarder's paradise, cranked in with too much furniture: three wardrobes, two chaise lounges, an enormous waterbed, and a multitude of small chests that housed who knew what. The seer was nowhere to be seen.

One chest wobbled as I approached it.

Merlin leapt back in alarm. "Don't do it."

I counted silently to three and opened it to a cascade of luminous green feathers, almost swallowing my tongue in fright as Babbu flew out. "How did you get in there?"

TO SAVE A SISTER

The parrot flapped around the room in a daze, landing on one piece of furniture after the other.

Molten-gold eyes glimmered in the dark. "Quick, put him back in it."

With a calming voice, I moved towards the parrot. "What's wrong, Babbu?"

He pecked the waterbed with his red beak, dishevelled and agitated.

"Get the parrot a bowl of water, Kiya, before we turn the seer's bedroom into a lagoon," said the hare.

"Dirty hare. She's gone. Gone. Gone," squawked the parrot, beady eyes on me.

My stomach plummeted. "What do you mean she's gone?"

"She's gone. They took her," the parrot said.

"Who took her? Where did they take her?" I asked urgently.

Babbu zigzagged across the room. "Who? Yes, who? She didn't foresee it."

A little under an hour later, Leena opened her palm and sent a thick vine with footholds creeping up the side of a dwelling in the heart of the kingdom, away from prying ears in the palace. I clambered up after her with the hare tucked in my jacket and hauled myself onto the rooftop.

We perched between a pair of gargoyles, taking in the view of Jalapashu. The scent of honeysuckle and jasmine filled my nose. The city was draped in a velvet blanket of night, illuminated by shimmering stars. Sleeping gargoyles guarded the red brick houses, their watchful stone faces etched in stillness. Further away, the marble palace loomed in the darkness, silent beasts moving in its sprawling gardens.

Sitara emerged at our side in a swirl of mist and darkness. "So the seer is gone?"

I pulled Merlin into my lap and caressed his silken ears. "Yes."

"We agree that Prem Kumar can't stay on the throne?" said Sitara.

"Yes," said Leena and I in unison.

A frisson of anticipation raced up my spine. This was about fighting for the soul of Jalapashu. A fight abandoned by our mother long ago. "Are we ready for this?"

In the rasping breath of the gargoyles, I already had my answer.

Acknowledgments

Embarking on a new story world is always a daunting task. There's a moment before I start when I worry whether I'll be able to translate my vision onto the page. Some days, the process is slow, and then suddenly, it can be like a dam breaking. Ideas multiply, words spiral into sentences, and all at once, characters feel like family.

I spent an oh-so-soothing afternoon at The Ceramic Garden researching pottery for this novel. Thank you, Mairéad, for always inspiring me to go on adventures and for coming along on this one with me. Thanks to owner Nikki for patiently showing us the ropes and letting us smush clay with abandon.

Through long writing days, I appreciated the support, sisterhood and cheerleading of readers and author friends. Paranormal Women's Fiction is such a vibrant, collaborative, kind community. Special thanks to Lynn, Louisa and my Divining Tales crew.

Writing is a solo activity, but publishing books is a team effort. A big thank you to my editors, Trish and Toni, for taking a scalpel and polishing cloth to my words with skill and wisdom. Thank you to Fay for the cover art that makes my heart sing. To Debbie and Sherry, my beta readers, who make time for me at the drop of a hat, you have my forever gratitude.

Thank you, Mum and Dad, for never making me second-guess my talents and for the food parcels the neighbours lust after. I still haven't forgiven you for the kebabs you sent in the post to uni.

To my husband, Jan and our beautiful children, thank you for never holding it against me when an errant thought weaves through my head, and I have to rush to write it down. Or when a deadline means I have to go into submarine mode. Writing might be my passion, but you are my dream.

SHARE YOUR READER LOVE

I hope you enjoyed *To Save a Sister*. Please take a few moments to leave a review online. Reviews are so appreciated. They tell authors which stories resonate and help readers discover our work.

In the next book in the series, *To Curse a Rival*, Kiya finds out how many people the raja has wronged and starts to plot against him. All the while, her feelings for Deven grow. Read on to enjoy the first chapter.

If you are a book blogger and would like to feature my books, please get in touch at www.NilluNasser.com.

N. Z. Nasser

xoxo

STAY IN TOUCH & GRAB YOUR SHORT STORY

Come and be part of my tribe and join my facebook reader group at Nasser's Book Nymphs.

To receive the short stories in the Majestic Midlife Witch world and keep up to date with my news, sign up for my fantasy newsletter at www.nillunasser.com.

For a close lens into my world, you can get early access to work-in-progress chapters and other goodies by joining my exclusive community: https://reamstories.com/nznasser.

Here's a coupon for the first time you make a purchase in my online store (it's so pretty!) at www.nillunasser.com: NILLU15.

TO CURSE A RIVAL
MAJESTIC MIDLIFE WITCH, BOOK 2

My magic stirs within me, both thrilling and daunting. Darkness wakens in Jalapashu. In this kingdom, silks are soaked in blood, and bones bend like boughs. To survive, my witch sisters and I must buckle up and learn fast.

The seer is gone. Her parrot warns that we must find her before time runs out. We unravel the raja's tangled web of corruption, discovering how many people he has wronged. None more so than the enigmatic general, whose terrible curse means he can't shift into his true form. I take refuge in his soft kisses, but our deepening chemistry is just another secret to keep.

With black magic closing in, the raja's wrath is one misstep away. He already suspects my innocence is a façade. He and his courtiers–including my grandfather–aren't afraid to fight dirty. But a woman in midlife stalks her own path. Will we find a way to take the raja's crown before he wises up to our treachery?

To Curse a Rival is the second book in a Paranormal Women's Fiction series. If you're a fan of stories about the strength of sisterhood, the allure of forbidden love, and the resilience of women in their midlife, you'll find yourself spellbound until the final page.

Also by N. Z. Nasser

DRUID HEIR

Midlife Dawn, Book 1

Midlife Tremors, Book 2

Midlife News, Book 3

Midlife Drift, Book 4

Midlife Portals, Book 5

Midlife Eclipse, Book 6

Midlife Battle, Book 7

Druid Heir Collections

MAJESTIC MIDLIFE WITCH

To Save a Sister, Book 1

To Curse a Rival, Book 2

To Trick a Raja, Book 3

To Hunt a Foe, Book 4

NEWSLETTER EXCLUSIVES

The Magical Grandmother, Druid Heir Short Story 0.5

A First Date in Paris, Druid Heir Short Story 1.5

Midlife Battle, Druid Heir 7 Bonus Epilogue

To Become a Witch, Majestic Midlife Short Story 0.5

Biryani Junction, a Majestic Midlife Witch Cookbook

About the Author

N. Z. Nasser is a writer of fantasy fiction. Her stories are about women who change the world, filled with magic and rooted in friendship.

A lover of barefoot walks along the beach, she is glad to have left behind her career in the civil service and to never wear heels again. Whether she is writing in her garden office or wrangling laundry, she is happiest with a cup of tea at her side.

She lives in London with her husband, three children, two cats and a fox-mad dog.

Printed in Great Britain
by Amazon